THE GREAT AMERICAN
BOYHOOD PROJECT

A dad. A boy. America.
What could go wrong?

A NOVEL BY
TAD SIMONS

The Great American Boyhood Project
Copyright © Tad Simons, 2022

Published by Pembroke Press

ISBN: 978-0-9961110-3-4

Cover Design: DaisyMaeDesign
Interior Design: DaisyMaeDesign

Printed in the United States of America

Don't let your kids
get the last laugh.

For my son, Hugh
Who turned out great, despite his parents

For Barbara,

ENJOY

PROLOGUE

Before reading *The Great American Boyhood Project*, you, the unsuspecting reader, should know that my wife and her legal team insisted that I call the pile of pages in your hand a "novel," in order to avoid being sued. Not only would she/they sue me, they said, but my publisher would also file litigation against me, along with every bookstore in the country, leading to a massive class-action lawsuit.

The wholly ridiculous gist of this legal assault would be that, in recounting the miraculous story of how I turned a helpless, illiterate blob of baby fat into a full-grown man, I may have distorted the "truth" by exaggerating certain details and reporting certain "facts" in a way that renders them "unfactual."

According to these know-nothings, my narrative is full of misleading hyperbole and "unreliable" interpretations of history—that my recollection of events has somehow been distorted by the fog of time, leading to a jumbled and twisted account of "what really happened." My wife even claims that I "made things up" to create a "better story," a charge so outrageous that I went back into the manuscript and removed some of the nice things I mistakenly said about her. My son hasn't read the book and says he doesn't care what I write about him (because who read books anymore?), as long as I spell his name right. To avoid that particular embarrassment, I took the precaution of removing his given name altogether, referring to him instead as "The Boy." For the sake of consistency, I also refer herein to my wife as "The Wife," though by the time you read this she may or may not be. It depends how the therapy goes.

After much discussion and fist-shaking, the compromise we reached was that I would pretend that this book is a work of fiction. The upside of this agreement for me is that I don't have to worry that some bored reporter is going to come along and claim that my son wore blue socks on a day when I said they were green, thereby sparking an international publishing scandal. Still, you should know that I have taken great care to represent the facts as they happened, regardless of how much I'd had to drink that day or the balance of my fluctuating mental state at the time. And in those rare instances when a note of skepticism might creep into the reader's mind as to the veracity of the account being offered, I only encourage the reader to recognize that it was parenthood, for chrissakes, so there was a lot going on.

Believe me or don't, but this is how it happened, no matter what anyone says. If someone else wants to "correct" the "record" for the sake of "accuracy," they can write their own goddamn book. This is my story, and I'll tell it my way, lawyers be damned.

—The Author

CHAPTER 1

Let me say at the outset that the whole baby-making thing was her idea. I was perfectly content to keep going through the basic and largely pleasurable motions of procreation, and would have been for some time to come.

But she wanted more.

She wanted to hold a squirming infant in her arms, to smell the sweetness of its newborn breath, to nuzzle its satin skin, to hear the blissful symphony of its gurgles, burps, and sighs. She was the one who wanted to "be a parent," to "start a family," to leap the chasm of social respectability and participate more fully in "the community." She was the one who thought it would be "fun" to raise a child. And it was she who wore skimpy negligees to bed and neglected to tell me when she was ovulating; she who preyed on my weaknesses and seduced me with her sly little smiles; she who cooed that I should not worry, that everything was going to be all right, that we were going to be great parents to a wonderful, magical, miracle child—the kind of child who would make our own parents proud and all the other parents jealous. The kind of child who might one day change the world.

It did not look promising in the beginning.

I had my concerns the moment it slipped out of her womb. Red, wriggly, and small, even for a baby, it had skinny arms and legs and couldn't even open its eyes. The thing was totally helpless. An entire team of nurses was needed to clean it, swaddle it in a blanket, and present it to us, the proud and groggy parents. They said it was a boy, but I had my doubts. Trust but verify, that's my motto.

After a thorough examination of its people parts, it was determined that the wiggling wad of people-flesh in my arms was indeed a boy. Which was a relief, because the last thing I wanted to do in this world was raise a girl. I have a sister. I saw what she did to my parents. I watched her manipulate my father into giving her whatever she wanted. First it was a tricycle and roller skates, then a fancy ten-speed bicycle, and then a horse, and finally a car. It did not escape me that most

3

of the things she cried and threw tantrums over were various means of locomotion, each faster than the next. It would not have surprised me if my sister had become an Air Force fighter pilot or an astronaut, so insatiable was her need for speed. Then there were all the clothes and jewelry, and her wacky girlfriends, and her loser boyfriends, and all the rest of it.

And let's not forget all the wounded animals she brought home in hopes of saving them. Once, she brought a dead cat into the house and asked my father if he could help her resuscitate it. My dad did what any sane parent would do in that situation—he grabbed it away from her, tossed the carcass into a plastic trash bag and yelled, "What the fuck is wrong with you?!!"

My sister cried, of course—not in teardrops, but in gushing rivers of heartbreak and betrayal. The fact that my father could not bring a dead cat back to life was evidence to her that he was not the man she thought he was, the man he pretended to be—the man who would do anything to make her happy. Anything, apparently, except bring a dead animal back to life! My father desperately wanted to be the any-thing man, so he spent the next six months trying to convince her that he had not lost his fatherly magic—that he was that man.

Watching a ten-year-old girl pout for months on end, and watching my father reward her relentless dissatisfaction—well, it was all very chilling. The experience taught me at an early age that girls combined the compassion of a saint with the cunning of a sociopath, a terrifying combination of attributes if there ever was one. So, given the choices, I knew it could have been worse—I could have been holding a baby girl in my arms.

But a boy was bad enough.

For me, the delivery of a baby boy meant that I was going spend the next eighteen years trying to teach him how to be man. In those early days, I didn't realize how difficult a project that would turn out to be. I am a man myself, so I figured all I had to do was teach him everything I had learned about life. But it quickly got more complicated.

Right out of the gate, they hit you with a question that has lifelong implications: Do you want your son to be circumcised? This isn't what they're really asking, of course. What they're really asking is: Do you want us to strap your newborn son to a table and have a large man with wrinkly hands and lip sweat use a sharp, shiny scalpel to slice off part of his penis?

There aren't many times in life when a man wishes he was Jewish, but this is one of them. If you're a Jewish father, tradition makes the decision for you, so you don't even have to think about it. Unfortunately, I am not Jewish, but I am circumcised. Furthermore, I like the way my penis looks, even if we sometimes disagree about how it should behave. Nevertheless, the pleasing aesthetics of my own member mean that my father, when faced with the same decision, could have said, "that's okay, we'll take him the way he is," but instead chose the path of unnecessary pain and disfigurement. Unless he allowed my mother to make the decision, that is, in which case many things in my life might make much more sense.

Not bound by tradition, but faced with a yes-or-no decision whose outcome was irreversible, I did what any reasonable man in that situation would do: I flipped a coin. It was the only way I could think of to have plausible deniability if the little bastard ever tried to call me on it.

As it happened, fate and luck determined that yes, my son's foreskin should be hacked off for no good reason. And that, I figured, is as good a life lesson as any.

CHAPTER 2

When we got The Boy home, he turned into a devil child. He wailed and whined and would not sleep. He filled diaper after diaper with his filth. He did not seem to care how his behavior affected other people, particularly me. I've never met a more selfish person. All the kid cared about was his own needs, and he made damn sure we met them. In those first few weeks, I wasn't at all certain we were ever going to get along, and feared that the whole arrangement—him sleeping in the same house, that is—was a huge mistake.

My wife, however, was ecstatic. She saw nothing but goodness and light in the little cherub we brought home from the hospital. When he cried, she smiled and said it was his way of communicating his needs. When he filled a diaper, she took it as a sign that all of his internal organs were working properly. When he fussed, she saw it as an opportunity to comfort him. When he threw up, she was happy, because it might be a clue that he was allergic to something that might kill him later in life—a calamity that could be avoided if we could deduce what the offending substance was from the chunks of undigested foodstuff the dog was trying to lick up off the floor.

She had read all the baby books, and had learned from them that most of the baby behaviors that annoyed and disgusted me were, in fact, signs that our son was the picture of health. Even the worst temper tantrums were, according to her, signs that our son knew he was loved, and that no matter how miserable he made us, our son knew without a doubt that we would continue to love him. How he knew this, I do not know, because in the early days it was not at all clear to me that "love" was the emotion I was feeling. At 3 a.m., awoken once again by The Boy's untimely wails, the emotion closest to the surface of my psyche was homicidal rage. I wanted to throw him into a dumpster and close the lid. I wanted to stick him in the oven and roast him. I wanted to hurl him into a wood-chipper and use his remains for mulch.

These feelings would eventually subside, of course, and be replaced by feelings of futility and resignation. In that foggy frame of mind, I would trudge to The Boy's crib-side, lean over, and wave a plastic fish in his face. He would smile and look at me with wide, wet eyes—eyes that seemed to be saying, "I love you, daddy." In those moments, when the bond between father and son was being formed in its own odd way, I would think to myself, "You are lucky, little man, because it looks like I am not going to kill you today."

CHAPTER 3

f The Boy and I were going to survive this ordeal, I knew I needed a plan, a roadmap to get him from his current state of perpetual need to, eighteen years from now, independence and, eventually, manhood. My initial thought—that I'd just teach him everything I know—began to disintegrate when, upon thinking about it, I realized that I don't necessarily know what I know, and I don't exactly know how I know it. Likewise, I'm not always aware of what I don't know, so there might be things I should be teaching The Boy but can't, because I don't know anything about them. Bridge, for instance. People say it's a great card game, and that it keeps your mind sharp, especially as you age, but I have no idea how to play bridge. Poker I can handle, but bridge? He'd have to learn that from someone else.

I also don't know how I survived my own childhood to become the model husband and citizen I am today. I don't know how any of us survived it. Yet we did, and now it was my job to convey to my son some of those childhood survival secrets, so that he too might survive. If he didn't, it would almost certainly be my fault, so there was a great deal of pressure to approach the whole boy-to-man project strategically, with a clear sense of purpose and direction.

I knew what the end product should look like: tall, strong, clean cut, with clear eyes and a winning smile. But how one molded a man from the raw material in that crib was a bit of a mystery.

To begin with, I started a spreadsheet to record various milestones and achievements. Then I added a column for body measurements to keep track of his growth—height, weight, hair length, blood pressure, body temperature, glucose levels, sweat production, tooth loss, etc.—and then added a few more columns to keep track of his food and drink intake, digestive efficiency, behavior, mood, attitude, speed, endurance, pain tolerance, shower frequency, chores, grades, and job potential.

Unfortunately, The Wife made me delete the whole thing before I ever got started. Nobody is fully prepared to be a parent, she told me, so I shouldn't get all wrapped up in the details. I should learn to enjoy the moment, she said, because, hard as it was to believe, his childhood was going to whiz by pretty fast. All that's expected of us as parents is that we do the best we can, she said, because no matter what sort of plan we try to put together, no matter whatever system we try to implement, no matter how much we want him to be one thing or another, that little fucker is going to screw it all up. No matter what we do, he's going to be his own man, she said, and there's only so much we can do about it.

Still, I had to try.

CHAPTER 4

I waited patiently for The Boy to reach an age when I could begin passing my wisdom on to him, preparing him for the challenges ahead. He spent several months gurgling and crying and lying in his crib waving his arms and legs, getting absolutely nowhere. For a long time his main interests seemed to be breasts, food, and sleep, and in that respect he was no different from the average teenager, I suppose. His inability to crawl or walk for some time was convenient as far as getting things done around the house was concerned, but not much else. I could park him in the corner and let him watch me patch the ceiling plaster, or angle him in such a way that he could see how the wires on a new light switch were properly connected, all of which would be valuable information someday. His slow developmental progress and apparent lack of ambition troubled me, of course, but my wife kept reminding me that he was "just a baby," so I was going to have to be patient before I could begin teaching him everything he ought to know in order to survive in this world.

On The Boy's first birthday, I could wait no more. It was time, I felt, to start his training for manhood in earnest. He'd mastered many of the basic infant skills—babbling, crawling, peeling daddy's eyes open during a nap—and was entering what the books called a "skills development phase." His manual dexterity needed some serious work, though, and his vocabulary was pitiful. According to my mother, I was scaling cabinets by the time I was six months old and reading the words on my father's gin bottles by the time I was one, so by this standard my son was already behind. My wife was not concerned about his development, but I could already see that if the little tyke hoped to be a man in a mere seventeen years, we were going to have to pick up the pace.

He was doing fairly well with the so-called "pincer grasp," which is what they call it when kids pick up a Cheerio between their thumb and forefinger. But all a kid has to do in order to master the pincer grasp is pick up a Cheerio off his feeding tray and put it in his mouth. How difficult is that? Not very. Practically any kid can do it.

What I found astonishing is that nowhere in the literature on child development is there a comprehensive program for developing manual dexterity beyond the pincer grasp, and there are no tests or benchmarks available to help parents assess their child's progress in this area. It's as if, once they've mastered the pincer grasp, the assumption is that they will somehow "get it" with respect to other ways in which they might utilize their opposable thumb, and that further training in this area is not required. Just keep dumping Cheerios in front of them, the thinking seems to be, and in no time they'll be tying double half-hitches with spaghetti and tapping out their dessert demands in Morse code. In other words, it's an area of child development crying out for innovation.

Being a man means being able to use your hands to exert some degree of control over the physical world. And, since ninety percent of a man's physical world consists of the land between his house and the hardware store, it made sense to start there. One of the most useful skills a man can have is the ability to thread a small screw into a tiny nut using a variation of the pincer grasp to hold the screw and twist it until the threads catch. A grown man can usually perform this feat of manual dexterity in eight or ten tries, so I figured it would take the kid maybe fifty to a hundred attempts, easily killing an hour or two—all for about thirty-nine cents of hardware.

What I didn't anticipate was that the kid would use the pincer grasp to expertly grab these items, put them in his mouth, and swallow them. He seemed incapable of understanding that the screw should be threaded into the nut, no matter how many times I demonstrated it for him. Each time, I would pick up a screw with my right hand, a nut with my left, and show him—right in front of his face—how the two components fit together. And each time, he would pick up a nut, put it in his mouth and gulp it down. On about the dozenth try, my wife walked in and asked what I was doing. I explained that I was trying to teach him some practical, alternative uses for the highly touted pincer grasp. She looked alarmed. "I hope you're not letting him play with those," she said, pointing at the array of hardware on his dinner tray. "He could choke on those things."

I reassured her that I had just watched The Boy swallow more than ten of the little hex nuts, and he had handled them just fine. I explained the same thing to the on-call doctor at the urgent-care clinic, but both of them acted as if I had done something horribly, stupidly wrong. I explained that our son's motor skills needed some drastic improvement, and that I was simply trying to address a situation that, in all fairness, did not receive nearly enough attention in the medical literature.

"So you decided to let him eat a motor?!" was how my wife put it.

"They were half-inch hex nuts," I explained. "That's smaller than the average Cheerio. I measured."

But there was no convincing them. The doctor said it wasn't necessary to pump The Boy's stomach—that the metal would likely pass through his digestive tract and he'd poop it out—but I got a stern lecture anyway. Apparently, new fathers are just supposed to "know" these things, and that "common sense" should have told me it was a dumb idea.

"At this age, anything smaller than a grape can be a dangerous choking hazard," the doctor explained. I nodded to indicate that I understood what the doctor was saying.

Having learned my lesson, I went to the grocery store and bought a bunch of grapes. I figured I couldn't get in trouble if I started with an actual grape, because then, by definition, no one could claim that the object I allowed my son to play with was *smaller* than a grape, and therefore a choking hazard. To be safe, I bought extra-large grapes— grapes the size of eyeballs.

I had my reasons. Cheerios are easy to pick up because they're round and kind of rough around the edges. It's like picking up a little handle—hardly any challenge at all. A grape, on the other hand, is round and smooth, and the best way to pick them up is with three fingers, not two, thereby extending the skill of the pincer grasp to one more finger—what I call the "Tyrannosaurus grasp." The only problem with grapes is that they're a little too easy to pick up, owing to their massive size compared to a Cheerio or hex nut. To make them more difficult to handle, I took a small bowl of grapes and slathered them in 10W-30 motor oil—the manliness of which no one can question. The side-benefit of this approach, I thought, was that when The Boy reaches the age of seven or eight, and someone in a Halloween haunted house makes him stick his hand in a dark bowl of disgorged "eyeballs," he would not completely freak out because the feel of oil on grapes would, in his subconscious mind, be familiar.

The grapes were a good idea, but it only took The Boy two or three tries to pick one up, and when he popped one in his mouth, he immediately spit it out. The taste of motor oil evidently didn't agree with him, and after that he just started throwing grapes all over the room.

Then I hit on the idea of using canned peaches instead. The ones doused in heavy syrup are extra slippery, and almost impossible for babies to pick up with their chubby little fingers. That's because when a syrup-covered canned peach lies flat on a baby tray, it creates a small amount of suction, adhering the peach to the tray. Since there's no easy way to grasp the peach, even the most industrious baby will spend hours pushing the suctioned slice around on the tray, trying in vain to pick it up. Some kids will try to cheat by trapping the peach against the tray with their mouths and sucking, but that's okay. It doesn't necessarily mean that their hand-eye coordination is lacking, only that they have excellent problem-solving skills. If a child can successfully suck several peach chunks off a baby tray, there's every reason to believe he may have other as-yet-untapped aptitudes as well.

CHAPTER 5

A couple of years went by during which The Boy was entirely unreceptive to my teaching. Sure, I tried to show him things, but no matter how many times I yelled at him, "No! That's not the way to do it!," he would just laugh at me and go about doing it his way.

So, frankly, I gave up. Anytime he started to get fussy, I'd tell him to go bug his mother. If she told him to go bug me, I'd give him a gummy worm, which made him happy, because at that stage in his life he was basically like a puppy, albeit one that refused to obey. Several times I tried explaining to him that I was waiting for him to say or do something interesting, but he didn't care. Usually he just stuck his tongue out at me and ran away.

Somewhere around the age of three, however, The Boy brought a game of Candyland out of the closet and set the box on the coffee table in front of me. He said he wanted to learn how to play it, and would I teach him? It was a rainy Saturday, one of those drippy, do-nothing days that makes playing Candyland with your kid sound like a good idea. I warned The Boy that I was a Candyland master in my day, so he shouldn't expect to win any of the first ten or twenty games. Undeterred, he insisted that we play. Now.

The Boy was learning a lot at that age, mostly because he asked a lot of questions, most of which began with the word "why." "Why" questions are particularly difficult for me because I often have no idea why things happen the way they do, or why people do the things they do. But in my limited experience, these are also the sorts of things children are interested in and won't shut up about. No one ever says it out loud, but sometimes the scariest thing in the world is a child with a question.

So we were playing Candyland that rainy afternoon when The Boy suddenly moved his piece from the Peppermint Forest all the way up to the Lollypop Woods, even though the card he had chosen from the deck only allowed him to move forward to the nearest purple square.

In order to teach my son the lesson that games have rules, and rules must be obeyed, I, the responsible father, said, "You can't do that. That's cheating."

"What's cheating?" The Boy asked.

"Cheating is breaking the rules," I answered. "Cheating is what bad boys do. Good boys follow the rules. You want to be a good boy, don't you?"

The Boy considered the question, then asked, "Why?, daddy. Why should I be a good boy?"

I sensed a trap. I knew what I was *supposed* to say in this situation: that it is better to be good than bad, because good is better than bad, and good people live better lives than bad people, and even if they don't, goodness is a generally helpful quality for a human being to have. But I also know that the world beyond the perimeter of the Candyland game board does not necessarily reinforce this message. Goodness is great and all, but these days it's all about competing in the cutthroat jungle of the global marketplace, where survival depends on being an aggressive, shrewd, relentless warrior, preferably one who is handsomely groomed and exceedingly well-dressed. The winners of this game—CEOs, investment bankers, lawyers, politicians, lobbyists—are all people who gleefully cheat the system and exploit every possible legal and ethical loophole to ensure that they come out on top. They are people, in other words, who do not care about the rules of the game, or why they should obey them. In fact, they believe it is "smart" to ignore the rules, because if you can just pick up your piece and declare yourself "King Candy," why shouldn't you? Why wouldn't you? After all, if these people had to be conscientious and ethical while they were crushing their competitors to make millions, the game would be that much harder to play.

I knew I was supposed to say something about the virtue of good sportsmanship, and how it doesn't matter whether you win or lose—it only matters that you work hard, try your best, and follow the rules, even if you happen to fail in a rather spectacular and humiliating way that haunts you for the rest of your life.

So that's what I told him. He could learn later that playing by the rules is for suckers, and that lots of bad people live really well by breaking them.

The news that he had to move his piece all the way back to the Peppermint Forest was not received very well. And, after he'd lost the first eight or nine games, The Boy was ready to quit.

A good parent recognizes when their child's spirit is being crushed, and the better ones try to do something about it. I put myself in the latter camp, so, during the next game, as The Boy was falling behind yet again, I decided it was time to let him win. So, pretending that the card deck needed to be re-shuffled, I thumbed through it, found the Snow Queen, and snuck her out of the deck and hid her in the palm of my hand.

For those who don't remember their Candyland, the Snow Queen card is the one that can magically launch you from the bottom of the board to the top, just a few squares away from King Candy. No matter how far behind you are, if you draw the Snow Queen, you're probably going to win. My plan was to save the Snow Queen for a strategic moment in the game when The Boy thought he was going to lose again, then sneak her onto the top of the deck so that The Boy would pick her up on his turn, launching him to the top of the board, eventually allowing him to beat me. As life lessons go, I thought, this would be a good one: because it would show The Boy that no matter how hopeless the situation is, there's always the possibility of drawing the Snow Queen. The game is never truly lost until your opponent's piece lands on the final square and he hollers for joy, does that little dance, and pokes you in the ribs.

I didn't think The Boy was watching, but when I palmed the Snow Queen out of the deck and secreted it under the table, The Boy asked, "What did you do there?"

"What do you mean?" I said.

"You took a card out of the deck," The Boy said. "Can you do that? Is that part of the rules?"

"I did not take a card out of the deck," I lied.

"I saw you!" The Boy cried. "You took it right out of the middle and put it in your lap," he said, looking under the table.

"I did no such thing," I protested.

"Then what's under your hand?" The Boy said, peering under the table.

"My leg," I said.

"Between your hand and your leg," The Boy clarified.

I tried sliding the card in my right hand up my leg and into my left hand without The Boy seeing, then showed him my right hand, which was empty.

"You just put the card in your other hand," The Boy said, wise to my trick. "Let's see it."

Sheepishly, I showed him the Snow Queen card and started trying to explain. But he wouldn't listen.

"That's cheating!" The Boy screamed. "Here you are talking to me about how I have to follow the rules, and you're the one who is cheating!"

I tried to explain that I wasn't cheating—that, if anything, what I was doing was the opposite of cheating.

"Mom, dad's cheating!!" The Boy yelled. My wife, who was in the kitchen, came out to see what all the fuss was about.

"Look, mom, he took the Snow Queen card for himself so that he could use it to win if I got too far ahead."

I gave my wife my "this is not what you think" look, which she took to be my "I'm guilty as hell" look.

"That's pathetic," my wife said. "Do you have to be so competitive? Would it really bruise your ego if The Boy won a game or two?"

"No wonder I always lose," The Boy pouted. "How can I win if I'm playing against a cheating cheater?"

"Really dear, The Boy has a point," my wife chimed in. "Think about what kind of example you're setting. He watches you very closely, you know, and wants to copy everything you do."

Under the pressure of these false accusations, I pleaded my case by explaining that I wasn't cheating for myself—I had taken the card out of the deck to make sure The Boy won a game. "Intention is everything in the law," I said, "and my intention was to let him win."

"That's even worse!" The Boy cried. "That just means you think I'm so bad at Candyland that I can't beat you."

"Statistics would seem to bear that out," I said.

"Well, I think you should both take a break," my wife advised. "I just took some chocolate-chip cookies out of the oven. Somebody needs to eat them while they're warm."

It may come as no surprise that I never won a game of Candyland again. Not because we didn't play; on the contrary, we played hundreds of games, maybe even thousands. And I lost every last one of them. Why? Because before every game, The Boy made a point of sneaking The Snow Queen out of the deck, and, at the most strategic possible moment, he would play it and leap ahead, ensuring his victory. The worst part is, there was nothing I could do about it. I never actually saw him steal the Snow Queen, and even if I did, who was I to accuse him of cheating? My job now was to be the Washington Generals to his Harlem Globetrotters, and lose graciously every time, until the end of time.

CHAPTER 6

As The Boy grew, one of my main frustrations was arguing with my beloved over which toys were appropriate for a growing young man to play with. Personally, I did not think it was necessary to invest in all kinds of expensive electronic entertainment devices, because a boy can turn anything into a toy. In fact, they often prefer to amuse themselves with everyday objects around the house, especially ones that make a lot of noise or shatter when thrown to the ground.

As every parent soon learns, however, the toy boys like to play with most is a gun. Why? Because guns are fun. You point them at things, pull the trigger, and suddenly there's a loud boom and the thing you are pointing at either explodes, disappears, or dies. What could be more fun than that?

It horrified my wife that whenever our son would eat a graham cracker, he would bite out a corner, grip the graham cracker like a German Luger, and start firing. Or, when he was in the yard, he would pick up a stick, snap off a branch, grip it, and start spraying the yard with imaginary bullets. If he didn't have an object to fashion into a gun, he would simply use his hand. The opposable human thumb makes an excellent firing pin, and an index finger is very easy to point, so very little instruction is necessary. With my son, I didn't even have to teach him how to make gunshot sounds with his mouth; it came naturally. About the only assistance I provided was to point out that when a real gun is fired, the recoil kicks the barrel back and up, a motion that's easy to imitate and adds a satisfying sense of verisimilitude whenever a finger-weapon is fired.

Unfortunately, whenever our son pointed his finger at his mother's head and started making machine-gun noises with his tongue and teeth, she would scold him. "Don't point that thing at me," she would say.

"It's not loaded," I would remind her.

"Oh yes it is," she would reply.

"No, it isn't" I would insist. "In fact, as deadly weapons go, the finger-pistol is about as safe as it gets."

"You couldn't be more wrong," my wife would argue. "It is loaded—loaded with *metaphor*."

For the uninitiated, a metaphor is something that stands for something else, which means that, by definition, it is not the thing it seems to be—a confusing semantic sleight-of-hand that, as far as I can tell, can only be explained by a combination of highly complex wave-particle quantum physics and whatever goes on inside a woman's mind. Put them together and you have a metaphor.

"When you allow him to point his finger at me that way and make those noises, you're allowing him to symbolically eliminate me," she would say. "It is an unacceptable form of aggression. It also implies that we, as parents, embrace this country's reprehensible gun culture, and encourage the use of firearms—rather than reason and judgment and communication—to solve our problems. It also suggests to me that even at this young age, our son has already begun to glorify guns, and I will not have my son pining for an NRA membership before he is in kindergarten. As far as I'm concerned, that pow-pow finger-thing is what's wrong with this whole country."

Being a man, I am of course unequipped to argue in the ethereal realm of symbolism and metaphor, so I don't. Whenever the metaphorical monster rears its ugly head, I simply say, "Anything you say, dear," and let it go. Why? Because I know, deep in my heart, that she can rant and rail and object all she wants, but there is no way she is going to prevent the boys of America from using their fingers, or whatever else is handy, to make a gun.

That said, we did come to a sort of compromise on other household items that might double as toys, organized by the level of parental supervision required. The list looked something like this:

Parental supervision unnecessary: toilet paper roll, saucepan, wooden spoon, plastic lid, cardboard box, blanket, pillow, washcloth, sponge, tennis ball, hockey puck, baseball, gym weights, tire gauge, tire iron, car keys, hammer, dog leash, toilet-bowl brush, shaving cream, mother's purse.

Parental supervision suggested: bottle openers, beer cans, bottle caps, jewelry, DVD player, small power tools, umbrella, vacuum cleaner, mild solvents, toaster, microwave, electric guitar, golf clubs, pocket knife, BB gun, road salt.

Parental supervision required: Kitchen knives, handgun, rat poison, lighter, matches, explosives of any kind, road flares, nail gun, chainsaw, ice pick, most types of acid, pitchfork, crossbow, lawnmower, ice auger, barbed wire, bolt cutter, pneumatic drill.

All of these items, when used improperly, can of course become metaphors for something else. But with the correct level of parental supervision and a strict "no moms in the play area" policy, the danger of this happening can be minimized.

CHAPTER 7

Somewhere around the age of four, I can't remember exactly when, The Boy started whining that he was lonely and wanted a brother or sister to "play with." Friends of ours were popping out babies right and left, procreating at a frightening rate, populating the neighborhood with little screamers on plastic tricycles. It would have been a good time to be in the baby business. Every week there was a shower or a birthday party. My wife was spending hundreds of dollars a month on presents, and a friend of mine who owned a bouncy-castle rental franchise told me business had never been better. My guess is that The Boy looked around and saw he was the only kid in the neighborhood who didn't have a sibling—and, kids being the selfish little weasels they are, he thought he was getting gypped.

I get it. From a four-year-old's perspective, a younger brother or sister seems like a good idea. It's something they can play with and boss around. Having a younger sibling around also means there's someone to blame when trouble strikes. And depending on the age gap, the elder sibling can usually maintain their advantage in the areas of strength and intelligence for a decade or more.

The problem is, four-year-olds don't bother to think these things through. They only see the benefit, and fail to weigh the cost. For instance, The Boy thought having a younger sister would be fun, but what he failed to consider were the hundreds of ways in which having a younger sister would make his life a living hell. My wife and I had decided long before that The Boy was going to be an only child, because neither one of us wanted to risk the possibility of saddling him with a younger sister. Both of us had suffered childhoods trapped in houses with a younger sister, and neither of us was willing to inflict that kind of pain and torment on our own child.

I didn't know quite how to explain all of this to The Boy, but I felt I had to try. So, one afternoon, I sat him down next to his boo-boo bear and said: "Son, I know you think you want a brother or sister, but that's never going to happen, and here's why: In economics, there's a principle called 'opportunity cost.' Essentially, it means that every time you make a decision, there is a hidden cost in the alternative decision you choose not to make. If your mother and I were to make you a baby toy-friend, for instance, that would be an irreversible decision whose 'cost' would be all the benefits you would lose by suddenly having a younger brother or sister around. How would that work?, you ask. Well, for one thing, you'd have to share all your toys. Do you want that? Of course not. For another thing, you'd have to watch the movies and television shows they want to watch, and play the games they want to play. Does that sound like fun? No, it doesn't. You'd also have to split all your food and desserts with them, and when you outgrow your favorite pajamas, they'd get to wear them. Does that sound fair? Heck no. And let's say you wanted to play a little game of "chase the pirate" with me. Would I be able to? No, because your little brother or sister would be crying and needing their diaper changed. There would be no time for you. Basically, you'd be on your own. So you see, having a younger brother or sister really means that you would be deprived of all the great things about being an only child."

I don't know how I could have put it any plainer. But The Boy did not look convinced. He just looked at me with that weird blank stare that sometimes made me think he was autistic. So, just to make sure he understood what I was saying, I broke it down even further for him: "You also need to be aware of the concept of risk and reward," I explained. "As we go through life, we make decisions by weighing the risks and rewards, to determine if the risk of doing something is worth the reward. If it isn't, it's not a good decision. If we're analyzing the decision to have a young sibling, for instance, there is inherent risk right out of the gate. If your mother and I decided to have another child, there would be a fifty-fifty chance of it being a boy or girl. If it was a boy, that'd be fine. But—and here's the part you need to pay attention to—there's also a fifty percent chance that it would be a girl, and that's a risk your mother and I aren't willing to take. The danger of getting a girl is just too high, and trust me, having a younger sister is unrewarding in the extreme. You want to know what the reward for having a younger sister is? First, they're big crybabies. They cry over everything, and they spend most of their time pointing out all the ways in which life isn't fair to them. Then they cry about it. Parents hate crying, so they give little sisters whatever they want. You, as a boy, can try crying like that, but it won't work. No matter how hard you try, you can never match the gush of tears or volume of hysteria a little girl can produce. And they can do it anywhere, anytime, at the flip of a switch. Second, little girls are expensive. You think you've got a lot of toys? That's nothing compared to all the stuffed animals and dolls and castles and unicorns and horses and little elf clothes and tiny tea sets and balls and bracelets and craft kits and other crap that little girls require. You can make do with a few nerf guns and some Lego. But look around. A little girl needs to have a miniature version of the entire world in her room. And it doesn't stop there. They also need a miniature version of two or three fantasy worlds, which include the aforementioned unicorns as well as an entire army of fairies, gnomes, witches, goblins, and sprites. It's ridiculous. And all of that stuff costs money—money that could be going to your college savings fund or into a well-diversified stock portfolio. Trust me, bringing a girl into this house is a one-way ticket to poverty for all of us. Little girls are also fascist do-gooders and tattletails. That means they watch everything you do, and if you break a single rule or step out of line in any way, they run right to your parents and tell on you. It's like having a video camera strapped to your back. You can't get away with anything. Leave the cap off the toothpaste and she'll tell. Miss the toilet when you're peeing and she'll tell. Steal a cookie out of the cookie jar and your ass is fried. And it just gets worse as you get older. The question you have to ask yourself is: Do you want to spend your whole life looking over your shoulder to see if your little sister is spying on you? I'll answer that for you: No, you don't! Because I guarantee you she will. The worst part is that little sisters aren't just annoying, they're devious. What do I mean by that? Well, they watch your every move, as I said, but in reality what happens is that they don't tell your parents *everything* you've done wrong. No, they keep some information to themselves, and use it against you whenever they want something. So let's say one day you catch her doing something she isn't supposed to be doing, like squirting whipped cream into her mouth straight from the can. Can you get her back by tattling on her? No, you can't. Because she knows something worse about you, and if you tattle, she will threaten to expose the even worse thing you've done. It's called blackmail, and little sisters are very good at it—much better than you could ever be. That's why, for your own good, you're not going to have a sibling. The chances are simply too high that it might turn out to be a girl, and we can't have that. You understand that now, don't you?"

Again with that autistic stare. But it was a good talk, and it had to be said. Otherwise, he'd go through life thinking that somehow he was missing something. I wanted him to know that he wasn't really missing anything—that, in reality, he was dodging a bullet. The weird thing is that when I phrased it like that to him—in terms of firearms—he perked up instantly.

"You mean like a superpower?" he said, excited.

"Exactly," I replied—and we never spoke about it again.

CHAPTER 8

Among other things, being a modern father means taking responsibility for certain daily rituals that, in another time and place, were traditionally performed by women. Rather than resist this inevitable shift toward modernity, I chose to think of it as an opportunity to teach my son some lessons that my forebears may have neglected, simply because they were not in charge of bath time.

Bath time is a particularly rich environment for instruction, because it involves one of the essential elements of nature—water—and all kinds of visual aids. The Boy loved bath time. What he seemed to like best about it was the opportunity to splash water everywhere while shrieking at the top of his lungs and forcing rubber animals to engage in violent and squeaky duels to the death. I knew better, of course. I knew that when my progeny was engaging in this type of behavior, he wasn't just splashing water and making noise: he was learning valuable lessons about the physics of water and the acoustic limitations of the average American bathroom.

For many months, our bathing ritual included spirited battles between Mr. Duckie and Professor Penguin, followed by a blitz attack from SoapZilla, which was thwarted by mild-mannered Wally the Washcloth—who, when rubbed on human skin, turned into Super Scrub, a washcloth so powerful that he could exfoliate several layers of skin in one powerful swipe.

Inevitably, however, the shout would come—"Hey, keep it down in there!"—and The Boy and I would have to revert to taking a simple bath. Apparently, the water from the bathtub was also dripping down the walls and ruining the kitchen ceiling.

One day, I decided to take the necessary measures to both rectify the situation and prolong bath time as long as possible.

First, I obtained several-hundred square feet of plastic sheeting from the hardware store, which I used to cover the walls and floor before bath time began. Empirical evidence suggested that very little of the water in the bathtub made it down the drain in the bathtub itself, so I installed a second drain near the center of the room, and surrounded the tub with drain tile and a sump pump. I also knew that, during an especially good bath, the bathtub often needs to be refilled several times, which taxed the capacity of our water heater. To solve this problem, I installed a second water heater as a backup—and, to save money, negotiated with our water-utility company to divert more treated wastewater to our house in the evening, rather than use precious well water from the local aquifer. To prevent my own clothes from being soaked every night, I invested in a pair of waterproof dungarees and some hip waders. Swim goggles were also necessary, of course, along with rubber gloves and a snorkel.

This setup solved almost all of our problems, transforming bath time into one of the most educational parts of the day. To new parents struggling with this very problem, I can only say that yes, bath time can be challenging—but with the proper equipment, it doesn't have to be.

CHAPTER 9

Although bath time can be a lot of fun, eventually kids need to learn how to swim. Fortunately, the proper time to teach a child how to swim is about the same time that bath time stops being so much fun.

Most parents in our acquaintance choose to outsource this particular duty to a team of teenage girls at the community pool. There, the moms gather in the bleachers to drink coffee and chat while these slim-legged, smooth-skinned debutantes instruct their babies to blow bubbles and churn the water into foam with their chubby little feet. How anyone ever learns to swim this way, I don't know. But week after week they go, seemingly pleased with the glacial progress their kids are making toward the day when they might not drown in six inches of water. It seems to me, however, that the conventional suburban swim class is an inefficient, ineffective, and fairly expensive way to teach a kid to swim. There has to be a better way, I thought, and when The Boy was ready to learn, I set out to find it.

I will admit up front that I had ulterior motives. Having witnessed the amount of time and money people were spending on swimming lessons, I figured that if I could devise a cheaper, more efficient way of teaching kids how to swim, I could single-handedly upend the whole kiddie swim-class business model. It was a market ripe for disruption, and I saw an opportunity. Knowing how to swim is something every kid needs to learn, so—like weddings and funerals—it's a market that continuously renews itself with paying customers. And, as far as I could tell, no one had developed anything new in the area of swim instruction for about fifty years, so it was also a market ripe for innovation.

My own father taught me how to swim the way they did it before teenage girls needed summer jobs. Which is to say, he threw me into a lake and let my survival instincts kick in. Sink or swim, that was his philosophy. "If you drowned, it was just one less mouth to feed," he once explained to me as we were waiting in line for a hamburger. Then he added, "Now that you're a teenager, and eating us out of house and home, I see the error of my ways: I shouldn't have tossed you in the water so close to shore."

The virtue of my father's sink-or-swim strategy was its brutal efficiency. It taught me how to swim in about twenty seconds. From a business standpoint, unfortunately, that's far too efficient. I knew that even if I could teach kids how to swim in twenty seconds, no one would pay for it. That's one of the ironies of capitalism. People will pay hundreds of dollars to send their kids to swim classes that might teach them how to tread water in a year or two. Why? Because if it takes a long time, people feel like they're getting something for their money. It never occurs to them that the instructors might be incompetent and the process flawed. But if I charged a hundred dollars for twenty seconds of brutally efficient but highly effective swim instruction, they'd think they were getting ripped off. There were also insurance issues to consider for those fortunate few who might actually sink. So, even though I knew it was technically possible to whittle years of gentle swim instruction down to a few terrifying seconds, the practicalities of building a business around that model required me to stretch out the process. All I had to do, after all, was make my method more efficient and cheaper than the current method. It didn't have to be perfect, it just had to be better.

The Boy was about five years old when I started teaching him how to swim. He wasn't very enthusiastic about the idea, what with his obsessive viewing of "Shark Week," but I managed to convince him that there were no sharks in the lake where we were going, only tiger muskies and northern pike. The biggest piece of a person's body these fish could eat was a toe or a foot, I explained, and he took that to mean that the water where we were going was only slightly less deadly than lunchtime at the Great Barrier Reef.

In reality, the lake I had chosen was a remote, relatively small blob of water where motorboats weren't allowed and not many people fished. We were entering the experimental phase of my swim coaching, and I didn't need a bunch of strangers around second-guessing my teaching methods.

"If I die, what will you say to mom?" The Boy asked on the way to the lake.

"You're not going to die," I reassured him. "But if you do die, I will simply explain to her that you turned out to be a lousy swimmer."

"What if I get attacked by a muskie?" he asked.

"Muskies are just like sharks," I explained. "If one attacks you, all you have to do is punch it in the nose."

"Where's a muskie's nose?"

"Okay, you got me there," I said. "They don't really have noses, so I guess you just bang them on the head."

"Have you ever been attacked by a muskie?" The Boy asked.

"No."

"Then aren't you due?"

"What do you mean?"

"Well, you're an old man, so if you've gone this long in life without getting attacked by a muskie, it must mean you're due—that you're going to get attacked soon."

"Getting attacked by a muskie is not inevitable," I explained. "Heck, there are people who spend half their lives *looking* for muskies and never see them."

"But that doesn't mean you're not going to get attacked."

"Well, it could happen," I conceded. "But it's unlikely."

The Boy thought about this for a few seconds. "Still, I'd be worried if I was you," he said. "You never know when your luck is going to run out."

I parked the car in a spot well away from the main road, near an old fishing dock that my brother and I used to frequent. I picked this particular place to start our lessons because the water was relatively shallow, and it was secluded enough that a modest amount of yelling and screaming would likely go unnoticed. My teaching aids on this occasion were a long piece of nylon rope, a pair of arm floats, and pellet gun.

We walked down to the edge of the water and then out along the dock to the platform where my friends and I used to fish. Once, my buddy Charles caught a large catfish off this dock, but it swallowed the hook so far down that we couldn't get it out. Charles thought we should just cut the line and throw the fish back, but I thought that was cruel, because the fish had just swallowed a hook and would probably suffer a horrible, agonizing death, writhing in the muck at the bottom of the lake. Charles said the fish's stomach juices would dissolve the hook, but I didn't believe him. I thought that if we threw the fish back, he would die. An old, bearded guy at the end of the dock heard us arguing and offered to buy the fish from us for a dollar. Problem solved. I don't know what we would have decided to do if that man hadn't bought our fish, but it taught me that the invisible hand of the marketplace sometimes works in mysterious ways.

At the end of the dock, I instructed The Boy to stand still and raise his arms while I tied one end of the nylon rope around his waist. I explained to The Boy that this was a precaution—that this was going to be his lifeline, so whatever happened, he was safe. For an extra measure of security, I blew up the arm floats and slid them in place above the elbow on his small, white limbs. These would keep him afloat even if he did nothing, I explained, which was a damn sight more considerate than anything my father ever did for me. I did not explain that I was going to hurl him over the railing and into the water, but he's a smart boy, so he figured it out pretty quickly.

"You're not going to just toss me in the water, are you?" he asked.

"You make it sound like that's a bad thing," I said.

"But I don't know how to swim," he said.

"That's why we're here," I replied. "And it's why we've outfitted you with so much state-of-the-art safety equipment."

"Could you warn me before you do it?" The Boy said. "You know, so I can prepare."

"Prepare? Prepare for what?"

"In case I die."

"You're not going to die," I reassured him. "Not today, anyway."

With that, I grabbed him around his ribcage, hoisted him up over the railing, and tossed him into the water. The splash was huge. He went underwater for a few seconds, then bobbed to the surface, coughing, with his arms stretched out to his side.

"You okay?" I asked.

"Yeah, I just swallowed a little water," he said, coughing the last bit up.

"First lesson: Hold your breath whenever you go into the water," I said. He was only a few feet from the dock, so I reached down and pushed him away. Slowly, he floated away from the dock, motionless and silent, out into open water.

"Move your arms back and forth," I shouted.

The Boy waved his arms back and forth, but all it did was make splashing sounds.

"Try scooping the water with your hands," I suggested.

"I can't," The Boy said. "I've got these balloons on my arms."

"No problem," I said, and grabbed the pellet gun.

Before you go getting all judgmental on me, know that I wasn't shooting some bargain-basement BB spitter. This was a Walther CP99 BB Pistol with a twelve-gram, handle-loaded CO_2 cartridge based on the very model that our boys in the Special Forces use overseas. I knew for a fact that I could fire that weapon accurately up to fifty feet, and The Boy was only thirty feet away from me, tops. So I took aim at the float attached to his left arm and fired. The BB hit its intended target with a soft pop, and the float slowly started to deflate. Then I fired at the float on the other arm. I missed on the first try, but my aim was true on the second attempt, and the float on his right arm began to deflate.

"Hey, what are you doing?" The Boy asked.

"Teaching you how to swim," I said. "It's now or never." "I'm sinking," The Boy said.

"You're sinking slowly," I said. "Trust me, when my dad taught me how to swim, I was sinking a lot faster than you are right now."

"What should I do?" The Boy asked, as he began thrashing his arms around. As his shoulder sunk below the surface of the water, he tried to keep his chin above the water line. He did not look pleased.

"That's it, keep your head above water," I said. But even as I said it, water began to swallow The Boy's neck and chin, until only his nose and part of his forehead were visible. Just before his nose was about to go under, I tugged on the nylon line and brought him back to the surface.

"Kick your feet and try to get your body horizontal," I suggested. "You can't swim very far with your feet dangling down like that."

Scared his head might go underwater for good the next time, The Boy started whirling his arms and legs with an impressive amount of fury and determination. It looked like some sort of insane water ballet, or like he was being shocked with five-thousand volts of electricity, depending on whether you think watching someone thrash around in the water is art or torture. He slapped at the water with his arms and kicked at the water like it was attacking his feet and he had to fight back. He gurgled and screamed. He cried and yelled. I made a mental note that this particular approach to swim training was turning out to be quite noisy, and it did not escape me that someone watching it might mistake what I was doing for criminal negligence of some sort, even though the rope in my hand was tested up to five-hundred pounds, so, technically speaking, The Boy's safety line was over-engineered by a factor of ten.

Then, in a manner as miraculous as it was clumsy, The Boy somehow began clawing at the water and making some forward headway, albeit slowly. Away from the dock he sort-of swam, toward the center of the lake. He wasn't sinking anymore, in any case, and seemed determined to keep on going.

I figured I'd let him swim for a while and refine his technique, then pull him back with the rope attached to his waist. I watched as he progressed farther and farther away from the dock. I fed the line out gradually as he went, gauging his distance by the length of the rope, which was rapidly coming to an end. When the rope ran out, I decided it was time to pull him back. I tugged on the line and felt it go taught, then began reeling him in, precisely as if he were a fish.

Then I suddenly felt the line go slack. Alarmed, I kept pulling on the line, but there was no resistance. After a few seconds, I found myself holding the end of the line in my hands, while The Boy continued to move away from the dock toward the center of the lake.

I knew what I had to do—I had to jump in immediately and rescue him. But just as I was about to dive into the water, I thought about what my son had said about the fact that I had never been attacked by a muskie in my entire life. For a split second I hesitated, suddenly frightened by the thought that this could be the moment—the moment when one of those razor-toothed monsters rose up from the muck and engulfed my foot in its mouth, preventing me from reaching my son, who—in that scenario—was sure to drown.

I looked out and saw that The Boy was struggling. He had stopped moving forward, and I could tell that he was disoriented and starting to sink. By this time he was about fifty yards from the dock—so far that I feared I could not reach him in time if he went under. So, instead of jumping in the water to save him, I got a better idea.

"Muskie!" I yelled. "Watch out for that muskie!"

I could see that The Boy had heard me, because he turned his head toward my voice.

"A muskie is coming to eat you!" I yelled, pointing at the imaginary fish. "Get out of the water!"

I could see from the terror in The Boy's eyes that he had heard me.

"It's a monster!" I shouted. "Biggest fish I've ever seen! Teeth like daggers! Get out now!"

Suddenly, with a sense of purpose and determination I had never seen before, The Boy aimed his little body toward the dock where I was standing and began to swim. As he moved toward me, his strokes got longer and more self-assured. He was no longer doing some improvisational version of the dog-paddle, he was kicking his legs like a frog and doing a fair facsimile of the American crawl. He was swimming fairly well, in fact, gaining confidence with each stroke. Smartly, he did not try to reach the dock and climb up; he swam to the tiny beach on the side of the dock and, once he touched land, crawled up out of the water on his hands and knees, gasping for breath.

I hopped down off the dock to greet him. As he kneeled in the sand, the deflated floats still attached to his arms, I patted him on the back and congratulated him. Then I looked at my watch. The entire episode had taken only four minutes and twenty-two seconds.

So yes, I had taught my son how to swim, and my entrepreneurial method of doing it had been a resounding success. But it had still been far too efficient to build a business around. On the way home, while The Boy shivered in the passenger's seat and ate a Twix bar to get his blood sugar back up, I thought about how I might break the events of the day into a four-week class rather than a four-minute lesson. I also thought about how, if I franchised the idea, I'd have to train an army of teenagers to shoot a pellet gun accurately. There were other logistical details to work out as well, such as how to tie a knot that releases at just the right moment. (I still didn't know how that had happened), or what to do if some smart-alecky kid didn't actually believe a muskie was about to eat him.

All in all, though, it was a successful day. Both my son and I learned something, though we both agreed that his mother did not need to know anything about our day. We went swimming, and we both survived—that's all that mattered. Everything else was just details.

CHAPTER 10

When my son was young, one of the most difficult things I had to deal with was his constant flow of tears. He cried about everything. My wife insisted that his crying jags were perfectly normal, and that our job as parents was to either comfort him or identify the unfulfilled need that precipitated the faucet-fest, depending on what was appropriate for the situation. Only occasionally is the crying of a child connected to a broken bone or a massive loss of blood, so over-reacting to a flood of tears is not what a responsible parent is supposed to do.

Underreacting is evidently frowned upon as well. When your kid cries about everything—the color of his food, the temperature of the room, the amount of oxygen in the air—it doesn't take long to grow some emotional scar tissue around the part of the heart that is supposed to give a shit about what's upsetting him so much.

Early on, however, I hit on the rather brilliant idea (I thought) of turning my son's tear production into a science project. From age one to eighteen, I began collecting my son's tears with an eyedropper and keeping them in a sealed Mason jar. I figured it would be instructive for him to see, when he was eighteen, the volume of tears he had produced during his childhood. In the interest of science, I considered cataloguing the total output of all his bodily functions, but a bout of stomach flu when The Boy was five forced me to abandon this phase of the project.

But the tears I kept.

It doesn't spoil any of the story to reveal that, when my son was eighteen years old, he had filled one-and-a-half Mason jars full of tears—for a total of roughly three cups.

From a scientific standpoint, however, this measurement was meaningless all by itself. So at the same time I began collecting my son's tears, I also began collecting my wife's tears every time she cried. For the purposes of my experiment, her tears acted as control data against which our son's tear production could be compared.

When our son turned eighteen, I compared the volume of tears he had shed to the volume of tears I had collected from her. After measuring her tears three times to make sure my readings were accurate, it turned out that over the course of our son's childhood, my wife had filled two-and-a-half fifty-gallon trash barrels with her tears—for a grand total of 124.6 gallons.

Admittedly, I was stunned. I knew there was an uptick in her tear production during the years when The Boy was taking violin lessons, but I had no idea the total would be that impressive. My guess was eighty to ninety gallons, tops.

CHAPTER 11

My wife did not find the big "reveal" on my tear experiment as fascinating or informative as I did. Her reaction was something along the lines of, "Tell me something I don't know." Which, of course, was the point—because how would anyone know the total volume of their tears over a period of time without measuring them?

The ultimate conclusion I have come to is that it is more important for men than women to quantify things. Certainly, in our son's early years, my wife was obsessed with making sure that our son met certain developmental milestones such as learning to walk, talk, and read. But it seemed to me that the milestones she was interested in weren't very important, because almost every kid in the universe learns all of these things by the time they're five. And when it came to comparing boys and girls, the experts seem to be in universal agreement that girls are smarter, better, faster learners than boys in virtually every area of childhood development.

Curiously, the literature is woefully lacking when it comes to developmental landmarks that mean anything to a growing boy. Using conventional benchmarks, it is impossible to determine whether a boy is thriving or not. Just because a boy does not know how to put his hair in pigtails by the age of four, or how to sell cookies by the age of seven, does not mean that he is "slow," it just means that he has other interests and priorities.

In order to fill this gaping hole in the literature, I devised my own checklist of watershed moments that every parent should be aware of and celebrate when their son achieves them:

Boyhood Development Checklist:
Directions: Record the date of each event when it happens, and be aware that every boy achieves these important milestones in a different order. Taking the first event as an example: some boys will pee in your face when they are infants, others may wait until they are four or

five, when it is less humorous for the parent, but exponentially more hilarious for the child.

—The first time he pees in your face and laughs.
—The first time he pukes on your leg and laughs.
—The first time he takes a header off the bed.
—The first time he swallows a penny.
—The first time he swallows a nickel.
—The first time he shoves a piece of Lego up his nose.
—The first time he smears dog poop all over himself.
—The first time he eats a piece of dog poop.
—The first time the paramedics pump his stomach.
—The first time he runs into traffic.
—The last time he runs into traffic.
—The first time he attempts to ride the dog like a horse.
—The first time he shoots someone else in the eye.
—The first time he breaks something valuable.
—The first time he gets in a fight.
—The first time he soaks a shirt in his own blood.
—The first time he cuts his foot open on a piece of glass.
—The first time the doctor says, "It's only a slight concussion."
—The first time he "accidentally" kills something.
—The first time he steals money from his mother's purse.
—The first time he lies to your face.
—The first time he denies lying to your face when accused.
—The first time he denies lying even though the proof is irrefutable.
—The first time he gives you the finger.
—The first time he crashes your car.
—The first time he gets a girl pregnant.
—The first time he asks you to bail him out of jail.

Astute parents may notice that this list of milestones differs considerably from the sort of list one usually encounters. For one thing, it's longer. For another, it does not include the words "inappropriate" or "unacceptable." That's because almost everything boys do when they are learning to be a man is inappropriate and unacceptable to the female half of the population, so including those words would be redundant.

The truth that nobody wants to admit is that transforming a young boy into a good man is an ugly process. The old saying, "You don't want to see how the sausage is made," applies here, because sausage-making is a twinkling ballet compared to the process of molding a boy into a man. As any decent man will tell you, the path he followed to become a respectable guy was full of disgusting acts of brainless nonsense, all kinds of thoughtless and stupid hijinks, several episodes of epically horrible judgment, and not a few instances of seemingly brilliant ideas that, in retrospect, could have got someone killed.

Simply put: Raising a boy is a nasty, brutish business. And yet it must be done, because the alternative is allowing them to grow up without experiencing a true, all-American childhood—a calamity that creates men who move to France to study art, or guys who don't know a pickup truck from a pickup line. Men, in other words, who don't quite know how to be men, and who spend the better part of their twenties and thirties trying to figure out what they should have learned by the time they were thirteen.

Tragically, some men *never* learn these vital lessons, and spend their whole lives wondering what they missed, and why regular guys don't invite them over to play poker or watch the game on Sunday. It's quite sad. Anyone married to one of these unfortunate un-men has seen the tears. Because that's what un-men do: they cry over stuff that regular guys don't think twice about, because regular guys cried buckets about it when they were, oh, eight years old. Grown men know how to choke their feelings down into a hot ball of anger that burns in their sternum, fueling their rage and motivating them to drink and yell until the police arrive. Such skills cannot be learned in a book or a classroom; they must be learned in the real world, where mistakes are made and regrets accumulated. True knowledge is derived from experience, and this is the knowledge boys crave—the sort of knowledge that can only be learned outside, with friends, while doing something illegal, immoral, or both.

CHAPTER 12

Much of what we think of as "raising a boy" is really trying to figure out how to curb their natural interests and inclinations in order to keep them alive. The path to that goal often leads in strange directions, however, and the logic that produces the parents' desired outcome is often counterintuitive. For instance, no one wants their adult son to have an unhealthy fascination with blood and guts, but in order to sate a boy's curiosity about blood and guts, they must become acquainted early in life with—you guessed it—blood and guts.

Now, most people are squeamish about the goo of life and the various ways in which it can be uncorked from the inside of a body, human or otherwise. If you talk too much about blood and guts at a cocktail party, for instance, some well-meaning busybody might report you to the police as a possible serial killer, and the cops might come to your house and seize all your guns and knives and duct tape, then ask you all sorts of uncomfortable questions about the contents of the freezer in your basement. (All of which can be settled peacefully if you can prove that the chunks of meat in your freezer aren't actually human.) Insane busybodies aside, however, an intimate familiarity with blood and guts is a necessary and unavoidable part of growing up.

The first time a boy encounters blood, it's likely to be his own, and it is most likely to be coming from his nose. It could be a common nosebleed, which happens all the time for no reason. But usually there's a reason. The Boy could have picked his nose a little too aggressively. He could have shoved a sharp object—like a thumbtack or a paper clip—up his nostril. He could have tried to pick his nose with a pocket knife or chopstick. He could have smashed his nose walking into a glass door. He could have fallen face first on the pavement. Another kid may have punched him in the nose. You get the idea: because it sticks out from the face and has not one but two orifices, the human nose is ripe for all sorts of ill-advised experimentation and abuse.

The other ways in which a boy is most likely to encounter his own blood are skinned knees and elbows, cut feet, and lacerations to the head.

Skinned knees and elbows are nothing to worry about. By the time a boy is eight years old, he should have skinned his knees and elbows so many times that a healthy patch of scar tissue has developed, protecting him for the rest of his life. In fact, if a boy hasn't skinned his extremities enough by the time he's eight, his father should—for the boy's own good—force him to go roller-blading and/or skateboarding, preferably on rough sidewalks strewn with lots of pebbles. If that doesn't work, dad should sign the boy up for little-league baseball and insist that he slide into every base knee first. In extreme cases, it may be necessary to make the boy dig a large hole in the backyard on his knees, or have him install a ream of carpet in the upstairs bedroom.

Unfortunately, it is now fashionable to have kids wear bulky pads to protect their knees and elbows, and to make them wear a helmet whenever they go outside.

This penchant for over-protection doesn't do kids any favors, because life is painful, and everyone knows it's important to learn that vital lesson early and often.

Cut feet are another common source of boyhood blood—but it happens more often these days because today's parents insist that their kids wear shoes outside. Thus, when they go barefoot, today's kids have soft baby feet that makes them far too vulnerable. All of this can be avoided if, on the first warm day of summer, you allow The Boy to take his shoes off and run around barefoot, everywhere, all summer long. A boy's feet are most vulnerable in those first few days after a long winter, when his soles are pink and squishy. It's important on those days for The Boy to traverse all kinds of terrain in order to build up thick, leather-like calluses on the bottom of his feet. Once those calluses are formed, he can walk anywhere without fear of injury. As I said before, the kids who run into trouble are the ones whose parents insist that they wear shoes all the time. When these unfortunate children try to go barefoot, as they inevitably do, they always step on a sharp rock or a piece of glass and end up in the emergency room, an embarrassment that results in further ridicule when they return to the playground shod in bandages and hiking boots.

As for lacerations to the head, they do tend to bleed a lot, but they almost always look worse than they are. That's why boys like them so much. No other injury has a higher blood-to-pain ratio. A small cut on the forehead can drench the whole left side of a boy's face in a sheet of glistening scarlet ooze. The dramatic effect is impressive. When I was a boy, if I fell out of a tree, or someone hit me in the head with a two-by-four, I'd wait five or ten minutes before going home—to allow the cut to open up, get the blood flowing and, if possible, ruin a perfectly good shirt. When I walked through the door and my mother screamed, it was worth every stitch.

Guts are more complicated than blood. But acquiring an intimate familiarity with the inner plumbing of many different types of creatures is an important part of boyhood. And, as long as the plumbing involved isn't one's own, the instructional value of a handful of guts should not be underestimated.

The first time a boy sees the insides of another creature, it's usually an insect—or hundreds of them—smashed against the windshield and bumper of the family car. On summer road trips, especially, windshield bug slime can end up covering more than fifty percent of the car's surface area. When I was educating The Boy, I'd use these occasions as teaching moments. When it was time to stop for gas, I'd dip a squeegee in blue wiper juice, hand it to The Boy, and say, "Remember, scrub then scrape." Then he'd spend the next fifteen minutes educating himself about the inner ooze of bugs.

The great thing about insect innards is that they come in so many interesting colors: green, yellow, blue, purple, black, silver, brown, turquoise—anything but red. After driving four-hundred miles through farm country at eighty miles per hour, the windshield of an average-size four-door sedan can look like a Jackson Pollock painting, only a bit less crazy and, if you happen to smash into a swarm of grasshoppers, more artistic. Or, if someone makes the mistake of trying to clean all that accumulated bug mush off with the car's windshield wipers, the resulting mess can look something like a Rothko or de Kooning. In any case, it should be The Boy's job to scrub and scrape as much bug gunk off as he can so that the family can get back on the road. And in so doing, he will inevitably learn that insects—while vitally important to a healthy agricultural ecosystem, and necessary as a food source for birds and frogs and other animals—are, for the most part, a huge pain in the ass.

After a boy has become well acquainted with the insides of insects, he's ready to learn about the plumbing of other animals. Fish guts are a good starter. A first encounter with fish guts should happen at least by the age of seven. If it hasn't happened naturally by then, a responsible father should engineer a way for it to happen as soon as possible, before the natural childhood fascination with internal organs begins to dissipate.

I did it this way, and you are welcome to follow my lead:

The Boy and I were fishing off a dock at a nearby lake one day and not having much luck. The sun was hot, we'd used all our worms, and I was working through a container of grubs, just trying to catch *something* so that The Boy didn't get the wrong idea and start thinking that his dad was a lousy fisherman, or that the activity of "fishing" involved nothing but sitting around and waiting for nothing to happen.

For some reason, on this day, not even the sunnies under the dock were tempted by my bait, which kept getting nibbled down to the bare hook by swarms of ravenous minnows. Why minnows aren't bigger, I don't know, because they sure do a lot of eating. Finally, I got a bite, and pulled up a smallish bluegill. The Boy got very excited.

"Is that a lunker?" The Boy asked.

"No," I said, "that's a bluegill."

"But you said we were going to catch a bunch of lunkers today."

"Yes, I did, but this isn't it," I said. "Lunkers take longer to catch."

"How much longer?"

"That's hard to say," I said. "Lunkers don't experience time the same way we do. What may seem like a long time to you is nothing to a lunker. So lunkers often make people wait a long time."

"Why do we care?" The Boy asked. "I mean, why do you want to catch one?"

"Because, as you've no doubt observed, standing around on a dock is pretty boring all by itself," I explained. "But throw in the possibility that you're going to catch a lunker, and suddenly it's very exciting. That's why fishing is so popular."

"What can we do to catch a lunker faster?" The Boy asked.

It was then that I saw my opening. I tossed the bluegill to The Boy and said,

"Here, find out what it's been eating. If we know what the fish are eating, we can improve our chances of catching them by giving them what they're hungry for."

"But didn't you catch it with one of those little wormy things?" The Boy said, pointing to the container of grubs. "Doesn't that mean that the fish are eating those?"

"You might think that, but fishing is both an art and a science," I explained. "This is the science part. What you just did was make a deduction—but it was a deduction unsupported by empirical evidence. And in order to get empirical evidence of what the fish was eating, you have to slice that fish's belly open and examine the contents of its stomach. That's what your pocket knife is for."

I could tell by the look on The Boy's face that the thought of getting his precious pocket knife coated in fish slime was not an appealing one. Nor did he seem very enthusiastic about slicing open a creature that was still alive. What The Boy didn't know was that finding out what the fish had eaten was only the secondary purpose for cutting it open. The primary purpose was to get The Boy accustomed to handling fish guts, since he was going to be spending the next ten or fifteen years gutting and cleaning all the fish we were going to catch on the many camping trips I planned to take him throughout his childhood.

"Here, I'll show you," I said.

I took out my own knife and inserted the tip into the fish's belly, then made a lengthwise incision along its white and shiny underside. Then I demonstrated how to remove the fish's guts by sliding my thumb along the inside of the fish's belly cavity and separating its organs into a teaspoon-worth of innards, which spilled out onto the dock and glistened brown and green in the sun. I showed The Boy which glob of fish gizzard was the stomach, and instructed him to cut it open with his knife. After some hesitation, he tried, but didn't so much cut it open as jab it until it liquefied.

After cutting the fish's stomach open, I said, "Now tell me what's inside? What's he eating?"

The Boy examined the pile of mush carefully, spreading the contents of the fish's stomach out so that he could examine each little bit of forensic evidence. "It's hard to tell," he said, "but it looks like he swallowed one of those wormy things."

"Excellent!" I said. "We now know for a fact that these fish are eating grubs."

"Didn't we know that already?" The Boy asked. "Because isn't that the bait you caught him with?"

"Yes, but now we have irrefutable empirical evidence," I countered. "Before, we were just guessing. Now science has confirmed what we suspected. Now all we have to do is keep feeding them what they want to eat."

We fished for another half hour or so, loading our hooks up with grubs, but didn't catch anything bigger than a baby perch.

"How come we're not catching anything?" The Boy asked.

"I don't know," I replied. "There are a lot of other factors involved in catching fish than just the bait. There's the line test, the type of knot you use, how you present the bait, the time of day, angle of the sun, the ratio of sun to clouds in the sky—all kinds of things."

"But none of them are working."

"No, they're not," I had to admit.

"Maybe we should try the other side of the dock," The Boy suggested.

"Good idea."

Unfortunately, our luck that day did not improve. After another half hour or so of futility, we'd run out of grubs and decided to go home. On the way to the car, The Boy said, "I need to wash my hands. They stink."

I stopped The Boy right there and put my hand on his shoulder. "You can't wash your hands—not yet," I explained. "The one thing you can't do after fishing is wash your hands or your pocket knife before you go home."

"Why not?" he asked.

In this particular instance I gave The Boy the standard, "Because I said so" dad answer, because I didn't think The Boy would understand. But I had my reasons. The stench of rotting fish is a smell every boy must get used to, and the best way to make that happen is to let the smell on his hands ferment in the hot sun for as long as possible. The worse the smell, the better. Your goal, as a parent, should be to make The Boy's hands smell so putrid that whenever he gets a whiff of fish funk in the future—when, for instance, you ask him to clean all those fish you've caught—it won't seem so bad.

CHAPTER 13

Another good way for boys to learn about blood and guts is through road kill. America's roads are lined with all kinds of unlucky critters—squirrels, raccoons, skunks, rabbits, possums, beavers, turtles, coyotes, deer, and the occasional cow—all of whom have discovered, in the worst possible way, how fast those creatures with the big white eyes and little round legs are running.

The problem with dead animals lying on the side of the road is that most of them are mammals, which means there is a considerable amount of blood mixed in with their guts—and, because of the nature of road kill, it is sometimes difficult to tell the difference between the two. But you wouldn't want to, anyway, because examining road kill up close is not as much fun as it sounds.

Boys are naturally interested in dead animals splattered on the side of the road, however, so—though road kill is disgusting in the extreme—one cannot allow a queasy stomach to get in the way of a boy's education.

The smartest thing to do is make a game out of identifying the animals encountered during a road trip. To keep boys busy during long drives, encourage them to record as many details as possible, including the location, distance from the road, estimated time of death, relative degree of smush, etc. Most states have a website for recording road kill, so after the trip, sit The Boy down in front of a computer, log into your state's department of natural resources, and allow The Boy to enter the data himself. Fairly soon it will dawn on him that the more information he records, the more work it is to enter it into the computer. After a few hours of data entry, his enthusiasm for road kill is likely to wane, as he will begin to associate it with the most boring job in the world.

The one exception to the above advice is deer. In many states, if you hit a deer with your car, it is legal to haul it home, cut it up, and eat it for dinner. If you live in middle America, there's a better than even chance that you drive a pickup truck, which makes the task easy. But if you're driving a ten-year-old Ford Focus, say, taking a deer home is exponentially more difficult. One doesn't just throw a fully grown deer into the trunk of a car, after all. No, one ties it to the roof. Indeed, the process of securing a deer to the top of a mid-size sedan provides a multitude of teachable moments, so no parent interested in their boy's education should pass up the opportunity if, in the middle of night, it tragically presents itself.

The impact of a moving motor vehicle hitting a full-grown deer is sudden and terrifying, but if you happen to survive it, and you're thinking clearly enough that the idea of venison steaks on the grill still appeals to you, the first thing you're going to want to do is make sure the deer is dead. In the Midwest, where I live, people are accustomed to keeping a disaster-preparedness kit in the trunk of their car. Simply remove the twelve-gauge shotgun from the kit, pump one well-aimed blast into deer's head, and you can be fairly certain the animal will not get up and run away.

A full-grown deer can weigh up to 300 pounds, so it's imperative that the whole family get involved. The task of lifting the deer onto a tarp, hoisting it up onto the roof of the car, and tying it down can be presented as a "fun" challenge, in which everyone plays a part. Mothers are particularly good at worrying if the knots are tight enough to prevent the deer from sliding off into oncoming traffic, and small children are excellent at wiping unwanted drops of blood off the car's exterior. The Boy's job is to help dad make sure the ropes are tight, and that blood from the head isn't dripping all over the windshield.

Once the deer is secure, and mom has stopped hyperventilating, the law in many states allows you to take the deer home and eat it. A mature buck will typically yield between seventy-five to one-hundred pounds of meat, which means that a reminder of the "adventure" that night will appear on the family's dinner plates for at least a year to come, maybe two. If The Boy is looking for a thoughtful Christmas present to give his mother, a venison cookbook is an excellent choice. Just make sure the book has a chapter in how to cook the "gaminess" out of the meat, because that makes the meat usable in many more recipes—which she will of course want.

CHAPTER 15

There are many ways to stunt a boy's education, quite a few of which include the word "school." I didn't care much for school myself, and honestly can't remember a thing I learned during all those years sitting in a classroom doodling on the side of my notebooks. The important things I learned all happened outside of school, in the classroom of personal experience.

Still, that didn't stop The Wife from outsourcing The Boy's education. The summer he turned five, she announced that he would be starting kindergarten in the fall, so if there were any vital lessons I needed to teach him beforehand, now would be the time.

Before The Boy started getting indoctrinated by the local school system, I felt it was important for him to know that he was different from other children—in ways that would eventually become apparent to him, especially if he decided to compete in the Olympics someday—because he was born in America. That made him an American, which is something billions of other people on the planet wish they were but aren't, because they were born in some godforsaken part of the world like Angola, Venezuela, or France.

Being an American comes with certain responsibilities, one of which is knowing without a doubt that you live in the greatest country on earth, and because of that you are better than other people. When you read about folks from Cuba trying to get to Miami by floating in an inner tube, it's because they've heard how much better Americans are than Cubans, and they want to find out for themselves. When they get to America and finally have an ice-cold Budweiser in their hands and a half-pound cheeseburger in their stomach, they realize that all the stories they've heard are true. America is better. Then they decide that they want to stay, because they want to be more like the nice Americans around them. You never read about these people climbing back in their inner tube and heading back to Cuba. No, the next thing you read about is how their family, after hearing how great America is, piled into a life raft and got rescued by the Coast Guard. It's the same with Mexicans, only they prefer to dig tunnels or cross the Rio Grande river into Texas. I don't know why you don't hear more about desperate Canadians crossing our border to the north, but you know they do. It's just human nature to want to be American.

There's a lot to learn about America, though, and it's never too early to start. So, before he started kindergarten, I decided it was time for a family trip to one of the most important places in the country, a monument to democracy that every American must visit at least once in their lifetime: Mount Rushmore.

The only problem with Mount Rushmore as a vacation destination is that it is located in South Dakota. Approaching from the east, from Minnesota, that meant we had to drive across the entire state of South Dakota, which is like driving across the moon, if the moon were eight-hundred miles wide and littered with billboards for the Corn Palace and Wall Drug.

For the uninitiated, or those approaching Mount Rushmore from the West, the Corn Palace is exactly what it sounds like: a palace made out of corn. It's impressive, in an I-can't-believe-anyone-would-go-to-the-trouble-to-build-this kind of way. The Corn Palace looks like the Taj Mahal, if you shrunk the Taj Mahal and made it all kinds of different colors and constructed it out of corn cobs. Sure, they could have named it something fancier, but this is a no-nonsense part of the world, and they evidently didn't want to confuse anybody by calling it something clumsy like the Colossal Corncob Castle of Mitchell, South Dakota. The place gets a lot of visitors though, because it's the only thing to see for three-hundred miles in either direction. And if nothing else, it is an important monument to American ingenuity and innovation.

Wall Drug is another South Dakota invention that's cleverly situated in the desert about a gas tank away from Minneapolis, the nearest big city. Just as your fuel gauge is inching toward "E," and you're starting to imagine what it would be like to run out of gas in the middle of the desert and die and have your carcass picked clean by vultures, Wall Drug looms up out of the sand like an oasis—one where you can get a decent burger and shake, and buy any one of ten-thousand "authentic" Indian artifacts, most of them made of plastic.

But Wall Drug doesn't just commemorate the history of the native people in the region. It also pays homage to the wildlife that once roamed the land around it. One of the oddest creatures is a thing called a "jackalope," which is basically a rabbit with horns. The Wife says there is no such thing—that the jackalope is a "made-up" creature that's just plausible enough to fool the tourists. But I don't believe her. A jackalope is no weirder than a platypus or an armadillo, I told her, and besides, if you were going to make up an animal just to sell stuff, wouldn't you put a little more imagination into it? Like maybe a turkey-goat, or a buffalo snake, or a gopher dragon? Besides, there's the actual physical evidence to consider, because I'm pretty sure I saw a few jackalopes squashed on the side of the road during our drive.

Dinosaurs used to roam these plains as well, back when it was a jungle and before it was an ocean. As proof, in the corner of the Wall Drug video arcade stands a scale-model Tyrannosaurus Rex robot, which, for fifty cents, roars and waves its arms and flashes its laser-red eyes of death. It is terrifying, but not in the way you might expect. The T-Rex is just tall enough that if it fell over, it would crush a small child—and, if you look at its feet too closely, you can see that the bolts holding it into the ground are gradually loosening over time. I haven't read about any child-crushing catastrophes in Wall Drug since our visit there, but mark my words, it's a disaster waiting to happen.

In any event, The Boy loved Wall Drug, The Wife hated it, and I paid the tab. That's what fathers do on family road trips: they listen to the griping and pay for everything, secure in the knowledge that the memories of a Great American Road Trip will last forever. I'm not complaining, mind you. It's just that dads tend to do all the driving too, so there is a limit to our infinite patience.

It doesn't matter which direction you approach South Dakota, though, because every two-bit rest stop and roadside teepee is just a preamble to the main attraction: Mt. Rushmore.

When I visited Mt. Rushmore as a kid, I'll admit I thought it was kind of stupid. My father did not do a very good job of explaining the historical significance of the place, so I was left with the impression that it was just the faces of four old guys carved into a mountainside. They don't move. They don't talk. They don't wink at you when you arrive. They don't do anything. So, to a kid, the novelty lasts about thirty seconds, which is not much novelty after a ten-hour drive. As I recall, however, the novelty only lasted about a minute for my father, so we were out of there pretty fast. He wanted to go buy whiskey and pan for gold instead, an activity he claimed was a lot more "authentic" than Mt. Rushmore, which was just a "tourist attraction." The quiet majesty and historical importance of the place were lost on him, and so they were lost on me as well.

As we drove up the winding road to the sacred monument itself, I vowed not to make the same mistake with my son that my father did with me. The entire reason I brought The Boy was to familiarize him with our founding fathers and start educating him about American democracy. One day he would be able to vote, and he needed to know what sort of miracles federal tax dollars used to be able to create, but no longer can. So, after we paid the entrance fee and parked the car, I began educating The Boy about this most historic of monuments.

"Did you know, son, that it took fourteen years and four-hundred men to carve Mt. Rushmore?" (I visited the website before we came, so I had such facts and figures at my fingertips.)

The Boy did not know this, he said, but wondered, "Did anyone die?"

"That's a complicated question," I replied. "If you believe the government, the answer is no. But if you believe common sense, the answer has to be yes. Lots."

My wife suggested that I not complicate matters by bringing politics into the equation, but it's pretty hard to look at the stone faces of four presidents and not bring up politics. The 'official' story from the government is that no one died during the construction of Mt. Rushmore, but that is of course impossible. The thing was carved with dynamite by a bunch of miners dangling off a cliff with nothing but a piece of rope between them and certain death. Hell, people die every day tripping over cracks in a sidewalk. Do they really expect us to believe no one bought the farm blowing up a mountainside with dynamite or dangling from a rope trying to get the perfect curvature in Thomas Jefferson's left nostril?

Clearly, it's a lie, and a clumsy one at that. What I don't understand is why? It's one thing for the government to lie—everyone expects that—but why does the government have to lie so badly? (And by "government," I of course mean the cabal of criminals that ran America before Ronald Reagan was elected.) In any case, why not admit that several men sacrificed their lives to build Mt. Rushmore? It makes for a much better story, anyway: patriots giving their lives to enshrine our founding fathers forever in granite. Why pretend that no one died, since it's so hard to believe anyway, and makes it sound as if carving Mt. Rushmore was no big deal? My guess, of course, is that the government's lawyers got involved, and they came up with the "no deaths" lie to make us, the taxpayers, believe that no one filed a worker's comp claim during the construction of Mt. Rushmore, or that anyone's family filed a wrongful death suit.

After I explained to The Boy that the base of Mt. Rushmore was probably littered with the bones of dead construction workers, he wanted to know why there were only four faces on the mountain when there have been so many other presidents—a pretty good question for a five-year-old.

"Well, you'll notice that the last face up there is the face of Abraham Lincoln," I explained. "The reason they stopped there is that Abraham Lincoln is the last president anyone in this country trusted. 'Honest Abe' they called him, and no president since has been called 'honest'—far from it. Ronald Reagan came pretty close, and there has been talk of putting his face up there as well, but Ronald Reagan was so good-looking that some people are afraid he'd make all the other presidents up there look bad."

Five-year-olds ask a lot of questions, most of which begin with that dreaded word "Why?" But I was determined to answer The Boy's queries as accurately as I could. Why, he wanted to know, did they build Mt. Rushmore in the first place?

"Well, there was a time when no one had any reason to go to South Dakota, so they needed to give people a reason to come here," I explained. "Think about it. Would we be here if Mt. Rushmore wasn't here? No. But one of the great things about America is that tourists will go to all kinds of godforsaken places if you give them a reason. Las Vegas is in the middle of the desert, for instance, but millions of people go there every year to gamble and pretend they're not married. It's the same with Mt. Rushmore. So, as we stand here and look at it, those faces remind us of what's great about American ingenuity: that if you can imagine something sufficiently insane, and have the guts to make it happen—by blowing up a mountain, say, or building a bunch of casinos in the desert—you can make one heckuva lot of money. Turning a mountain into a monument that attracts millions of people every year—that's what economists call 'added value.'"

As for what it all meant, and why those people were up there, I didn't want to numb The Boy's mind with a lot of historical facts. George Washington was easy: Father of our country, period. I'd already told him about Lincoln, and what can you say about Teddy Roosevelt? Not much, so I skipped him.

Thomas Jefferson was a little more difficult. I explained that he was the "pursuit of happiness" guy, but I regretted it as soon as I said it, because The Boy wanted to know what that meant? I didn't know what to tell him, because I never quite understood it myself. Americans should be happy that they're Americans, period. Why complicate it by suggesting that happiness is something people need to "pursue"? Not only is it unnecessary, in my experience, as soon as you start pursuing happiness, that's when unhappiness sets in. If you're chasing happiness, after all, the implication is that you are unhappy, which is totally un-American. Thomas Jefferson also failed to specify how much happiness people had a right to pursue—which, in my opinion, was a dangerous oversight. There are laws against being too happy, and people ought to know that. Some people achieve maximum happiness after drinking half a bottle of Jack Daniels and punching someone. Some people are extremely happy when they're high on drugs and doing unmentionable things in a public park, during the day, when children are playing nearby. Other people find a great deal of happiness driving a hundred miles per hour on the freeway, or fooling old people into giving all their money away. Plus, if you're too happy—if you walk through a shopping mall singing and dancing, for instance—they will lock you up for disturbing the peace and acting like a wacko.

So there are definitely times when the pursuit of happiness is not a good idea, and those times tend to coincide with times when, on purpose or by accident, you end up finding more happiness than you bargained for. Thomas Jefferson could have spared people a lot of agony and confusion if he had just spent a little more time on that sentence to clarify things.

A better way to put it would have been, "We hold these truths to be self-evident, blah, blah, blah . . . that Americans have the right to be moderately happy, but not deliriously so, lest people from other countries be consumed with jealousy and hatred."

That way, people would know what to expect from living in America (a decent but not unreasonable level of happiness), and they'd know that if they suddenly found themselves in a state of way too much happiness, the sound of the police knocking on their door wouldn't be such a surprise. It would also communicate to Americans how lucky they are relative to people living in other countries, and warn them that bragging too much about how moderately great Americans have it could lead to war.

Not that I'm second-guessing the founding fathers—I just think that if they'd put a little more effort into things, they could have spared Americans a lot of confusion and headaches down the road.

For these and other reasons, I felt it was unnecessary to go into the whole pursuit of happiness thing too deeply. Instead, I told The Boy, "All you need to know is that no matter how unhappy you are, there's some miserable kid in Kenya who thinks he'd be happier living your life than his. So don't take your life for granted, because if you whine and complain too much, I'd be happy to trade you."

As interesting as Mt. Rushmore is, it only took about five minutes for all of us to get bored and wonder what else there was to do in South Dakota. Still, that's five times longer than me and my father lasted. And who knows, maybe when The Boy brings his son to Mt. Rushmore, they'll last even longer.

I briefly considered re-enacting the gold-panning adventure with my own father, but I didn't think The Wife would approve of letting The Boy drink whiskey at such a young age. Besides, she was more interested in the history of the "region" and how the U.S. government had "taken" the land for Mt. Rushmore from the Lakota Indians. She wanted to go see Crazy Horse, the giant monument the native Indians are carving into a mountain twenty miles to the south. I didn't understand why she wanted to go see some copycat monument that isn't even done yet. She said she thought it was important for The Boy to see "both sides of the story," but I told her there is only one side that matters: ours.

"Look, those Indians have been working on their monument for seventy years, and it's only about ten percent finished," I pointed out. "We did ours in fourteen years, top to bottom, and that pretty much sums up the relationship between Indians and Americans, as far as I'm concerned. We get the job done; they don't. Therefore, we win."

The Wife chided me for being so short-sighted, racist, and patriotic. So, to make her happy, I agreed to drive down to Crazy Horse and see what all the fuss was about.

I have to admit, I was pleasantly surprised and even a little impressed by the many ways in which native Americans have embraced the customs and rituals of actual Americans. First of all, they charge for parking, which is customary at all American landmarks. They also have a visitor's center and gift shop full of useless stuff people can buy, another essential element of the American tourist experience. What they don't have yet—and this is the most impressive part—is an actual monument. Instead, they have part of a monument, the face, and it's about a mile away from the visitor's center, so you can only see it decently through binoculars. They make a big deal about how the "finished" monument will be so much bigger than Mt. Rushmore, but that just tells me the Indians bit off more than they can chew. At the rate they're going, it's going to take another five hundred years to finish it. I told my wife that when it's done, they should call it Mt. Rush-less, because they're obviously in no hurry.

No one was working on Crazy Horse the day we visited, which disturbed me at first. But the more I thought about, the more I realized how clever the whole thing is. After all, there's no reason to see Mt. Rushmore more than once or twice in a lifetime. But with Crazy Horse, they've stretched out the construction of it to create a moving story about how the Indians can't raise enough money to buy picks and shovels and backhoes. This means that people could visit Crazy Horse ten or twenty times during their life to check on its "progress," and fool themselves into thinking they are seeing some, dropping a small fortune every time they visit. It's kind of brilliant when you think about it. The Indians could stretch the whole Crazy Horse project out for a few thousand years if they wanted to. Every once in a while they'd have to add a finger or a few strands of hair, of course, but otherwise the Indians can sit back and let the cash flow in.

At first, I thought they had the whole thing backwards. We, after all, carved a monument, then put in the gift shop and visitor's center. They did it the other way around. From a cash flow standpoint, though, it's hard not to wonder if their way might be better. Of course, the Indians couldn't do it their way until we did it our way, so in that sense we are still the pioneers. Still, it looks to me like the Indians have been taking business lessons from the Japanese: steal our idea, then figure out how to milk it for even more money. There's nothing crazy about that, of course; what's really crazy is that we let them.

The Boy was plenty happy we visited Crazy Horse, since he got himself a nice little bow-and-arrow set complete with little suction-cup arrows that stuck quite nicely to our car windows. I had to teach him how to lick the suction cups so that they'd stick better, and The Boy never had a problem generating saliva, so he caught on pretty fast. Meanwhile, the Mt. Rushmore snow globe we bought him disappeared somewhere under the seat of the car, never to be seen again.

CHAPTER 16

Now that I have successfully raised a son, young parents facing the same challenge often ask me what the most important lessons I, as a father, learned during my son's all-important formative years. These parents are anxious to make sure that their child's first few years on earth are as nourishing as possible, in the belief that a healthy, happy toddlerhood will lay the foundation for the child's future success and happiness. Furthermore, they believe that traumas and difficulties incurred when a child is young can grow into developmental road-blocks as the child grows older. So, for instance, a child who is forced to watch too much PBS or the Learning Channel might develop an unhealthy interest in the humanities, jeopardizing any hope he might have of getting a decent job as an adult.

Consequently, new parents tend to be anxious about how their children are developing. More to the point, they are anxious about how their kid is developing *relative to other children their age.* In a capitalist society, competition for jobs begins before conception, when, before copulating, parents-to-be mentally calculate the genetic and economic consequences of not using birth control. Ninety-nine percent of the time the parties involved conclude that having a baby is a bad idea, because the genetic/economic calculations yield a net negative.

Once the deed is done, however, there is no turning back. Parental anxiety shoots through the roof when the child being contemplated is no longer imaginary. Soon, the calculations become more complex and the numbers involved grow exponentially. The cost of diapers alone can make a grown man hyperventilate. Add in the cost of getting them for the baby too, and the whole thing can feel like it's spinning out of control. Then, one day, you might find your son sitting in the corner chewing on the dog's Nylabone, because he doesn't know any better. Every couple's fear is that their son may *never* know any better, which means they could have stopped at getting a dog, saving thousands on day-care expenses and video games.

Because competition for jobs is so fierce, parents need to reassure themselves that their child will one day be employable. During the baby years, when optimism about a child's future is at its peak, parents are constantly on the lookout for signs of marketable abilities in their progeny. Indeed, no developmental sign is too small to justify a new parent's conviction that their child is special. If a baby rolls over on its own, parents inevitably conclude he is a naturally gifted gymnast whose Olympic training has just begun. If a baby manages to shove a triangle-shaped plastic cube into a similarly shaped hole in a plastic ball, parents will attribute this amazing feat to his sudden mastery of Euclidian geometry. If he spills a bag of marbles on the floor, it is because he is studying their dispersion pattern on his way to becoming a theoretical physicist. And if he bangs on a pot with a wooden spoon, they immediately buy him a tiny drum set and start researching the logistics of renting Madison Square Garden for a three-night run eighteen years from now.

This sort of wishful thinking is understandable. The hope is that by some miracle of genetics, the parents' demonstrably mediocre genes will somehow combine to produce a child of superior intelligence and ability—an infant superhero of sorts who will redeem their own unremarkable DNA by someday earning enough to allow the parents to retire. This fantasy begins to erode rather quickly, however.

By the time all the kids in daycare have learned to walk, talk, and pee with some degree of accuracy, the creeping realization that your kid is not so special after all inevitably starts to take hold. And by the time they reach kindergarten, it can often disappear altogether.

CHAPTER 18

I remember our first meeting with The Boy's kindergarten teacher well. Ms. Wheaton was one of those young, energetic women whose enthusiasm for teaching had yet to be beaten out of her by the act of teaching itself. She had neatly cropped blond hair, and teeth so white and straight that they could have joined the Republican party. When she smiled, she radiated such a relentlessly positive attitude that I figured she must be fiddling with the dosage on her medication.

Her classroom was a happy jungle of construction paper and glue, with the alphabet spelled out across the ceiling in the guise of dancing animals—A for Ant, B for Bear, C for Caterpillar, etc.—and plastic bins full of blocks, books, and other educational aids were arranged with military precision in shelves along the wall. Each bin had a child's name on it. My wife scanned the shelves to find The Boy's bin, and seemed gratified that he had one, though I don't know why. Of course he had a bin. We bought it at Target ourselves, and stuffed it with $150 worth of classroom supplies, per instructions provided by Ms. Wheaton herself.

I scanned the room for clues about Ms. Wheaton's teaching philosophy and was alarmed to see a poster with a quote from Dr. Seuss that read: "Today you are you, that is truer than true. There is no one alive who is you-er than you."

This is where it starts, I thought—the blind acceptance of ideas that are not necessarily backed by concrete evidence. How does she know, for a fact, that there is no one out there who is "you-er" than you? Maybe there is. Who's to say there isn't a kid out there somewhere who is better at being you than you are? And what if you happened to meet the better you at a party? If you were under the false impression that no one in the world could out-you you, you'd be in for a huge disappointment.

Also, if you are already the best you there is, where's the incentive to get better?

And what if you don't like yourself? What then? Does that mean you're stuck with your essential you-ness, and that dissatisfaction with the icky, ugly self you despise is all you have to look forward to in this life?

To me, it didn't seem like the sort of quote one should feature prominently in a kindergarten classroom. A kid who reads that kind of thing every day might start to get the idea that he really is special.

Ms. Wheaton instructed us to sit in one of the tiny, kid-sized chairs, which I immediately recognized as a strategy to humiliate us. She then stood over us, as if we were the students, and spoke in a sing-songy voice that I interpreted as a cry for help—as in, "Help, I am stuck in a room all day with snotty five-year-olds and have forgotten how to talk to adults."

She explained that The Boy was doing well in school, that he played well with the other kids, and that his behavior was excellent. "He's very polite," she told us. "He always raises his hand, never interrupts, and he is the only child in my class that has never had to sit on the red 'X,'" she said, pointing at an X in the corner marked out on the carpet with masking tape. The red X is where kids who are disruptive go to have a "time out," she explained, and our son had never misbehaved to the point where sending him to the red X was necessary.

I was horrified.

"You mean to tell me that every other kid in your class has done something bad enough to get the X treatment, but my boy hasn't?"

"That's right," Ms. Wheaton said, beaming. "He's one of my best students."

"How is that possible?" I asked.

"Good genes, I guess," she said, laughing.

"Well, he can't go on like this," I said. "This has to stop."

Ms. Wheaton looked confused. "No, it's good not to sit on the red X," she explained. "Only children who are being bad have to sit on the X."

"It's not good, not good at all," I objected. "No one wants their child to be the goody-goody kid who follows all the rules. If he can't break the rules in kindergarten, what hope is there for him later in life?"

"I don't understand what you're saying," Ms. Wheaton said. "Are you saying that you *want* your son to break the rules?"

"Every now and then, yes," I said.

"That's interesting," she said, but I could tell she was lying.

"Tell me this, does he also color inside the lines?" I asked.

"Why yes, he does," she answered.

"It's worse that I thought," I said, turning to my wife, who had remained uncharacteristically silent since we'd entered the room. She nodded, as if she understood my concerns and might even agree with them. Then she changed the subject.

"What about his socialization skills?" she asked. "Is he getting along with the other children?"

"Yes, wonderfully," Ms. Wheaton reported. "He's such a trooper. Even when some other boys pushed him on the playground the other day, he just took it like a little man—got up, brushed himself off, and removed himself from the situation."

"What!?" I cried. "That's no way for a little man to act. A little man needs to stand up for himself—and, when some other kid pushes him, he needs to kick their snotty little ass!"

Ms. Wheaton took a deep breath and said, "That's not the way we resolve conflicts here. We think it's important for children to have non-violent strategies for resolving conflict. Toward that end, every child is required so sign the "Kindergarten Pledge," she said, handing us a piece of paper that looked like a contract. On it was written:

"As a child at Randolph Heights Elementary School, I promise to treat all other children with kindness and respect. I will try to be a good friend to all and to make no one sad or angry by my words or actions. If I am angry with another child, I will use the deflection skills I am taught to make the situation better, and will refrain from behaviors that have a negative impact on the classroom environment. I will also strive to be a good student, an active participant in class, and a positive contributor to the community of learners at Randolph Heights."

Below this paragraph was The Boy's signature, scrawled in green crayon.

"What the hell is this?" I asked.

"Language," Ms. Wheaton tisked, waving her index finger back and forth like a little windshield wiper.

"What exactly are 'deflection skills'?" I asked.

"They are ways to de-escalate conflict and resolve potentially hurtful situations without being pulled into destructive behavior patterns," Ms. Wheaton explained.

"Fighting, in other words."

"Yes."

"And how does it work?"

"Well, if one child does something to another child that they think is unfair or makes them angry—takes away their blocks, say, or cuts in front of them in line."

"Or pushes them on the playground . . ."

"Or pushes them on the playground, yes—they are taught to take the other child's feelings into account and understand that while the other child's behavior might make them angry, it is probably coming from a place of hurt and pain—so, rather than fight or argue, they should seek to have empathy and compassion for the other child, and to re-double their efforts to treat them with kindness."

"Are you kidding?"

"I am not."

"And this works?"

"Yes, it does," Ms. Wheaton said, "and your son is a shining example of how well it works. He could have fought with those boys on the playground, but instead he chose the more difficult path—he rose above it and chose the path of compassion and respect."

It went on like that for a while, but I'd heard enough. The next day, I enrolled The Boy in a Karate class and explained to him that it's a lot easier to get other kids to respect you if they know you can kick their ass. The trick is, if you ever get challenged, you really do have to kick their ass, but good. You only have to do it once, though, I told him. After that, no one will have the guts to mess with you, and you can radiate all the compassion you want.

In the basement, I created a training area with several punching bags, plenty of boards to snap in half, a life-size mannequin of a five-year-old child (to help him better aim his blows), a wall of corkboard for hurling ninja stars, and a box full of num-chucks, blowguns, a samurai sword, a bullwhip, and an assortment of tactical knives for any situation. To build The Boy's strength, I installed a set of free weights in the corner, and bought a crate of Muscle Milk protein drinks that he could substitute for the useless carton of non-fat milk he got with his lunch. And to make sure he understood the historical and philosophical context behind the training I was providing him, I bought him a birthday subscription to Warrior magazine, and instituted "father/

son movie nights," during which we watched all of Bruce Lee's movies, both *Kill Bills*, plenty of Steven Segal, and his favorite—Chuck Norris.

"Hey dad, what's Chuck Norris's blood type?"

"What?"

"AK-47!"

"Hey dad, do you know who Waldo is hiding from? Chuck Norris!"

"Hey dad, did you know that on a high-school math test, Chuck Norris got an A+ for answering each question with the word 'violence,'—because that's how Chuck Norris solves all his problems."

"Hey dad, did you know that there isn't a theory of evolution—just a list of creatures Chuck Norris allows to live!"

I was justifiably proud of the progress my son was making. A month into his Karate class, The Boy had learned some basic kicks and several useful defensive maneuvers. After every class, I encouraged him to show me what he had learned.

One night, before a Jackie Chan double feature, The Boy wanted to show me a new move he had just learned in class. He wouldn't tell me what it was—he wanted to surprise me—so I got down on my knees to closer approximate the size of one of his future foes. The Boy instructed me to keep my arms by my side and not to move, because he had just learned this technique, and if I moved I might "ruin it." He then adopted the traditional karate fighting stance known as "The Crane," and I waited. Then, with a speed that belied his small size, he yelled and jammed the tip of his hand into my throat, right below the Adam's apple. I immediately fell to the floor and was unable to breathe.

The paramedics said he collapsed my windpipe, and that I could have died if the strike had been any harder. At the hospital, The Boy said he was sorry, and was glad that he had not added the "other move" he'd learned that day—namely, using the heel of his hand to jam my nose cartilage back up into my brain to render me unconscious. I told him I was proud of him, and that it wasn't his fault. In fact, all it proved was that he was picking up some useful skills—skills that would soon come in handy on the playground and, later in life, business meetings.

CHAPTER 19

That wasn't the end of it with Ms. Wheaton. Near the end of kindergarten, at the final parent-teacher meeting of the year, Ms. Wheaton informed us that, despite the incident on the playground some months earlier that sent a young bully home with a nosebleed, our son had performed above and beyond his age level in almost every category. He was particularly good at spacial relations, she said, and even though he was technically what she called a "kinetic learner," he also listened well and could name several different types of dinosaurs off the top of his head.

All of this added up to the subject of our meeting. "I want to let you know that I think your child is gifted," she told us.

"Gifted?" I said. "What does that mean?"

"That he is exceptionally smart and talented, and that he could go on to do great things," she answered.

"What kinds of things?"

"Well, that's impossible to say," she said. "Only time will tell."

"So you don't really know."

"No, but he has so much talent. I'm sure you'll be very proud of him one day."

"What talents does he have?" I asked. "Because I have to tell you, I've been looking for them and I don't see them."

"But he has so many."

"Such as?"

"Well, you'd be surprised. Not every child in my class can handle a pair of scissors like he can. And sometimes I hear him humming, but I don't recognize the tune, so I assume he's making it up. Maybe he's a composer at heart," she offered.

"Wait a minute," I said. "You're not trying to tell us he's some kind of little genius, are you?"

"Well, I . . ."

"Because the last thing we need on our hands is a little genius," I said. "I mean, who wants to raise a genius? I know a lot of people want their kid to be a little Mozart, but not me. Let's face it, Mozart was a thin, pale, neurotic little man who couldn't make a buck and died at the age of thirty-five. Oh sure, he wrote "Twinkle, Twinkle" when he was five, but the last thing any parent needs is a kid who sits around all day dreaming up catchy little melodies. If my kid started whistling a tune like "It's a Small World" all day long, trust me, you'd have a triple homicide on your hands. Besides the annoyance factor, there is also the very real danger that a child genius might grow up to be an artist—which is of course the ultimate nightmare for any parent. So please tell me he's not a genius."

Ms. Wheaton may have been taken aback by the "triple homicide" reference, because she took a while to gather her thoughts. "I'm not in a position to judge true genius," she said carefully. "But I wouldn't be surprised if he skips second or third grade, because, as a I said before, he is definitely gifted. At some point, you may want to consider en-rolling him at the gifted and talented magnet school."

My wife did not have a problem with the whole "gifted" thing, and even said she expected it. "Have you seen some of the other kids in his class? It's not like there's a whole lot of competition," she observed.

I, however, was not convinced. Ms. Wheaton was a well-meaning teacher, I thought, but her lack of specificity made me suspicious. She said The Boy was gifted, but at what she could not say. So, was this "gifted" label designed for children who show a small degree of apti-tude for nothing in particular, which may or may not develop into a talent or skill, depending on circumstances that cannot be predicted and factors that cannot be controlled? Or was it something worse?

I suspected the latter after learning that several of our friends' chil-dren—children who I knew for a fact were clueless as a cucumber—had been deemed gifted as well. Calling a child "gifted," it seemed, was just a polite way of informing parents that their kid wasn't en-tirely normal. Furthermore, sending them to a school for "gifted" children—separating them from the normal kids—was just a way to allow parents to save face in the community while they came to grips with their child's conspicuous lack of normalcy.

Though my wife thought sending The Boy to the gifted and tal-ented school might be a good idea, I strongly disagreed. Stranding The Boy in the developmental limbo of a "gifted" school was rather cruel, I thought, because instead of schoolwork, such schools tend to encourage kids to do all kinds of projects aimed at improving the world and generating pity for the less fortunate. These types of projects tend to instill in boys the unrealistic expectation that they can and should change the world, which leads to disappointment later on in life, when they learn how screwed up the world really is, and how little difference one person can actually make.

In the car, on the way home, I let my wife know what I was thinking. "Don't you see, the sooner we abandon our insane expectations for The Boy's future, the better it will be for everyone," I reasoned. "This whole gifted thing is a trap," I said, "and I for one am too smart to fall into it."

"Well, considering that half his genes are connected to you, you might be right," she said. "Let's see how he does in first grade before we start making any big decisions about his future."

I considered that a victory—a gift, you might say, from a woman who usually takes a little more convincing.

CHAPTER 20

Once the giftedness genie has been let out of the bottle, however, it's difficult to stuff it back in. The Boy's mother, especially, was suddenly attuned to his every move, looking for signs of exceptional ability in everything he did. If he microwaved a burrito, she'd project thirty years ahead and declare that he might be a famous chef one day. If he cracked his knuckles, she thought he might be a budding chiropractor. If he made a paper airplane, she thought he might be developing an interest in aviation or aeronautical engineering.

But the truth is that years went by without The Boy showing any particular interest in, or aptitude for, anything. He did however have an active disinterest in many things, especially things that ended with the word "lesson." Music lessons, swimming lessons, tennis lessons, chess lessons—these were all viewed by The Boy as traps designed to force him to learn something constructive, against his will, so that his parents did not succumb to despair over his lack of prospects for the future. Karate was the only sort of class he would consider taking, and he only did that because, once or twice a week, he learned a new way to incapacitate me.

All of our efforts backfired. My wife tended to get overly excited about whatever The Boy did, often offering him some bizarrely enthusiastic encouragement—"Awesome job with that burrito, honey!"—which creeped The Boy out. He also got tired of hearing suggestions about how he might develop his microwaving prowess into a lucrative and rewarding career. When she started Googling things like "chef schools for six-year-olds," The Boy took it as a cue to leave the room and eat his snacks in the basement, alone, where his parents weren't around to ruin the experience.

That said, parents are hard-wired to observe anything their child does and project decades ahead to determine if they can make a living at it. Parents are then obligated to offer whatever support and encouragement they can, if only to defend themselves against charges of neglect when, as a young adult, the child goes to therapy and learns how his parents have squashed his ambitions, crushed his dreams, and ruined his life. I was not about to allow that to happen, so I kept a careful watch on The Boy's activities to see if I could identify an area of interest that, with some gentle parental assistance, could be nourished and developed.

For years I waited and watched, but, hard as it is to believe, The Boy demonstrated no special skills whatsoever. In fact, he had an uncanny ability to drift through life, day after day, without showing much of an interest in anything. Even when he played video games, he did it dispassionately, sighting a rifle scope on an enemy's forehead and blowing their brains out without so much as an eye-twitch of excitement. When I offered encouragement—"Nice head shot—way to save your ammo, son!"—he would shrug his shoulders and say something like, "A knife kill would have been cleaner," or "It doesn't matter, dad, I've got unlimited ammo," then shake his head like I was an idiot.

This went on until about the age of nine, when, one day, I happened upon The Boy and his friend Zacc in the backyard at the very moment that they had dropped a pack of Mentos candy into a sixty-four-ounce Coke bottle. In a matter of seconds, a geyser of brown foam shot ten feet into the air and splattered all over the lawn. Both The Boy and Zacc laughed and hooted for joy as the plume of soda spewed upward for several seconds, then slowly subsided and died.

"Let's do that again, man!"

"Let's do three at once!"

"No, how about ten?!"

I'd never seen my son so happy. This gave me the idea that he might be interested in chemistry, and that he might enjoy finding out what happens when other compounds and materials are mixed together.

I immediately went and bought him a chemistry set full of colorful crystals and powders that, the box said, could be used to conduct hundreds of experiments. I should have known from the outset that the promise on the box—that all the experiments were "safe and non-toxic"—would immediately suck all the fun out of it.

Initially, The Boy was only interested in one of the experiments—the one that involved burning sulfur in a test tube to make the stinky-egg smell. The first time we did it, he went into the kitchen and pretended he'd farted, and to watch out, mom, because he had apparently eaten some sketchy mystery meat at school that day.

I have to admit, it was funny—the first time. But by the time we burned through all the sulfur, even The Boy admitted that the joke was getting old and the smell was getting to him.

It quickly became apparent that The Boy had no interest in learning anything about how molecules and compounds interact to create new substances, or how the principles of physics allow us to predict natural phenomenon. We made slime and goo and things that glow in the dark. We dropped dry ice into water, turned liquids different colors, grew crystals, and started seeds in little wet sponges. I tried to teach him about the "scientific method" and explain why it was better than the "unscientific method." But he didn't care about any of it. In the end, all he cared about was finding ways to make things explode, and nothing in the chemistry set I bought him was helping him explore his newfound passion.

When I complained to the manufacturer about the conspicuous lack of chemicals like glycerine, ammonia, chlorine, potassium carbonate, and gunpowder, a service representative explained to me that the modern chemistry set has been neutered by a well-meaning but entirely evil cabal of lawyers and insurance executives. Fear of terrorism and the popularity of methamphetamines are the main culprits, I was told—because, while we want kids to be interested in science, we apparently don't want them to be too interested. This is unfortunate, because back when I was a kid, chemistry sets came with all kinds of great chemicals that could create plenty of small explosions, not to mention toxic gases and eerily colored flames. But now, you're lucky if you get a set that will allow you to use any other liquid than water. How is a kid supposed to learn about liquids like gasoline, turpentine, acetone, and paint thinner if he doesn't have a chance to play with them? It's really a shame. Every once in a while you hear about one of these meth kitchens blowing up and the people inside getting incinerated. When you read about that kind of thing, you have to wonder—if their meth cook had a decent chemistry set when he was a kid, might they be alive today?

Now, it's no secret that boys like to make noise and destroy things, so they have a natural affinity for things like firecrackers and bombs. If you know anything about household chemistry, though, you know that while mixing vinegar and baking soda creates a satisfying volcanic foam, it does not make much noise. The Coke and Mentos trick, too, is disappointingly silent. A potato cannon made out of a tennis-ball can has a nice pop and hurls a projectile, but getting just the right size potato can be a challenge. Fireworks like the classic M-80 or a pack of Black Cats are practically impossible to get without driving to a state like Wisconsin, and the "safe" fireworks they sell in the stores in our state do nothing but shoot colored sparks into the air, which is very—I don't want to say "gay," because that would be prejudice—so let's just say "feminine."

What's a boy to do?

Well, if you're an enterprising self-starter with an entrepreneurial streak, and you live in America, the land of opportunity, you do what you have to do: you build it yourself, then try to sell it to your friends.

As it turns out, The Boy and all his friends were frustrated by their lack of access to small explosives and things that could injure or kill them in the course of friendly horseplay. Yes, they had AirSoft guns that shot soft rubber pellets, but they longed for the days, recounted by their elders, when they could shoot a friend's eye out during a BB-gun war. Yes, they could build bike and skateboard jumps, but the amount of protective gear they were required to wear made it practically impossible for them to skin a knee or break a bone. And yes, they got to light off fireworks every year, but watching plumes of blue and red sparks fly into the air gets old after about thirty seconds, and the only things in their fireworks kits that exploded were those little balls of paper that make a sissy little snap when they hit the ground.

The problem with not allowing boys to indulge their inherent interest in explosive destruction and dangerous horseplay is that these impulses do not go away; they fester and build. Killing and destroying things in video games isn't quite the same thing, because even boys understand that when they barbecue someone with a flamethrower or fire a rocket launcher at an enemy combatant, they are just tossing pixels around. They're not really killing or destroying anything, so their lust for destruction is incomplete.

To my son's credit, he identified a "need"—for explosive devices that a ten-year-old could operate—and filled it. So, in that sense, his actions were guided by sound business principles. It must also be said that he made a nice little profit, which should have counted for something with the judge, but didn't.

As it turns out, the general lack of a decent chemistry set in this country has turned the Internet into a veritable encyclopedia of fascinating workarounds. All a curious boy has to do these days is a quick Internet search for "how to make a homemade bomb," and all the information to fuel weeks of amusement and experimentation is there for the taking.

My son started small. Per the instructions provided by one of his peers on YouTube, he filled a plastic water bottle with pellets of tin foil, added a cup or so of toilet-bowl cleaner, sealed the cap, shook it, and waited. After about thirty seconds, the inside of the bottle began filling with smoke as the toilet-bowl cleaner interacted with the metal, and pretty soon the thing exploded with a nice, fat boom. The problem with this bomb, from a business standpoint, was that it was extremely time-intensive to make the foil pellets, and once the cap was sealed, the product destroyed itself in a matter of minutes. So, while it was fun and easy, there was no way to package and sell it.

Of the bombs it is possible to make with easily obtained materials, pipe bombs deliver the best bang for the buck. So that's what The Boy built next. Fortunately, our garage is well-equipped with hacksaws, wrenches, drills, C-clamps, pliers, and other useful bomb-making tools. I took him to the hardware store to buy a length of two-inch water pipe and some fitted end-caps, and we got a decent supply of gunpowder from the local sporting-goods store, which sells it to people who like to make their own shotgun shells. We bought a spool of fuse from an army surplus store, and got some aquarium gravel from the pet store to pack inside so that the bomb itself had some destructive punch.

Don't get me wrong: It's not like I just gave all this stuff to my son and let him make a bomb. Certainly not. I carefully supervised the entire project to make sure he was doing it right, and that all the pieces fit tight enough to create the necessary amount of compression inside the pipe. We cut the pipe into several one-foot lengths, and made a few of them—with different amounts of gunpowder and shrapnel to find out what the optimal combination was. Then we took the bombs out into a nearby field and tested them.

The first one was, admittedly, more powerful than we had anticipated. It blew a six-foot crater in the ground, and I got hit in the leg with a few pieces of blue gravel. The wound didn't bleed much, though, so

I just pulled my sock up and told The Boy it was nothing. When we set the other two off, we moved to the edge of the field and hid behind a tree. Which was a good idea, because all kinds of ball bearings and nails and rocks and things ended up embedded in that tree trunk. Both of us knew that stuff could have been embedded in us—which was, of course, what made it so much fun.

As it turned out, the first pipe bombs we built were too powerful and dangerous for the rest of the kids on the block to enjoy. The explosions could be heard around the neighborhood, of course, so word got around about what we'd done. And once everyone knew about it, there was intense pressure to develop a bomb that would be fun for everyone. As a result of our experiment, all of the boys in the neighborhood—and one very strange girl—also developed an interest in learning how to make their own pipe bombs. As the adult "in charge," however, I felt it was irresponsible to teach them, because the ends of the cut pipe can be very sharp, and someone could cut themselves if they weren't careful.

This gave my son the idea of creating a somewhat less powerful bomb made out of safer material—namely, plastic PVC tubing. Using the same basic design as the larger pipe bomb, my son developed a similar device by cutting one-inch PVC tubing into five-inch lengths. The explosive force of the resulting device was somewhere in between an M-80 and a full stick of dynamite—not exactly a bomb, but perfect for setting off controlled explosions that yielded spectacular results.

For instance, if you set off an M-80 inside a mailbox, the resulting damage is often very slight. Maybe it'll blow the door open and darken the inside. One of my son's patented PVC pipe bombs could blow just about any mailbox to smithereens, and do it in a way that allowed kids to observe the whole thing from a safe distance of about fifty feet. Likewise, if one of his bombs was exploded in a school locker, it would easily blow the door off, but not destroy all the lockers around it, making targeted mischief that much more effective.

But fun was the goal. My son and his friends stuck one inside a watermelon, which spewed a red cloud of pulverized fruit juice ten-feet high. They learned, too, that those seeds can sting if you're standing too close to the detonation. Another good effect came from submerging one in a tub of lime jello. The results were fantastic—green globs everywhere.

There were practical uses as well. In our backyard we had a stand of buckthorn that needed to be removed. Instead of doing the usual chopping and digging out of the root ball, we planted a few of my son's PVC bombs underground and bam, no more buckthorn. They also proved useful in loosening the asphalt on our driveway when it needed to be re-paved.

Though I supervised the development of the PVC project, I must say, in my defense, that I had no idea how enterprising my son could be when given the right motivation and resources. I learned after the fact that he had made dozens of those little PVC bombs, painted them different colors and sold them to his friends for five dollars apiece. He even came up with a name for them—Kabooms!—and designed a logo that he drew on the side in fun cartoon lettering. What kid could resist?

None of them, as it turns out. In a matter of days, every boy in the neighborhood had four or five Kabooms! at their disposal, and suddenly little bombs were going off all around town. Jeff Lansing set one off in the cantaloupes at the farmer's market. Doug Plant put one in his father's briefcase. Juaquin Sandoval blew up one of his sister's American Girl dolls. Several toilets in the boy's bathroom at school were destroyed, creating an awful mess, and for a few evenings there, you could hear one of my son's devices go off every half hour or so.

The destruction was fairly harmless, and no one had actually gotten hurt—until Mark Zander decided to duct-tape one to the bottom of the propane tank outside of the local Fill and Feed. Long story short, the tank exploded, the store burnt down, and Mary Louise Felder, the nice old lady who worked the counter on the six-to-two shift, was hospitalized with third-degree burns over forty percent of her body. Some thought it was a poor decision on her part to try to save the ice from melting, but Mary Louise was nothing if not dedicated.

Security cameras caught the Zander kid red-handed, and when the authorities questioned him, he folded like a greeting card. Said he'd bought the "incendiary device" from my son, and that he never would have blown up the propane tank if the other boys on his block hadn't started a betting pool for the person who created the biggest, best explosion. Once the challenge was issued, his lawyer explained, his competitive nature took over. Losing the betting pool was not an option; he had to win. Though the outcome was unfortunate, Mark

Zander, the argument went, was motivated by an intense inner drive to succeed. What good would come from squashing that drive by punishing him too harshly?

Amazingly, the judge agreed, noting that Zander was the school basketball team's star player, and that if the team's win-loss record was ever going to improve, Zander's competitive drive needed to be nurtured, not crushed. Another consideration was that Zander was only in seventh grade, so he had five more years of sports development ahead of him. Such promise at such a young age was rare.

Mark Zander had learned his lesson, the judge declared, and simply piling on the shame and humiliation was not going to do his current or future basketball teams any good.

The judge's ruling on my son was not quite as generous. Arguing on my son's behalf, I explained that injury and destruction were not my son's intention—all he wanted to do was embrace the great American entrepreneurial spirit and build a business. The product he sold just happened to be a small explosive, but it could have been anything—beer, cigarettes, drugs, whatever. The important thing was, my son had identified a need in the community, developed a product to fill that need, and had branded and marketed it to the best of his ability. He wasn't a "terrorist in training," he was a budding businessman—an entrepreneurial visionary in the tradition of Steve Jobs, Bill Gates, and Robert Oppenheimer. Whatever the consequences of his actions were, he was simply trying to be a good American. His mastery of the free-enterprise system at the age of ten indicated that The Boy had a bright future ahead of him, and to punish him for it would be hypocritical in the extreme. Besides, I said, today's chemistry sets suck, so what did he expect?

The judge had only one question: "Does your son play a sport?"

"No," I said, "he plays the violin."

"In that case, I sentence your son to one-hundred hours of community service," the judge said. "Making music is a communal act that requires people to work together toward a common goal. Grandstanders are not welcome, especially in chamber music. Your son needs to learn that."

"But . . ."

That's as far as I got. The judge then informed me that my wages were going to be garnished for as long as it took to pay for all of the property damage caused by my son's Kabooms!. Also, that my name had been added to the Homeland Security Department's "no fly" list, and I was not allowed to leave the country. Not that I would ever want to leave America, the greatest country in the world. I mean, where else on the planet can you get a Culver's butter-burger at three o'clock in the morning? Why would anyone want to go to a place where such a tasty and marginally nutritious meal isn't available any time, day or night? It doesn't make sense. Still, freedom is really about knowing you could leave if you wanted to. The great thing about America is that there is no reason to leave. Everything is here—except, apparently, a chemistry set that will actually spark a boy's interest in science.

CHAPTER 21

After the whole pipe-bomb fiasco died down, The Boy began assessing the political lay of the land at school more strategically. Mark Zander had gotten off easy because he was a basketball player, so, to ease his path through junior high and high school, The Boy reasoned that maybe he should take up a sport as well.

But which one?

It was spring, so football was out. Basketball wouldn't work because my son won't let anything but cotton touch his skin, and basketball shorts are made of a shiny synthetic material that gives him a rash. Soccer might have been acceptable with the right shorts, but The Boy thought it was a lot of running around for not much reward in the scoring department. "Soccer is why they invented basketball," The Boy told me, "so players can use their hands and score more often. Not that I want to play either, you understand—I'm just making an observation."

Nothing in the track-and-field world held any interest for The Boy either, except perhaps the javelin throw. Otherwise, track and field is all about speed and strength and endurance, none of which The Boy had much of. We considered tennis and golf, but those are sports that require actual skill to play, and my son did not want to practice any more than he had to. That left only one logical choice: baseball.

Baseball turned out to be the perfect sport for The Boy. Unlike other sports, in which every player needs to have some ability, baseball includes at least one position—right field—that requires almost no skill whatsoever. All the player has to do is stand out in a patch of grass, far away from the main action, and hope no one hits the ball to him. At age ten, there are only one or two boys on any given team who are strong enough to hit a baseball that far, so the odds were heavily in The Boy's favor. Another aspect of baseball that my son enjoyed was that not all of the players on the team could play at the same time. This meant that several of the kids on the team didn't even have to play. Instead, they got to sit on "the bench," while all the other kids had to stand out in a hot, dusty field—and, if the ball was hit to them, the rules of the game required them to put their bodies directly in the path of a tiny comet and risk getting a "bad hop" that could knock their front teeth out or rattle their testicles. Considering the risks involved, The Boy preferred to sit on the bench and watch, and felt privileged that, when his team was in the field, he pretty much had the bench to himself.

The whole point of joining the baseball team, however, was to pave a smoother path through middle school and high school. In the off-season, during the fall and winter, The Boy reported seeing no benefits or advantages whatsoever from his hours on the baseball field. After the season was over, most of boys on the team ignored him, or pretended not to know him. The girls in school were as indifferent to him as ever. And, even though he wore his baseball cap to school every day to let everyone know that yes, he was on the baseball team, no one seemed to care.

"It's not working, dad," The Boy complained. "Honestly, I'm not seeing a return on my investment. I don't think I'm going to play next year."

I did not like the sound of that. It sounded like quitting. I tried talking to him about it, but the old "winners never quit, and quitters never win" speech didn't work. "That might make sense if I cared about winning," The Boy said, "but I don't. The score of any given game is irrelevant, because there is always going to be another game, and then another and another. It's all so redundant and stupid."

I didn't like the sound of that, either. It was about this time that I started having concerns that my son might not have what it takes to succeed in this world. Not succeeding meant of course that he might be a failure, and failure, as everyone knows, is not an option. I had to do something—but what?

When confronted with such knotty problems, I often find it comforting to talk to my next-door neighbor, Larry-something. Larry is a writer of some kind—mystery novels, I think, but maybe it's horror stories. All I know is he spends a lot of time researching bizarre mental illnesses and different ways to torture and kill people. He once told me that he always wanted to write "real books," but there was no money in it. "Nobody wants to read about the psychological complexities and challenges of living in a country that has sold its people a false dream of prosperity and who are finding out that pursuing 'happiness' is a fool's game. They'd rather get right to the violence and sex. So I give 'em what they want, cash the checks, and that makes me moderately less depressed than I would otherwise be."

When I explained to Larry what was going on with The Boy, and how he was ready to give up on baseball, his response was quick and certain.

"Sounds to me like The Boy needs a coach," Larry said.

"He already has a coach," I explained. "Bill Chapman—who also happens to be his math teacher, but that's beside the point."

"No," said Larry, "that could very well be the point—and the problem."

"What do you mean?"

Larry put his meaty hands together and struck a thoughtful pose. "Well, as you know, the best way to kill a boy's interest in anything is to make it come from a teacher," he said. "To boys, teachers are just parents with a chalkboard. Both parents and teachers want boys to 'learn' and 'grow' and develop a 'positive attitude,' none of which boys have any interest in. They also represent authority—authority being anyone who tries to prevent boys from doing whatever they want, whenever they want, with whomever they want. The truth is, the only authority figure a boy will respect is a coach."

"What's the difference between a teacher and a coach?" I asked.

"Coaches are different from teachers in that they wear shorts and a whistle, and they yell more," Larry explained. "To boys, coaches are more like a cool big brother or scary uncle; they're people boys want to impress, but who secretly terrify them. And while a boy's mother might not be able to motivate her son to get up off the couch, a coach can motivate a boy to run until he pukes, or shoot free throws until his arms collapse. It's not fair, but there it is."

"But like I said, he already has a coach," I said.

"No, he has a teacher who is doubling as a coach," Larry clarified. "What he needs is a *private* coach."

"Private?"

"Yes, one dedicated to developing his skills on the baseball diamond. Any parent these days who wants their son to succeed in the highly competitive world of grade-school sports hires a private coach.

If your son doesn't have one, it could explain why his attitude is so poor."

I thanked Larry for his advice, and set about finding my son a private baseball coach—one who could help him field sizzling ground balls, throw with strength and accuracy, hit with authority, and fearlessly slide on dirt in a way that tore holes in his uniform and turned his knee into a bloody crust of scar tissue and pus.

Finding a baseball coach who is not also a teacher is easier said than done, though. Schools do not hire people simply to coach baseball, and "baseball coach" is not a profession many people will admit to having. Outside of school, in fact, almost all little-league baseball teams are coached by fathers of boys on the team. My son had absolutely no interest in playing little-league baseball, mainly because one of his friends who did told him that "everyone gets to play." To The Boy, setting foot on the field was the least interesting aspect of baseball, so the prospect of constantly playing struck him as counterproductive. According to Larry, however, The Boy's inability to throw, hit, or field might be eroding his confidence. A coach could help him develop the skills he needed to succeed, boosting his self-esteem to the point where his innate competitive drive—if he had any—would naturally kick in.

Most of the other boys on my son's baseball team were playing little-league baseball on the side, however, and this, I surmised, was how they were outpacing my son's development. That and the fact that my son's hand-eye coordination seemed limited to the thumb dexterity required to operate various weapons in Call of Duty, Halo, and Gears of War.

Since I couldn't find a suitable private baseball coach—and since all the other coaches in the area seemed to be fathers—the most logical thing to do was take on the coaching duties myself. True, it had been twenty-five years or so since I played the game. But baseball is timeless, and I remembered the fundamentals—think ahead, keep your eye on the ball, spit downwind, don't yawn during the pitch, run counter-clockwise—so I felt confident in my ability to pass this knowledge on to my son.

For our first practice session, I felt that we should concentrate on throwing and catching. Right field is a wonderful position for people who have very little interest in playing the game. The only problem is that in the unlikely event the ball is hit to right field, the player must suddenly switch gears from bored onlooker to engaged participant. If the player can catch the ball and throw it back into the infield with practiced nonchalance, he can return to his semi-hypnotic state of boredom in a matter of seconds. But if the player cannot perform these basic tasks, the shame and humiliation the player was trying to avoid by embracing the relative anonymity of the position are suddenly and unwittingly thrust on him.

My son had endured this very torture during a game late in the season. Runners for the opposing team were on second and third. The score was 7-6, and the runner on second represented the winning run. A double would bring him home. As fate would have it, the batter at the plate chose that moment to swing a bit late and send a looping fly ball out into right field. The timing could not have been worse, as my son had chosen that exact moment to investigate a bumblebee crawling on a dandelion bloom on the ground at his feet. Oblivious to the crack of the bat and the roar of the crowd, my son was not aware that he was suddenly "in" the game, because that had never happened before. The ball landed with a thud ten feet away from him. When he looked up to identify the noise, he didn't quite know what it was at first. Gradually it dawned on him that the white sphere rolling past him was the game ball, and that all those voices in the distance were screaming at him to do something.

But what?

He scampered after the ball, and while he ran he recalled from his training that the players standing on the dirt part of the field needed it as quickly as possible. Why, he wasn't certain. But he was determined to return the ball to the infield as quickly as he could. He had never quite mastered the overhand throw, however, so he decided to throw the ball back underhanded. But he couldn't throw it very far that way, either, so he calculated that the ball might actually reach the infield faster if he didn't throw it so much as roll it, like a bowling ball. My son interpreted the eruption of noise that greeted this idea as the crowd's enthusiastic approval. Since the ball only traveled about ten feet before nestling down into the long grass, The Boy trotted up to the ball and rolled it again—and again he received a roar, this one even louder than before. By the time he got the ball to the edge of the infield, he judged by the level of chaos in the bleachers that he was suddenly the star of the game—the hero being cheered by his adoring fans.

"It wasn't my fault," The Boy insisted after he learned the truth. "If the lawn had been properly mowed, that bee never would have been there in the first place, and my concentration wouldn't have been broken. Also, if the grass had been shorter, the ball itself would have rolled farther and faster, increasing the likelihood that it might reach the infield before the opposing runners scored. And let's not forget the dubious coaching involved. I mean, what madness led the man to take me off the bench in the first place? It was like he was begging to lose. So no, I don't feel bad about it. After all, I'm the victim here."

But all sports involve a learning curve, I reasoned, and as every coach knows, when an athlete begins to falter, it's time to get back to the fundamentals. At the very least, I figured, learning how to catch and throw would spare The Boy (or at least me) another such embarrassment. So we grabbed our gloves and a ball, and went into the backyard to play some catch.

To begin with, I taught The Boy how to slam his fist into his glove to let his opponents know that he was serious. Then I taught him how to arch his right eyebrow and spit—not in a glob or spray, but in a steady, even stream. After mastering those skills, we moved on to the mechanics of gripping the ball and throwing overhand. The Boy's grip was excellent, but he had difficulty with the idea of letting the ball go at just the right moment to ensure its forward trajectory. This problem stemmed from a fear that if he let the ball go, it would fly over the fence, through a window, or into my face—all of which turned out to be legitimate concerns. "Wild" is the word coaches use to describe pitchers whose accuracy is somewhat unpredictable. Better words for my son's throwing might be "berserk" or "tornadic." There was no telling where that ball might go or what it might do, so the smart strategy was to duck and take cover until it was over.

When it came to catching, my son was a bit more defensive. He preferred to use his glove to protect his face rather than catch the ball. I tried to persuade him that if he used the glove correctly, he could catch the ball and protect his face, but convincing him was not easy. I cajoled and encouraged him; begged and pleaded; empathized and affirmed—but nothing worked. The Boy just cowered underneath his glove whenever I threw the ball toward him, and let it hit him—in the shoulder, arm, hip, or leg—rather than attempt even the most furtive catch.

Then I remembered what Larry had said about the special authority coaches had that teachers and parents did not. Upon reflection, I noted that I was wearing long pants, did not have a whistle around my neck, and had not yelled at The Boy even once. I realized then that I was still playing the role of "parent," not the role of "coach." It wasn't The Boy's attitude that was standing in the way of our progress, it was mine.

To change that dynamic, I went back inside and put on a pair of khaki shorts and a green Polo shirt, and borrowed my wife's "rape" whistle out of her purse. Thus equipped, I went back outside and we started over.

This time, rather than trying to coax The Boy into doing what I asked, I did what a true coach would do and yelled, "Get that glove off your face, maggot!"

Taken aback at the abrupt change in my tone, The Boy lowered his glove enough to see that I had donned the uniform of a coach. He didn't know quite what to make of the new wardrobe, but I could tell by the wary look in his eyes that he was almost ready to respect me.

"What are you, some kind of beauty queen?!" I yelled. "Is your face so precious that you have to protect it from an itty-bitty baseball?! Would you rather be practicing for the Miss America pageant?!"

Stunned, The Boy looked at me with a mixture of terror and confusion.

"How do you expect to catch the ball if you can't see it?!" I screamed. "Are you some kind of psychic? Can you somehow sense where the ball is with the power of your mind?!"

I then threw the baseball at him and hit him in the stomach.

"You're going to need a bigger glove if you want to keep the rest of your body looking nice for that beauty pageant!" I yelled—then picked up the ball and threw it at him a few more times. "You can't win the swimsuit competition with bruises all over your body. So man up and catch it!" I screamed. Then I walked up to him and blew the whistle into his ear as loud as I could.

These tactics may work for other coaches, but they did not work for me. Instead of obeying my instructions, The Boy simply crumpled into a ball on the ground and cried. Big, heaving sobs. Wails of pain and indignation. His mother heard the cries—connected as those two are by some invisible tear duct of the soul—and rushed out of the house to see what was the matter.

"What did you do?" she said as she knelt by his side and began stroking his forehead.

"I was trying to teach him how to catch a baseball," I explained.

"Did he get hit or something?"

"Well yes, several times," I said.

"What are these bruises and welts?" she asked.

"Those are indications of progress," I explained. "If he gets hit with the ball enough times, he will no longer be afraid of it—and that's the goal."

"Why were you blowing my whistle?" she inquired.

"It's what coaches do," I explained. "I don't quite know how it works, but the shrill tone of the whistle somehow motivates boys to push themselves harder than they would otherwise."

"Well, I think he's been pushed far enough for one day," my wife said as she cradled The Boy in her arms and guided him inside. "And take those stupid clothes off," she added. "You look like you're going to play golf."

Later that afternoon, I told Larry what had happened. He listened without judgment, and, when I was done, offered his perspective.

"If it's any consolation, most coaches are no better at motivating their own children than other parents," he said. "It turns out that when coaches apply the magical techniques that work so well on the football or baseball field to their own kids, the police tend to get involved. You're lucky you weren't arrested."

As usual, Larry's counsel was both wise and comforting. After that day, The Boy never played baseball again, and I gave up on trying to "coach" him at anything. Being his dad was enough of a headache.

CHAPTER 22

otivating children to do things they don't want to do is every parent's biggest challenge. This wasn't always the case, of course. Back in the days when parents were allowed to spank their kids or beat them with a stick or shove a bar of soap in their mouth, motivating children was simply a matter of how much physical pain to administer. Parents ruled with fear, and they backed up their words with punishments that were legitimately terrifying. It was a good system.

But, like all good systems, it was broken by a bunch of well-meaning people who "knew better," and wanted to improve it. Unfortunately, now that beating children into submission is culturally unacceptable, there is nothing for children to be afraid of. Deprived of their most potent weapon, parents are now powerless and must try to motivate kids through persuasion, coercion, and other passive techniques that do not work very well.

One school of thought that doesn't work at all is the "people of praise" approach. People of Praise advocates think children are no different from dogs, and that kids can be guided toward the right behaviors by ignoring their mistakes and heaping praise on them whenever they do something right. You see this at parties a lot. Parties put people's children on public display, and kids like to misbehave at parties, so parents must try to stop them without resorting to violence. Consequently, you'll hear things like, "Good boy for not hitting Jimmy again," or "Thank you for screaming with your inside voice, Suzy, and not your outside voice," or "You're such a good spitter, Billy—let's see if you can hit the ground this time."

What most modern parents don't understand is that there's a difference between empty, toothless praise and praise that leads to the sort of outcomes parents really want. For instance, inane encouragements like "Atta boy, Johnny!" or "Way to go, Hank!" do absolutely nothing to motivate boys to try harder. That's because boys are naturally lazy, and they interpret such mindless, unconditional enthusiasm as proof that they've done as well as they need to at that particular moment, so why try any harder?

More effective forms of praise communicate that a boy can always do better, and the praise is framed in a way that lets the boy know it. Suppose the boy has come in third place at the school science fair. Parents who want their praise to motivate a boy to work harder on his next science project shouldn't say, "Way to go, Boy. " Instead, they should say something like, "Hey, you tried your best—it just wasn't good enough," or "Don't worry, lots of third-place finishers go on to live, happy productive lives."

The key is to couch the praise in the form of what sounds like a comforting consolation, but really says: "You didn't do your best. You know it, and we know it. We are not impressed." On the surface, The Boy is allowed to save face, but deep inside he experiences the shame of knowing that his parents are right—he hardly even tried—and he shouldn't be fishing for praise he doesn't deserve.

Consider another real-world example from the fascinating world of baseball:

Though my son never actually got a hit when he played baseball, I observed the fathers of many boys who did make contact with the ball, and was dismayed to discover how clueless these men were when it came to doling out praise for their child's accomplishments. If their son hit a double, for instance, most dads would give their son one of those empty "atta boys" and clap a few times. Nothing could be more useless. What I could never understand is why these men didn't seize these golden opportunities to teach their son an important lesson about effort and expectations.

If my son had ever hit a double, I would have handled the situation like this: As The Boy ran into second base and everyone else was cheering, I'd yell, "Holy cow, with a little more hustle that could have been a triple!" This would have communicated to The Boy that he needed to work on his speed—because while a double is nice, a triple is better. The important thing to communicate would be that he came up a little short. To properly motivate a boy, the goal must be kept just out of reach. If The Boy had hit a triple, for instance, it could have been home run. If he hit a home run, it could have been a grand slam. If he hit a grand slam, he could have hit it in the bottom of the ninth to win the game. If he hit a grand slam in the bottom of the ninth to win a game, he could be proud, yes, but it's not like he did it at Yankee stadium. And if he ever did hit a grand slam at Yankee stadium, it would only be impressive if it was to win the seventh game of the World Series. Otherwise, it's just another fancy fly ball over the wall.

By doling out praise in this way, in tiny increments rather than full-blown explosions of unqualified adulation, parents can instill in their sons the valuable life knowledge that no matter how hard they try, it's never enough; no matter how well they've done, they can always do better; and even if they win, life isn't about competing and winning—it's about winning in a way that lets everyone else know you weren't even trying very hard.

CHAPTER 23

What the Parents of Perpetual Praise eventually discover of course is that their kids are not dogs, and that treating them like dogs only ensures that they will eventually shit and piss on everything, then bite you if you try to stop them. This is no way to raise a child. At some point, every parent must dole out some form of punishment—but if you can't hit your kid with a belt or a stick, what can you do?

What I've discovered is that in order to motivate a boy to do his best, it is important to implement a rational system of rewards and punishments that will serve as a foundation for guiding his behavior in the future. Many parents opt for the "carrot and stick" approach, but this method does not work on boys, because boys hate carrots and, while they will occasionally eat sticks, they are not afraid of being hit by one. My approach to discipline is based on a different theory of motivation altogether—a theory based on real-world knowledge of what boys actually hate.

One day, for instance, the phone rang and I answered it. On the other end was a police officer who informed me that my son had been apprehended trying to shoplift a can of Red Bull from a nearby Super-America, and that he was being held at the local police precinct. If I came down to pick him up, they would release him into my custody, they said, and if we promised to discipline The Boy appropriately, the store owner had promised not press charges.

"What does 'discipline him appropriately,' mean?" I asked the officer.

"That's up to you," the officer said. "But my advice is not to let him off too easy. It's his first offense, so now's the time to hammer some sense into him, if you can."

I thanked the officer and went down to pick The Boy up, as agreed. On the way over, I wasn't thinking about what type of punishment was appropriate for The Boy's crime—because nowadays, "appropriate" punishment is illegal. What I was thinking about instead was this: What could my wife and I do to The Boy that would inflict an enormous amount of pain, but not cause any physical harm? Sure, we could ground him and make him do a bunch of chores. And of course we could make him play classic board games with us, or take away his precious books. But the situation at hand required a more creative approach, one that would drive home the magnitude of his crime and deter such felonious temptations in the future.

The punishment we came up with was so clever and devious that we ended up using it on several occasions. Its virtue was its utter simplicity. And here I have to give my wife credit, because when it comes to doing devious things that don't look devious on the surface, she's the queen. So, rather than yell at him and threaten him and call him names like "degenerate criminal scum," or "thieving little monster" we—at my wife's suggestion—simply sat down and "talked" to him. And by "talk" to him, I mean we tag-team lectured him for eight hours straight.

I took up the topics of right vs. wrong, social responsibility, citizenship, karma, fate, and cosmic retribution. His mother talked about the importance of honesty and trustworthiness, and how, with this on his record, he would never get into Princeton—and that "boys like him" ended up going to state universities where the classes were taught by armies of over-worked, underpaid adjunct professors who couldn't win a Nobel prize if all they had to do was throw a dart at it. She also did a good forty-five minutes on the twin evils of sugar and caffeine. I explained the impact of The Boy's thievery by drilling deep into the economics of small-business ownership, inventory management, SuperAmerica stock, the social contract between buyers and sellers, and international monetary policy. She tried to make The Boy understand how badly he'd hurt the store owner's feelings, and how stealing from people—unless it's done by large corporations who have the blessing of the U.S. government—is unacceptable in a civilized society.

About five hours in, when I was running out of things to say, my wife delivered the coup de grace—the velvet shiv that made The Boy's blood run cold and turned his eyes into hollow holes of mortal dread.

In a tone so deviously sweet that you'd swear she was comforting a baby, she asked The Boy why he took the Red Bull? Was he tired? Was he getting enough sleep? Was he sick? Dehydrated? Did his friends make him do it? Was he aware that what he was doing was wrong? If so, why did he do it? If not, where did we go wrong, as parents?

How had we failed him? If he didn't know stealing is wrong, what else didn't he know?

The reason this is such a brilliant strategy is that the only thing boys hate more than being lectured at by teachers is being lectured at by their parents. For The Boy, each question feels like a punch, and sitting there for hours on end listening to his parents drone on in hushed tones of sincere concern is sheer agony. But before you try this technique yourself, here are a couple of tips, borne of experience:

—If you're not prepared to talk for at least three or four hours, don't bother. Anything less than three hours isn't long enough to wear down a boy's resistance.

—No matter how long the lecture goes, or how exhausted the topic at hand may seem, always end by saying, "We'll discuss this some more in the morning." This ensures that The Boy will spend a sleepless night imagining how his parents' concern will be expressed over breakfast.

—No two parents can talk for eight hours at a stretch without a little help. My advice, if you plan to talk this long, is to keep your own secret stash of Red Bull on hand, at the ready.

—After you've doled out the punishment, it's important to guide The Boy's behavior with an appropriate "reward." Post-lecture, the best reward you can give a boy is to tell him that in the future he can avoid a "talking to" by simply not screwing up. Normally, this is all the motivation a boy needs to get his act together and figure out how not to get caught next time.

CHAPTER 24

Of course, no disciplinary tactic will work unless the proper psychological groundwork has been laid. In order for children to experience a sufficient amount of guilt and dread to prevent them from disobeying their parents, or from doing something they know is wrong, they must be taught to feel the cold chill of fear in their bones. Indeed, a certain amount of paranoia goes a long way in the parenting world. But for it to work, children must be taught to believe, deep down, that their parents are omniscient, omnipresent, infallible super-beings who instinctively know what is going on in their psychopathic little minds.

The sort of pure terror that parents of our generation used to keep us in line is of course illegal now, so today's parents must be craftier. Besides, fear only goes so far. A more effective deterrent for today's parents is to instill a deep and foreboding sense of guilt—about everything. If something goes wrong, The Boy should immediately assume it's his fault. If he is tempted to engage in any sort of forbidden or illegal activity, he should immediately assume that he will be caught, prosecuted, and punished to the fullest extent of the law. Most boys think they are smarter than their parents, but deep down they fear that they are not. This weakness must be exploited at an early age. That way, in the future, after engaging in any type of unapproved activity, they will be haunted by the question of how they are going to get caught this time, especially considering that their parents are so stupid.

This type of guilt is extremely useful, and it can be achieved by setting up a series of simple situations around the age of five or six, when The Boy is old enough to understand the consequences of his actions, but not old enough to recognize a trap when he sees one. It works like this:

Situation #1: Mom bakes a batch of chocolate-chip cookies, filling the house with their delicious aroma. She leaves a pile of them on the counter, with a chair nearby so that The Boy can reach them. She then goes down into the basement, ostensibly to do the laundry, leaving the cookies unguarded. Naturally, The Boy sees the opportunity to steal a cookie, and quietly tiptoes into the kitchen. He pulls the chair close to the counter and climbs up. When he reaches for a cookie, mom jumps up out of the basement and screams, "Ha, I caught you!" Startled, The Boy jerks his head around, drops the cookie he is holding in his hand—which is now irrefutable evidence of his wrongdoing—and starts begging for mercy. Mission accomplished.

Situation #2: Dad is watching a football game, trying to explain the rules of the game to The Boy, and at some point gets up to get a beer. "I know Thomas the Tank Engine is on channel 245," he says, "but don't change the channel." In fact, The Boy did not know Thomas the Tank Engine was on, but now that he does, he cannot help himself. After a few minutes have passed and dad does not return, The Boy punches 245 on the remote, figuring the channel can easily be changed by pushing the "last" button when dad gets back. What The Boy doesn't know is that dad hasn't come back because he is sitting in his office, where he has installed a webcam attached to the TV The Boy is watching. When The Boy punches "245," it activates the webcam in dad's office and, instead of seeing a talking blue train on the screen, The Boy sees his the spectre of his father, who yells, "Boy, I told you not to change the channel! What the hell is wrong with you!?" Trust me, The Boy will never change the channel again.

Situation #3: You send The Boy up to brush his teeth, but don't hear any water running, so you know he hasn't done it. When you ask, "Have you brushed your teeth yet?" and The Boy lies that yes, he has, sit him down and tell him to close his eyes and open his mouth. Tell The Boy that you are making him take a "lie detector pill," and that if he is in fact lying, his tongue will catch fire. Then put a Flintstone vitamin on his tongue that you have dusted with cayenne pepper. In seconds, The Boy will confess and run screaming to the bathroom to brush his teeth. In addition to teaching him a valuable lesson, the minty coolness of the toothpaste will immediately make his tongue feel better, creating a lifetime of positive associations with teeth-brushing. (Note: if the idea of putting cayenne pepper on your son's tongue disturbs you, the same result can be achieved by using an Alka-Seltzer and telling him that he is foaming at the mouth because he is lying like a filthy, rabid dog.)

These are simple but effective tactics that pay multiple dividends later in life. Particularly sensitive boys may of course need a modest amount of therapy in their twenties to address issues of generalized anxiety and paranoia, but that's a small price to pay for a lifetime of blind obedience.

CHAPTER 25

Now, some readers might be tempted to dismiss the parenting tactics I've described above as nothing but deceit, trickery, coercion, and torture. And some well-meaning but demonstratively ineffective parents—the kind who want to be friends with their kids—might think the methods I am describing are unnecessarily cruel. Nothing could be further from the truth, of course, because when it comes to raising boys, a certain amount of subversive cruelty is sometimes the only thing they understand.

Doubts are understandable, though. Raising a boy is not for the squeamish, requiring as it does a commitment to results that many parents are reluctant to accept, let alone embrace. What most parents don't realize is that raising a boy is not a blissful boat ride down a river full of lotus blossoms—it is psychological warfare, pure and simple. The sooner parents realize that they are fighting a society that wants to turn their kids into sociopaths, and kids who desperately want to become sociopaths, the better it will be for everyone.

The problem is, it can take years to learn the complicated psychology of boys. Granted, it takes longer to understand girl psychology, but we're talking about boys here, so parents of girls, you're on your own. Good luck.

That said, there are a few simple guidelines that every parent can follow to ensure that life with their growing boy goes more smoothly:

—Never say anything is "educational."
—Never say anything is "good for you."
—Never say anything is an "opportunity."
—Never ask them about their grades.
—Never force them to eat green food.
—Never call them "cute" or "adorable."
—Never turn off their Playstation before they've "saved."
—Never express concern about their health.
—Never try to cheer them up.
—Never tell them to clean their room.

—Never go into their room, period.
—Never ask them about their friends.
—Never ask them if they are drunk or stoned.
—Never ask them about their feelings.
—Never hug or kiss them in public.
—Never offer unsolicited advice.
—Never try to solve their problems.
—Never tell them to get a haircut.
—Never ask them for help.

Follow these simple guidelines and life with your growing man-child will be much more pleasant.

CHAPTER 26

Boys and girls like different things, of course. What typically distinguishes a "boy thing" from a "girl thing" is the element of hazard involved, combined with the potential for pain and/or spilled bodily fluids, multiplied by the degree to which it drives mothers crazy.

In the category of "stuff boys love that mothers hate," owning a pet snake is it at the top of the list. As a rule, mothers hate snakes because when all mothers were little girls, some boy with a pet snake terrorized them by shoving a slithery serpent in their face, or sneaking it into their school locker. The girl-mother screamed, the boy laughed, and forever after there has been a clear gender divide on the issue of snake ownership.

I caught and kept snakes when I was a kid, so when my son expressed an interest in reptiles, I understood completely. An intense fascination with things that slither and chomp and eat their food whole is perfectly natural for a boy. It starts with dinosaurs, of course, which engage a child's imagination by being monstrously large and terrifyingly violent, often ripping their food to shreds in seconds. Boys love that sort of thing. It reminds them of their teachers at school, and their parents after a bad day at work.

Once the novelty of theoretical creatures from the past wears off, however, kids naturally turn their attention to the real world of the here and now. One day, I took The Boy to a local pet store run by a man covered in fish tattoos. The tattooed man carried all kinds of interesting reptiles, including a Komodo dragon, an albino boa constrictor, and a snapping turtle that could take an arm off. I don't know exactly how it happened, but one minute we were standing there watching a king snake flick its forked tongue at us, and the next minute the idea of owning his own snake suddenly popped into The Boy's head. Since I too had enjoyed snakes as a kid, I thought it might be rewarding to share this hobby with my son. What I didn't take into account was my wife's reaction to the idea of allowing The Boy to have an itty-bitty corn snake in a ten-gallon aquarium in his room.

"Absolutely not! There is no way you are starting him down that path!" she insisted the day the subject came up—the day, that is, that we brought the snake home. "I will not have a snake living in my house!"

"Technically, mom, you already have a snake living in the house," my son pointed out. "He's right here. His name is Flash."

Weirdly, my wife can do that same muffled throat-scream thing that my mother used to do. "This is your fault!" she growled, pointing at me. "You and your stupid snake stories. What is it with boys? Why this ridiculous fascination for the slimiest, most disgusting things on earth!"

"That Nastassja Kinski photo in the 1980s might have had something to do with it," I explained. "Then there was Britney and the boa constrictor. And Rihanna just did that snaky, sexy GQ cover."

"And snakes aren't slimy, mom," my son added. "They're really very clean. Here, feel him," he said, pushing the little red corn snake toward her.

"I don't care. Take him back!" she hissed in an ironically snake-like way.

As my son began to cry, and I shrugged my shoulders in helpless resignation to events already in motion, my wife re-assessed the situation and finally relented.

"Okay, here are the conditions," she said. "You can keep the snake if I never have to hear about it or see it again. Do you understand?"

We both nodded.

"And if you ever lose it, or it ever escapes, the subject of snakes will never come up, ever again, in any context, as long as you both shall live. Is that understood?"

Yes, we nodded.

"Furthermore, no one outside this house is ever to know that we have a snake residing under our roof. Agreed?"

Well no, because that would take half the fun out of it, we both thought—but we nodded yes anyway.

The first week with Flash the corn snake was fairly uneventful. He was only a foot long, and about as thick around as a Cheerio, so not particularly fearsome. He had nice red and rust markings, and my son enjoyed how Flash would wiggle around in his hand and wrap his tiny tail around The Boy's thumb and wrist. Flash lived in a ten-gallon aquarium adorned with wood shavings, a rock to hide behind, and a stick on which to climb. Corn snakes can grow to be six feet long and live for twenty years, but snakes grow slowly, so this particular enclosure would do for a while at least. The lid of the cage was a rectangle of screen mesh that fit tightly over the top, and a forty-watt light bulb clamped to the lid acted as the snake's sun. The Boy was only allowed to take the snake out of his cage when I was home to supervise, and if for any reason his mother had to enter the room, he was instructed to drape the cage with a towel so that she wouldn't have to see it.

Then came the day when, at last, Flash had to be fed. Unfortunately, corn snakes don't eat chunks of apple or little shreds of lettuce; they dine almost exclusively on a diet of mice. And since Flash was small, he needed to eat small mice. Baby mice, to be precise; little, pink, just-born mice that can't even see yet, to be even more precise; helpless, innocent little critters, that is, who come into this world unaware of the terrors that await them, and are fated to return to the void from which they came before they have even sampled their first nibble of cheddar.

One doesn't have to breed baby mice, however, because the pet store where we bought Flash carries them in abundance. How, I do not know. My guess is that they have a giant rodent ranch somewhere, a Ponderosa of procreation that produces all manner of mice and rats for the sole purpose of feeding them to slithery reptiles one notch up the food chain. On any given day, dozens of squirming little baby mice are available in different sizes. So, on the day we were scheduled to feed Flash, I stopped by the store and picked one up. A kid with black lips and a nose ring plopped the little guy into a paper bag like a gumdrop, and I carted it home for the ceremonial first feeding.

My son was excited to see his new snake eat its first meal. I knew from experience, however, that his excitement would probably not last very long. This perhaps connects back to the reason my wife did not want a snake in the house in the first place.

You see, when my wife and I first met, one of my roommates was a ten-foot-long Burmese python which I inherited when a previous roommate who, short on rent money and only half a step ahead of the law, skipped town and abandoned the snake with me. I considered it a windfall, though, because the python was far more personable than the former roommate—and, secretly, every boy wants to own a python someday, even if he has to wait until he's twenty-five years old to do it.

My python's name was Fred, and though Fred was relatively docile, even friendly at times, he was also what most people would consider dangerously large. He was somewhere between ten and twelve feet long (accurately measuring him was impossible), and at the thickest point in his long body he was as big around as my leg. In short, you would not want to leave a small child in the same room with Fred, because there was always the outside chance he might mistake the kid for a snack. In fact, I used to let Fred roam my apartment on his own periodically, and had to warn anyone shorter than five-foot-five to keep their distance.

Feeding Fred was an event. Among my circle of friends, there were always a few jacked-up macho types who wanted to watch Fred swallow a guinea pig or a rabbit, and who made a point of letting me know how eager they were to witness this spectacle of "nature in action." Fred only had to eat once a month, so I fed him on the fifteenth, religiously, and issued an open invitation to anyone who wanted to see it.

The dynamic was always the same. Rarely did anyone want to watch Fred eat by themselves, and women almost never did. The guys would always come in a group, armed with plenty of beer to stoke their blood lust, and, before the fact, would talk big and bold about how awesome it was going to be to watch ol' Fred devour a live animal right before their very eyes. What they didn't know, but soon discovered, is how slow and agonizing it is to watch a Burmese python go about its natural business.

Guinea pigs were the easiest meal to procure. So, when the time came, I would announce that the feeding was about to begin, and the guys would gather 'round, each one of them intensely eager to witness the dance of death between predator and prey. Then, I'd drop the guinea pig into the cage, and we'd wait.

The thing is, Fred was unpredictable. Sometimes, he'd ignore his dinner for an hour or two before waking up. Other times, he'd immediately fasten his eyes on his prey and move in for the kill. Either way, the poor guinea pig sensed what was coming and inevitably cowered in the corner, terrified, awaiting his fate, frozen with fear. The fact that guinea pigs are cute made the spectacle that much less enjoyable to watch. When Fred struck, he did so in a blinding instant, holding the guinea pig in his jaws while it wriggled and squealed. Then he would slowly coil his body around the guinea pig and start preparing his meal.

Pythons are constrictors, which means they kill their prey by squeezing it to death. What most people don't know is how long this process takes, and how brutal it is to watch. Constriction works like this: once the snake is coiled around its prey, it slowly starts squeezing. Each time its prey exhales, the snake tightens its grip, preventing its victim from inhaling again. Eventually, the prey dies from suffocation, then, in Fred's case, he would continue to squeeze until pretty much every bone in the guinea pig's body was crushed. This part of the process alone could take two or three hours, and I never knew anyone who could stand to watch it for more than fifteen minutes. Usually, the blood lust in our living room gave way in short order to sadness and pity, followed by horror at the grim "reality" of it, then varying degrees of shame and regret. Some guys wretched; others pretended to get bored; and others, to save face, checked in every hour or so to see "how things were going." The unhinging of Fred's jaw to work its way around the head of the guinea pig was another moment of high interest, but it could take Fred another couple of hours to swallow his meal, at which point all but the most dedicated spectators were usually exhausted by death fatigue. Rarely did anyone wish to witness Fred dine twice; once was enough for most people, because the truth is that, outside of TV and movies, death is not very entertaining.

So I knew what was coming the first night we fed Flash. He, too, was a constrictor, and he reacted to the baby mouse in his cage precisely the way Fred used to react to the guinea pig: body tense, eyes trained on the meal, then the strike, the kill, and the big gulp. All the same as Fred, but on a much smaller scale, and considerably faster. Much to my surprise, however, The Boy did not flinch or leave the room when Flash began to feed. Instead, he asked questions.

"How does he know it's food?"

"Do snakes have taste buds?"

"How long does digestion take?"

"What happens to the hair and bones?"

"How do snakes find food in the wild?"

"Will I be able to see him grow?"

"How big do you think he'll get?"

"Can I bring him to school?"

"Can I feed him next time?"

That's when I knew I had a true snake boy on my hands. It was one of the few times in his life when I could look at The Boy and know, for certain, that he was probably my kid after all.

Now, one of the unfortunate aspects of owning a pet snake is that there are only three possible outcomes: 1) the snake dies, 2) it escapes, or 3) you have to let it go. Snakes do not stick around for years like a dog or a gerbil; they tend to force the issue. Fred the python, for example, ended up as a gift to a local rescue organization, because he ultimately violated some ancient zoning law against harboring a deadly predator in a neighborhood crawling with tiny toddler snackables. Also, my girlfriend-cum-wife insisted that I get rid of him, arguing that she would not marry me if that "baby killer" came along for the ride. Though to be fair to Fred, he never killed anyone's baby—he just looked like he could, to people who don't understand a thing about snakes. Even in the Everglades, where pythons are as common as rabbits, you hardly ever read about them eating babies, because they prefer dogs, goats, and sheep.

For months, Flash flourished in his tiny cage, eating every week and molting now and then as he grew. As snakes go, he was quite likable, and did not mind being held or carried. In fact, he seemed to like the view, or whatever he could see of it through his little prehistoric eyes.

The thing about snakes in captivity is that they are very patient. They will wait for months or years, if necessary, for their chance to escape—and when it comes, they will take it and not look back. Snakes don't care. They are also too stupid to realize that if they just stay put, their lives would be a lot easier.

And so the day finally came, as I knew it eventually would, when we went to feed Flash and he was nowhere to be found. Upon closer inspection, the lid to his cage was slightly askew, and there was a tiny gap through which he must have crawled, because there was no other way for him to escape. Even worse, I was fairly certain it was my fault, because the night before I had opened Flash's cage to fill his pickle-jar lid with clean water. Had I forgotten to make sure the lid was completely closed? Probably. Would it be the death of me if I didn't find him? Most definitely.

Though my son was on the verge of panic, I instructed him to stay calm and search every corner of his room. "He couldn't have gone far," I said, even though I knew this wasn't necessarily true.

We searched everywhere—under the bed, in the closet, behind the bookshelf, under the sock pile—but could find no trace of our escapee.

"He'll turn up," I assured The Boy. "He has to be somewhere," I said, which was technically true, but that somewhere could be in the wall or ceiling, or in any of a thousand dark corners where we would never find him.

Then the call came from downstairs: "Dinner, you two!"

Alarmed—terrified, really—I warned my son that we both had to suddenly become extremely convincing actors and pretend that nothing was wrong—that indeed, everything was hunky-dory. He asked me what "hunky dory" meant, and I told him to look it up on his phone. He did, and said he didn't understand why we had to pretend like everything was like a David Bowie album from 1971. Who was David Bowie?, he asked. And what is an album? And, really, is anyone from 1971 still alive?

I reminded him what would happen if his mother found out that the snake had escaped, and he reminded me that it was my fault, and asked why he should be punished for my mistake, and what was I going to do about it if she did found out, because he wasn't going to go down with me if he could possibly help it.

"I'll cry if I have to," he threatened.

"You wouldn't."

"I would, and I will."

"That's not fair."

"We use the weapons we have," he said. "You have your guile and wit. I have my boyish charm and an arsenal of irrational childish feelings that no mother can deny."

Or something to that effect.

We composed ourselves and walked downstairs to the dining room. Knowing the stakes of the situation, we both forced ourselves to smile as if nothing was wrong.

"What's wrong?" my wife asked, the moment she saw us.

"Nothing," I said. "Nothing at all."

"Of course there is," she said. "You both have idiotic grins on your face, and when you're nervous you say something, then repeat it. So what is it?"

I glanced down at my son, and he glared up at me. Uh oh, I thought, he's going to betray me.

"Dad left the lid off of Flash's cage and he got away," The Boy blurted.

I didn't say anything, because there was nothing to say.

My wife leveled her eyes at me and bore into my soul with one of those laser-beam death-mom stares.

"How it happened isn't entirely certain," I backpedaled. "There will of course be a full investigation."

My wife breathed through her nose like a rhinoceros about to charge. "So you're telling me that the snake I never wanted in this house is now, at this moment, crawling around somewhere in it, we know not where?"

"That's about it," I said. "But I'm sure he'll turn up. Why don't we eat, and resume the search after dinner?"

"I've got a better idea," The Wife said. "Why don't we resume the search now, and neither of you gets to eat until you find it?"

"That works too," I agreed, retreating toward the stairs.

"Sure, mom. Anything you say," The Boy concurred.

Long story short, we never found Flash. I know you thought this story was going to end on a happy note, with us suddenly finding the wayward creature hidden in a cupboard or coiled up in someone's shoe. But no, it ends on a sad note in a distinctly minor key, because that's how most stories of snake ownership end. It ends with my son mad at me for ruining his dream of one day taking his snake to school. It ends with my wife furious that she has had to spend years wondering if this was the day the snake would show up out of nowhere, under the sink, in that pile of laundry, or anywhere else she didn't expect. It ends with me wondering how my good intentions could go so wrong, and whether there might be another time to do it right. It ends with my son still interested in snakes, but unable to call one his own.

Still, on rainy days when there is nothing else to do, my son and I often sneak out and visit that same pet shop, where the man with the fish tattoos and the boy with the eyeliner and lip ring are glad to show us any snake we want. Sometimes, they'll even let my son feed them, and they always invite us to stick around and watch. We usually do, for a while, then call it quits and head home, where the ghost of Flash the corn snake will likely live forever—or until the day he turns up, which I am certain he will.

Eventually.

CHAPTER 27

The Boy's favorite holiday was always Halloween. He loved it all, from digging out the goo inside a pumpkin to dressing up and going out at night to extort candy from the neighbors. Fortunately, we live in an excellent neighborhood for trick-or-treating, in that the houses are small, crammed close together, and laid out in a grid. In order to fill a couple of pillowcases full of candy, all an enterprising trick-or-treater needs to do is map out an eight-block quadrant, start early, and methodically hit each house on every block.

To maximize The Boy's haul, I also taught him the dangers of getting caught in a pack (too much wasted time); how to distinguish good trick-or-treating houses from bad ones based on the brightness of the porch light and number of pumpkins outside; the importance of tracking from year to year which houses are giving out the best treats; why it's important to keep moving, minimize interaction with candy-givers at the door; and to avoid getting distracted by so-called friends who want to try some other unknown, unmapped neighborhood "just for the fun of it."

I warned The Boy that deviating from these well-established Halloween rules leads to nothing but disappointment and regret, because the mythical house that gives away jumbo-size Snickers bars is never there, and then you have a long walk back, during which time you could be filling your pillowcase with the low-hanging fruit of a proven neighborhood like ours. Remember, three small Snickers bars is the same as a big one, I reminded him—and besides, his mother wouldn't let him eat a whole big Snickers bar anyway, so abandoning your whole plan to chase the big-bar dream is pointless. Other key points to remember: decline any fruit or soda (too heavy), and if anyone tries to give you something quasi-healthy like a box of raisins, some walnuts, or a bag of kale chips, close your pillowcase immediately and move on to the next house. If these pathetic non-treats also came with a sanctimonious lecture about the evils of candy and the importance of eating healthy, I gave The Boy permission to yell "Help, I've been tricked!" as he left their porch.

On a typical Halloween night in our neighborhood, we'd get at least ninety to a hundred trick-or-treaters, usually in a steady stream between 5 p.m. and 8 p.m. The traffic tapered off after that, but for those few hours, the neighborhood would be crawling with witches, ghosts, princesses, pirates, aliens, and superheroes. They'd travel around in packs (a mistake, tactically speaking, but charming nonetheless), swarming each house with a chorus of "trick or treat"s while their mothers patrolled the sidewalk, keeping an eye out for child molesters and drug dealers, and reminding their little goblins at each house to say thank you. On a typical Halloween night, we'd go through twenty or thirty bags of candy, easy. When the candy was gone, I'd shut things down and hang a sign on the front door that read, "Sorry, your competition got here first. See you next year."

Deciding on a costume for The Boy was always a delicate negotiation, because he never wanted to wear a conventional costume. From a very young age, he got it in his head (I don't know how) that his costume of choice would be based on the most evil person in the news that year. So one year it was Saddam Hussein, then Osama bin Laden, then Kim Jong Il. But after a few years, The Boy wanted a better criterion for "evil," so I suggested the monster's body count. How many people a person has killed is a good indication of how evil they are, I argued, a line of reasoning that The Boy enthusiastically embraced.

Choosing was always difficult, however, because there were all kinds of people like Syrian president Bashar Al-Assad and Zimbabwe's Robert Mugabe, who killed thousands of their own people during civil war, a gray area of mass extermination that made it difficult to assign blame. And, after some Internet searching, The Boy discovered that there were all kinds of other candidates as well. 200,000 people a year die from cigarette smoking in the U.S. each year, so the president of Philip Morris was up for consideration. About 35,000 people die in car accidents every year, so the presidents of Ford and General Motors were on the list. But I had to draw the line when, one year, after some extensive research, The Boy declared that he wanted to dress up as president George Bush.

"His body count is impressive," The Boy argued. "50,000 to 100,000 Iraqis and Afghanis by most estimates, and a few thousand of our own soldiers. No one else can beat him."

To divert The Boy, I encouraged him to broaden his search to more historical bad guys like Adolph Hitler and Benito Mussolini. That would give him some perspective. This turned out to be a brilliant move on my part, because The Boy uncovered all kinds of people who gave our president's patriotic efforts a more favorable context.

"Forget Hitler," The Boy told me after an evening of intense research. "He only killed seventeen million people. This guy Stalin wiped out twenty-three million, and Mao Zedong killed seventy-eight million, maybe more. Leopold II was a bad-ass, too, but not quite in their league. This year, it's gotta be Mao. Go big or go home, right?"

Dressing a kid as Mao Zedong isn't too difficult, as it turns out. If you get the hair right—black helmet hair with a lot of forehead—everything else falls into place. Explaining to other people who you're dressed as is a little trickier, because when people at the door ask, "Now, who are you, young man?," they don't really want a long answer with a lot of historical background. Also, when The Boy pronounced Mao's name it sounded like he was saying "mouse dung," so most people just nodded politely and gave him an extra piece of candy to go away.

CHAPTER 28

The year The Boy dressed as Mao was a strange one for other reasons as well. That Halloween night, I had noticed early in our rounds that the streets weren't nearly as full of trick-or-treaters as usual. I assumed the crowds would pick up as the evening wore on, but by six-thirty the streets were practically empty. The further we got away from our own home, we also began running into blocks where more than half the houses were dark. It was like a ghost town, but with no ghosts. No princesses, Spidermans, or Sponge Bobs, either.

It didn't feel right. I checked my phone to make sure it was actually Halloween, because I've made that mistake before. It was. So what was going on? Had the forces of political correctness managed to somehow eliminate one more holiday?, I wondered. Had the fear of flammable costumes and poisoned treats scared the timid parents of today's toddlers into keeping their kids at home? Had Halloween itself become a casualty of the global war on sugar?

As we ambled down yet another desolate block searching in vain for a few glowing pumpkins and an inviting porch light, another dad with two kids came around the corner.

"Pretty quiet tonight," I said as we crossed paths. "Where is everybody?"

"They're all down on Stratford Lane," the man said. "We just came from there. Every house on the block is decked out like Disneyland. There must be hundreds of people over there. I even saw a bus come by and drop a bunch of people off. It's crazy."

This was news to me. Curious to see what all the fuss was about, The Boy and I walked the half-mile or so over to Stratford Lane, a large cul-de-sac with a dozen McMansion-sized houses on it. What we witnessed there was appalling.

Every single house on the block was decorated according to a different theme. One house was a pirate ship, with mounds of glittering treasure in the front yard guarded by a crew of singing skeletons. Another was the lair of a deadly giant spider, which was eight feet across and outfitted with some sort of robotic engine that allowed it to crawl across the front lawn and pretend, just for a second, that it was going to eat a child. There was a graveyard with clouds of fog curling along the ground, a witch's coven with a burbling cauldron of trouble, and several different haunted houses with flashing strobe lights and the promise of a humorous but certain death inside.

Screams and cackles seemed to come from everywhere as people streamed in and out of the houses. And it wasn't just kids; the place was crawling with teenagers and parents, all marveling at the creativity and ingenuity that went into the block's "Halloween spirit." Worse yet, the homeowners themselves were dressed up as actors, animating their own living dioramas with all the enthusiasm and skill of a community theater run by people who always wanted to act but can't. One house re-enacted the Mad Hatter's Tea Party from Alice in Wonderland, employing a cast of eight people, including a caterpillar kid who sat in a tree and smoked a giant hooka.

I asked the guy playing the Mad Hatter what he thought they were doing, and he explained that everyone on the block had signed an agreement to restore what he called "All Hallow's Eve," to its true pagan origins as a celebration of spirits both living and dead.

"Halloween has become too much about candy and commercialization," he explained. "We think it's healthier to re-direct the emphasis away from all that and toward the holiday's original spiritual roots."

"By performing Alice in Wonderland in your front yard?" I asked.

"That was my son's idea," the Mad Hatter said, pointing to the hooka-smoking caterpillar in the tree. "We were going to do Through the Looking Glass—The Jabberwocky, specifically—but there weren't enough parts."

"What does any of this have to do with Halloween?" I wondered.

"Halloween is the new Christmas," the Cheshire Cat chimed in.

"Alice in Wonderland doesn't have anything to do with Christmas, either," I pointed out.

"The truth is, we all got tired of taking our kids trick or treating and dealing with the whole eat-candy-'til-you-puke thing," Alice explained. "So we decided to cut the candy out of it and make it more about having fun."

A pack of kids with their parents showed up on the sidewalk and the Mad Hatter cut Alice off. "Places, everyone!" he ordered. I walked away, not at all sure I understood the logic behind it all.

At another house, I remarked to a sodden gravedigger that the coffin he was preparing to bury was amazingly lifelike. "Found it on craigslist," he said. "Only cost me two-hundred bucks. Used the rest of my budget this year to upgrade my fog machine and get a better sound system. Next year I'm going to have remote-controlled skeletons that pop out of their graves and laugh."

The whole thing made me queasy. These people didn't seem to know or care that there were no trick-or-treaters within a mile of their block. It was as if all the fun of Halloween had been sucked out of the neighborhood and deposited on Stratford Lane, where the Disney-fication of yet another holiday was growing like some kind of orange, electric fungus. The worst part was that no one else seemed to care. Everyone around me seemed deliriously happy that this block of homeowners had gotten together and amped up the whole Halloween experience to the point where no one else could compete. Don't get me wrong: I'm all for competition. But these people suddenly had a monopoly on Halloween. And monopolies, as everyone knows, need to be broken up, especially when they threaten to destroy already established economies of scale that have worked for decades, if not centuries.

I called The Wife to explain what was going on. She reported that traffic at our door had been unprecedentedly light, and that she still had twenty-eight bags of candy left. Every kid who came to door from then on out was going to get a full bag of Milky Ways, she said, because for her own good she could not afford to have that much chocolate in the house for more than a day.

Clearly, something had to be done.

While I was gathering intelligence from the neighbors, The Boy had gone off to check out one of the haunted houses. He returned with glowing green stars on his face, clutching a Mylar balloon with a silver slice of moon and a black cat on it.

"What happened to you?" I asked.

"I went into that house," he said, pointing to a faux Tudor McMansion with a giant ghost peering out of the second-story window, its fat, inflatable arms flapping at the sky. "The whole house is haunted," he said. "Some of it's a little lame, but at the end this witchy woman draws on your face and gives you a balloon, so I guess it's okay."

I clasped The Boy on the shoulders and made him look me in the eye. "It's not okay," I clarified. "Don't you see what they're doing? By giving you a balloon, they're forcing you to hold something continuously in one hand so that it's more difficult to open and carry a bag of candy. It's a trick."

The Boy looked at the balloon and said, "Still, it's kind of nice to get something besides candy on Halloween."

That's how dangerous the whole thing was: Fifteen minutes on Stratford Lane and The Boy had already forgotten about the true meaning of Halloween. A mere hour earlier, he was focused like a laser on amassing as much candy as possible. He was aware of the limited time frame, knew the consequences of wasting precious seconds on houses where there was only a slim hope that someone was home, and he'd had the foresight to wear a costume that didn't restrict his movement and allowed him to run freely between houses. He had even asked me to carry an extra pillowcase, in the event that his first one got too full—a sure sign that, when we left the house, his priorities were crystal clear. Now, he was talking about witches handing out balloons and wondering if he could check out some other houses while I waited for him.

I broke the news to him gently. "Son, do you remember when we went to the fair and heard that man talking about how, behind that bright red curtain, there was a creature so fearsome and ugly that the mere sight of it curdled people's blood? And how, when we paid our money and went inside, we found out it was nothing more than a giant rat?"

The Boy nodded.

"Well, this is the same thing," I said, waving my hand to show that I meant the entirety of Stratford Lane. "All of this is just a bunch of smoke and mirrors and theater designed to distract you from the ugly truth about this place: that there is no candy here."

The Boy looked confused.

"Look around," I said. "Do you see anyone handing out candy? No, you don't. Why? Because these people don't believe in candy on Halloween," I explained. "They believe that if they put on enough of a show—if they distract you with all kinds of empty entertainment—you'll forget about collecting candy altogether. They're trying to brainwash you, to make you think that Halloween the way you've always known it is boring and unhealthy. And this isn't the end of it. Deep in their heart of hearts, these people want to prevent you from having any candy at all on Halloween—all for your own good! Or what they think is your own good. But the important thing is, what do you think?"

The Boy had a pained look on his face, so I could tell he was taking the question seriously.

"Well, I do like all the lights and costumes and things," he said. "But if what you're saying is true, and this is all we did on Halloween, I'd have hardly any candy at the end of the night."

"Exactly."

"But why do I have to choose?" The Boy asked. "Why can't we do both—trick or treat, and come here to see the haunted houses?"

I explained to him that it was human nature to want it all, but that—as we had observed on our way over—the mere existence of this block had depleted the neighborhood of participating trick-or-treat houses, and that in future years, the trend was likely to continue until there was nothing but Stratford Lane on Halloween. Is that what he wanted? No, of course not. So, I explained, we had to do something, or pretty soon Halloween as he knew it—with its familiar and beloved rituals and traditions—would be no more.

"What can we do?" The Boy asked.

"Let's think about that for a second," I said. "Sometimes it helps to look at things from a different perspective. You're dressed as Mao Zedong, so let's look at it from his point of view. If Mao were here, and wanted to put a stop to all of this, what would he do?"

The Boy thought for a moment. "Well, Mao got rid of people he didn't like mostly by starving them to death and taking away their resources," he said. "So I guess I'd start there."

"Okay," I said. "Look around. What's the biggest resource these people need to keep their heretical perversion of Halloween going?"

"Spooky sounds?" The Boy ventured.

No.

"Colored lights?"

You're getting warmer, I told him. "What do those two things have in common?"

"Electricity!" The Boy exclaimed. "The whole block runs on electricity!"

"Exactly!" I confirmed. "So, if electricity is the vital resource these people need the keep their sham Halloween party going, we—if we're thinking like Mao—need to figure out how to deprive them of it, right?"

The Boy nodded enthusiastically. "Yes, but how?"

"You leave that to me," I said.

"Okay."

"I am going to need one thing from you, however," I said.

"What's that?"

"I'm going to need your balloon. And I can't promise that I'll give it back. In fact, I'm pretty sure I won't."

The Boy looked up at the balloon floating over his head and reluctantly handed it to me. "Okay," he said, "if you think it'll help."

I took the balloon from him and, in return, handed him the pillowcase that was only half-filled with candy, the most pathetic haul we'd had in years. We ambled out of the cul-de-sac and down the street as if we were just another father and son enjoying the spectacle. But in reality, I was examining the block's electrical grid and attempting to locate the main transformer. We found it at the end of the block, on top of a telephone pole about thirty feet high. The transformer was a big green box with several fat electrical lines sticking out of it, and was located on a telephone pole that had no street light. Obscured by darkness, it was all but invisible to anyone on Stratford Lane itself.

At the end of the block was a tree decorated with spiders and stars and tiny little ghosts dangling from various pieces of fishing line. When no one was looking, I cut a few of the decorations down with my pocket knife and tied several strands of the fishing line together. I gave each intersection of fishing line a tug to make sure the knot was secure, and attached the end of the line to the balloon.

"What are you doing?" The Boy asked.

"The plan is simple," I explained. "These balloons are covered with a metallic substance. All we have to do to deprive this block of its precious electricity is hoist this balloon up into that transformer up there. When the balloon hits the transformer, there should be a small pop, so you'll want to stand back a little. Then poof, the lights will go out. Goodbye, super-stupid Halloween."

"That sounds dangerous," The Boy said.

"Not to us. The fishing line is plastic, so the electricity can't travel down the line and electrocute us. Also, we're wearing tennis shoes, so that means we're grounded—but in a good way."

"Are you sure?" The Boy asked.

"Absolutely. Trust me," I said. "This isn't the first time I've blown a transformer."

Slowly, I began floating the Mylar balloon upward toward the transformer, letting out the fishing line a few feet at a time. When the balloon was about three feet below the transformer and I was certain we had enough line to get the job done, I stopped.

"Before I do this, we need to be clear on one thing," I said. "You understand that this is not something your mother needs to know about, right?"

The Boy nodded that he understood.

"No matter how many questions she asks, you won't crack? You promise?"

The Boy continued nodding.

"Okay, then, here goes," I said, letting out the rest of the line.

The balloon bounced against the bottom of the transformer, but nothing happened. I tried pulling the balloon around to the side, but there was a slight breeze that made the balloon difficult to control. Time after time, I bounced the balloon against the transformer and it floated away. Then, when the wind subsided, I regained some control and tried again. I knew I needed to somehow wedge the balloon between the transformer and the wires going into it, so that the metal from the balloon was touching both the transformer box and the wire couplings at the same time. Each time I tried, however, the breeze came up, the balloon drifted away, and I had to start all over again.

After about ten minutes, The Boy was getting discouraged. "I don't think this is going to work," he said. "Should we just go home?"

"Patience, boy. We're almost there," I said as I positioned the balloon for one last attempt.

Then, out of the darkness, came a voice. "Hey, you there! What are you doing?"

The Boy looked to see who was yelling at us.

"Dad, it's a cop!" The Boy said.

A wave of panic rushed through me. Without thinking, I let go of the balloon and yelled, "Run!"

The Boy took off down the sidewalk and I followed directly behind him.

"Stop!" the officer commanded—but just as we heard him, we also heard a loud explosion followed by a bunch of fizzling, sizzling sounds.

I looked over my shoulder and saw a shower of sparks raining down from the telephone pole, and, in an instant, the entire neighborhood was plunged into darkness.

The Boy cut down an alley and I followed him. The alley was pitch black, but after our eyes adjusted we could see just well enough to make our way out the other end and onto another block. The police officer did not to follow us. I assume he elected to deal instead with the sudden emergency of a neighborhood full of suburbanites hopped up on Halloween madness hitting the darkened streets with mayhem on their minds.

The Boy and I doubled around to the street in back of Stratford Lane. The entire block was dark except for a few pumpkins and some people with flashlights. From our vantage point, we could see that the crowd was dispersing and that most of the people were heading home. Some stood around in the middle of the street, sipping unknown liquids from Styrofoam cups, waiting for the electricity to come back on. But I saw how that transformer blew, so I figured it was going to be a while.

"Mission accomplished," I whispered to The Boy. "Let's get out of here."

As we headed toward home, it became apparent that the blackout wasn't exactly localized. There was darkness as far as the eye could see. But the great thing about total darkness on Halloween, we soon discovered, is that the pumpkins don't go out, and a lit pumpkin is the surest sign there is of a candy-friendly house. On the way home, we hit every house with a pumpkin in front of it, and, because it was near the end of the evening, people were unloading their candy on The Boy by the handful. There were no other trick-or-treaters around at that hour, either, so it was The Boy who now had a monopoly on Halloween, and he who was reaping the rewards.

As we approached our own house, we could see that the lights were off and that our own pumpkin had already blown out. The Wife had lit some candles, and the glow inside was dim and cozy. The Boy and I walked through the door with two pillowcases full of candy, and he immediately dumped them both on the living-room floor to begin the traditional inventory of the haul.

"Thank god you're both safe," The Wife said as we arrived. "The power went out a while ago, and they say it's not going to be back until sometime tomorrow."

I assured her that we were better than safe; that we had, in fact, brought home the biggest, best Halloween haul ever.

"Wow, they must have been pretty generous over there on Stratford," The Wife said. The Boy and I agreed that, yes, Stratford Lane had provided us with quite a bounty.

The Wife shook her head. "I don't know why you two care so much about collecting all that candy," she said. "The Boy is borderline diabetic. He can't eat any of that," she said, pointing to the mountain of loot on the floor. "And you know that more candy just means there's more to carry and give away at work. Besides, we've still got twenty bags of Snickers bars and Milky Ways in the garage. If we don't get rid of them, that chocolate is going in my mouth, then on my hips."

The sad, final ritual of the evening was for The Boy to choose one, and only one, piece of candy to eat, and hand over the rest to his mother. He wisely chose a full-size Three Musketeers bar, then, in a gesture of uncommon gratitude, broke the bar in two.

"Best Halloween ever," The Boy said as he handed half to me.

I had to agree. And in retrospect, that Halloween has stood the test of time as the best ever. The Wife still doesn't know that we blew that transformer, plunging the neighborhood into darkness and forcing her to throw out everything in our refrigerator and freezer. For once, The Boy kept his promise and never told his mother what really happened that night. And as long as The Boy keeps his mouth shut, she's never going to find out.

CHAPTER 29

The first ten years of a boy's life are important, certainly, but the real man-building starts at ten or eleven. Unfortunately, something happens around this age that is beyond the reach of parents to address. Part of the reason is that this is the age when boys stop listening to their parents. It's also the age when boys need to test themselves. And rather than have them test themselves on you, it is preferable to find a way for them to test themselves somewhere besides the family living room. This requires outside help.

For better or worse, sports have always been the most constructive way to channel a boy's most violent and destructive impulses. Admittedly, baseball didn't work out for The Boy, but I had a suspicion that it was because baseball can be boring, involving as it does a lot of standing around and doing nothing. Football is different. Football practice is brutal, and football games are exhausting, which is why football is such a good sport for boys with an attitude. Boys can't talk back when they're trying to catch their breath, and boys secretly like to be yelled at by men who aren't their fathers. So, although baseball was a bust, I had hopes that football might shape The Boy up and give him something to do that involved breaking a sweat.

When I was a boy, trying out for the football team was a rite of passage all by itself, involving as it did a great deal of personal sacrifice and a certain amount of blood loss. The fun always began in August, when both the temperature and humidity were hovering around a hundred. The coaches would make us wear pads and helmets in that heat, and run us until we puked, then run us some more until dehydration and heatstroke rendered us unconscious. Then they'd yell at us for being pussies and tell us to be back on the field at three in the afternoon for another workout. It didn't matter if you were sick or in the hospital from the morning workout, because the only way to build a competitive football team was to work through the pain of "two-a-day" practices in summer. Only survivors of this torture got to play in actual games. Those who quit or died were immediately forgotten.

And we loved every minute of it.

The reward for making the football team was that you became a school hero, a warrior for the green and white envied by all. The mere possession of a letterman's jacket in football meant that you were superior in every way to the other kids, and when you wore it to school, the jacket was like a cloak of royalty. Boys bowed, girls curtsied, and teachers automatically gave you an "A" just for being cool.

But the best part was the violence on the field. You don't know what fun is until you've lined up a wide receiver who is ready to catch a pass, lowered your shoulder and smashed into him with such force that you can hear his ribs snap (or was it your collar bone?). The only place you can legally hit a person that hard is on a football field. And I'm guessing it's illegal because it's so much fun. Hitting someone that hard and causing them immense physical pain is incredibly satisfying. It makes you feel invincible. When the other kid is lying on the ground, holding his side and moaning for his mommy, it just confirms everything other people have been telling you about yourself: that you're a bad-ass, a monster, a fucking all-star!

I wanted that for my son. At school, he wasn't exactly knocking them dead in the popularity department, and both the color of his skin and his lack of muscle tone suggested that he spent way too much time inside, immobile, in front of a computer screen or reading a book. A season or two of football would toughen him up, I figured, and help pave the way for a bright future in the perpetual popularity contest that is high school.

So, at the earliest opportunity, I enrolled him in Pee Wee Football. Some parents don't let their kids play Pee Wee football because there's so much talk in the media these days about kids getting concussions. These are the same parents whose kids have peanut allergies and who lobby the school board to include gluten-free foods on the school lunch menu and ban selling soda pop. They're also the parents who want teachers to warn them if the stuff their kid is reading might make their kid uncomfortable, or who insist that all kids wear "safety glasses" in chemistry when they're using sulfuric acid. These are the parents who can't bear the idea of their child living in the real world, and who would prefer that their kid go through life inside a protective plastic bubble. What these parents fail to understand is that a giant protective plastic bubble is precisely what a football uniform is! No other sport—not basketball, baseball, volleyball, track, tennis, or swimming—provides the level of protective gear that football provides. Hockey comes close, but hockey players can take their gloves and helmets off whenever they get into a fight, so the protection is lost when they need it most.

A kid who plays football is basically encased in plastic and foam, so the chance they'll get hurt is actually pretty small. Sure, they might break a finger or snap a tibia, but all the vital organs are protected. The real worry, I submit, is that if their kid tries out for football, these parents might discover that their boy isn't very good at it, and their dreams of having a high-school football star, full-scholarship collegiate All-American and eventual NFL legend in the family will be crushed. Afraid of risking the dream, they'd rather take no risks at all.

To play Pee Wee football, you have to be ten years old and weigh at least eighty pounds. Three weeks before sign-up, The Boy only weighed seventy-six pounds, but after putting him on a strict regimen of pizza, burritos, and ice cream, we got him up to eighty-two for the weigh-in.

Now, I am aware that being at the bottom of one's Pee Wee weight class is not ideal. My son would be playing against some kids who were twelve years old and weighed a hundred and thirty pounds. And when a hundred-and-thirty-pound kid slams into an eighty-pound kid, the eighty-pound kid loses. That's just physics. In theory, the smaller, lighter boys should be faster than the bigger, heavier ones, so that they can get out of harm's way. But that's just a theory. In reality, the older, heavier kids are also faster and stronger, so that first year of Pee Wee can be tough on a kid. Or, as we used to say, "character-building."

Though he had not shown much interest in athletics up to that point, I figured The Boy was a natural judging from the killer instincts he displayed while playing his favorite video games. Wielding a sniper rifle or sub-machine gun, he could locate and destroy his enemy with alarming efficiency. He was also cool under fire. Blood and gore did not bother him. Neither did explosive noises or other diversions. In the middle of a combat shit-storm, he could tune out the chaos and pick off his opponents one by one in the most methodical manner imaginable. Those same skills would come in handy on the football field, I figured, particularly on defense. When you're playing defense, as I did, you have to react almost instantaneously to the play unfolding in front of you, deducing from the motion of the blocking patterns and receivers whether it's a run or pass play, then moving into position to tackle whoever is carrying or catching the ball. In terms of basic skills, it isn't much different from being swarmed by a bunch of armed insurgents and eliminating them, so I figured The Boy would be fairly good at it. And, judging from his bloodthirsty instincts on the electronic battlefield, I thought he'd enjoy the opportunity to hurt someone in real life.

His team was called The Wranglers. They sported helmets with a logo that looked a lot like the University of Texas Longhorns, including crisp white uniforms with orange letters and smart, tight pants with an orange stripe down the side. The boys on the team ranged between ten and twelve years old, but I had to admit, a few of the twelve-year-olds looked like they were ready for college. The Boy was one of the smallest players on the squad, which was to be expected in his first year. But by the end of the season, if we kept up the pizza and burrito regimen, I was confident I could get him up over a hundred pounds.

The first day of practice was in late August. The temperature was in the mid-eighties and the humidity wasn't bad, so first-day casualties were likely to be minimal. Their coach believed in getting right down to business, so that first practice was a full uniforms and pads affair.

The Boy did not like the uniform. But, to be fair, moving around in a suit of plastic armor does take some getting used to. His shoulder pads were a little big for him, but his helmet fit well and I double-knotted the laces on his cleats to make sure they wouldn't come loose out on the field. Then I slapped him on his shoulder pads and told him to go out and have some fun.

I can't tell you how proud I was of The Boy when he trotted out onto that football field in his orange and whites. It reminded me of my first day of football all those years ago, and the years of glory and heartache that followed. He'd win games and celebrate, I knew, and he'd lose games and cry. But through it all—the sweat and the blood and the tears—he'd learn what it means to work together as a team and compete as hard as you can to win. That feeling in the fourth quarter when your legs are numb and your lungs are burning and your stomach is clenched and you don't think you can take it for another second, then the other team snaps the ball and the play is in motion and instinct takes over, pushing you beyond the limit in your mind to a point of exhaustion you didn't think was possible—well, there's no way to experience that feeling other than having a colicky baby or playing football. Now The Boy was going to experience it, and then we'd really have something to talk about.

Everything was going fine until, mid-way through that first practice, The Boy got tackled by one of those twelve-year-old brutes and didn't get up. He just lay on the ground, with his hands splayed out to his side, staring at the sky.

I was on the sideline standing near the coaches when it happened, and I heard one of the coaches say, "Looks like he got his bell rung."

The other coach didn't think so. "There was no helmet contact on that hit," he said. "I think he just got the wind knocked out of him."

Concerned, I ran on to the field to the spot where The Boy was lying, and kneeled by his side. "You okay, son?" I asked.

"I'm fine," he said, his face framed by his helmet.

"Then get up," I said.

"No," he said. "If I get up I'll have to keep playing."

"You can't just lie here on the field," I said. "Everyone is waiting for you."

"Let them wait," The Boy said.

I knew that The Boy had never played football before, and was a little foggy on some of the rules, so I explained to him that taking a rest whenever he wanted, in the middle of the playing field, was not an option. When you get tackled in football, I explained, you have to get up as soon as you can. Even if you are in pain or feel like you're going to puke, you have to get up. Especially after you take a big hit like that, you have to get up as fast as you can to show the other guy that you're tougher than he is—that he can hit you with his best shot and you can take it.

"But what if I can't take it?" The Boy asked. "More to the point, what if I don't want to take it?"

"It's not about what you want," I told him. "It's about what needs to happen in order to keep the game going."

"But the game is pointless," The Boy said, staring up at me through his faceguard.

"What do you mean it's pointless?" I said, exasperated. "It's the farthest thing from pointless. It's football!"

"Think about it, dad. You play what, ten or twelve games a season? You win a few and lose a few. So what? All over the country, in thousands of Pee Wee football leagues, kids are winning and losing games. But what does it matter? Am I a better person if we win? Am I a worse person if we lose? Next year, no one is going to remember what happened this year, so what's the point?"

"The point is to play!" I screamed. "Do the video games you love so much have a point?! Don't you just play them for the sake of playing them? Football is the same—you just play it! Because it's a game!"

"Video games are entirely different, dad," The Boy said. "There's usually a mission, with clearly stated goals, and there's always a way to win. There's strategy involved. Playing them also develops your critical-thinking and problem-solving skills, and improves your reflexes. Studies have shown that they make you smarter, too. None of that is true about football, as far as I can tell."

"That's not true. Football involves lots of strategy," I countered. "And the goal is pretty simple: score more points than the other team."

"Maybe the coach gets to develop a strategy and come up with plays," The Boy said. "But the rest of us, the players, we don't get to decide anything. We're just supposed to do whatever the coach tells us to. Where's the fun in that?"

I grasped for a way to convince The Boy that playing football wasn't a waste of time—to get him to understand that there were valuable life lessons to be learned involving teamwork and sportsmanship. "The fun—and value—of playing football is working as a team to achieve a common goal," I said. "It's that unity of purpose that makes football special."

"We might as well be ants," The Boy said. "They're good at cooperating."

"Then what about the social part—the friends you'll make playing for the mighty Wranglers?" I begged.

"I don't want to be friends with any of these guys," The Boy said. "They're all stupid. And the second they put on their uniforms, they just get dumber and meaner."

"That's because in order to play football well, you have to be an animal," I explained. "You have to be aggressive. When I put on a football uniform, I remember just wanting to go out there and kill someone."

"Well, it didn't happen to me," The Boy said. "When I put this uniform on, I didn't get stupider or meaner. I also discovered that I don't like colliding with people."

"But that's the best part!" I said. "C'mon, there's nothing better than delivering a good hit! Just give it a try. You'll like it."

"I don't think so."

"But you love hurting and killing people in video games," I said. "It stands to reason that you'd like a little taste of it in real life."

The Boy sighed and said, "The people in video games aren't real, dad. No one actually gets hurt."

The coaches and other players were getting impatient. They could see that we were having a discussion, and that The Boy seemed to be conscious, or at least conscious enough to carry on a conversation.

"Did he break something?" one of the coaches asked.

"I don't think so," I said. "He's just a little slow getting up."

"Well, if he can't get up on his own, maybe you can pick him up and carry him off the field," the head coach said. "He can come back in when he's ready."

I looked down at The Boy and said, "So, are you going to lie there all day?"

The Boy sighed, rolled over, and pushed himself to his feet, then began walking toward the sideline.

"Where are you going?" I asked.

The Boy took off his helmet and threw it to the ground. "I don't think football is for me, dad." The words stabbed me like a knife. "I'm thinking maybe I'm more cut out for tennis or golf," he added, "something that only involves hitting a ball, not people."

"But, but, but . . . those are country club sports!" I gasped.

The Boy turned around and looked back at me as he approached the bench on the sideline and sat down. "Country club," he said, feeling the words in his mouth. "I like the sound of that."

CHAPTER 30

If you live in a place where one of the seasons is winter, you will eventually get into a heated argument with your spouse over the appropriate amount of outerwear required to keep The Boy warm and safe. Our family lives in Minnesota, where winter is actually two seasons long, so the disagreements are twice as intense.

These fights would be unnecessary if it weren't for the fact that women tend to think boys are fragile creatures who need to be wrapped in six layers of clothing and a heavy coat, puffy gloves, and boots so heavy they could anchor a ship. No boy wants to have that much clothing attached to their body, so they protest by pouting and screaming and flailing their arms to make it extra difficult for mom to put all those shirts and sweaters on. Mothers are undeterred by such antics; the fighting just makes them more determined. And if you, in a misguided attempt to mediate, suggest that perhaps The Boy could do without the waffle-net underwear or the triple-wrapped neck scarf, beware. Your well-intentioned suggestions will be interpreted as attacks on her judgment and indications that you do not care as much about her "baby" as she does.

And the truth is, you don't. No one cares more about their children than mothers. Fathers can pretend to care as much, but when the rubber hits the road, it's no contest. If a mother loses a child—to sudden-infant death syndrome, the flu, or cancer, say—she will be devastated for life, haunted by the specter of what she could or might have done to prevent the tragedy from happening. If a father loses a child, he'll be sad for a week or two, sure, but at some point he'll seal the pain inside a hot flaming knot in his chest and move on. Not so, mothers, which is one vital clue to their occasionally odd behavior.

The reason mothers insist that their kids "bundle up" so that they don't "freeze to death," is because that's what mothers are actually afraid of. A father figures the worst that can happen is that their boy's feet and hands will get a little numb, in which case it's his own damn fault. But mothers are programmed to fear that their kid is going to die if he doesn't take every possible precaution against every conceivable threat. Their basic assumption is that boys don't have a lick of sense in their heads, and, if given the opportunity, will spend their day walking into life-threatening situations just for the fun of it.

What mothers don't understand about boys is that they have extra-thick skin and highly oxygenated blood, which protects them from the cold and makes it possible for them to endure subzero temperatures and bitter wind-chills wearing comparatively little clothing. Even in Minnesota, boys can get through winter wearing nothing but a hoodie, jeans, and a cheap pair of sneakers. Anything more is overkill. But, since fathers and mothers differ so radically in their opinion about the amount of clothing needed to survive a trip to school in the snow, there is no point in arguing; other tactics are required.

In my case, I was trapped between my wife, who, when I questioned her judgment about the amount of clothes The Boy needed to wear, claimed that I was "second-guessing" her—and The Boy, who pleaded with me on the side to talk "some sense" into his mother.

"It's ridiculous, dad," The Boy told me. "When I get to school, I just have to take all these clothes off and stuff them into my locker, which is on the other side of the building from my classroom. There's not enough time to take everything off and get to class, so I'm always late."

My advice to him was simple: "Next time your mother insists that you wear all that stuff to school, don't be an idiot and argue with her. Instead, play it smart and say "yes, ma'am," then ditch the clothes, snow jacket, and boots in the garage and replace them with a hoodie and sneakers you've secretly hidden there. When you come home, just do the reverse and put the clothes back on, so that when you walk through the door, your mother will think you've been warm and safe all day long."

This strategy worked beautifully for about a month. But, as I said, we live in Minnesota, where it gets so cold sometimes that spit freezes by the time it hits the pavement. We're talking twenty to thirty below, with a wind chill of sixty to seventy below. For those unacquainted with the term "wind chill," it's a measure of what the temperature outside actually feels like to human skin. Wind makes it feel colder outside, so it might only be twenty below outside, but add the wind chill and it feels like old man winter is shoving his icy digits into every orifice of your body, then twisting them around and laughing at you.

The problem is, even the hardiest of boys can be affected by the cold when it dips that far below zero. More to the point, their skin can freeze and their fingers and ears can turn black from frostbite.

When this happened to The Boy, he didn't actually feel it—it just happened. He and his friends decided to take the bus to school instead of walking, and the bus was late, forcing them to stand outside for half an hour in the bitter cold. You'd think it'd be possible to sue someone in that situation—to make the school or the bus company or the governor take responsibility for the pitiless cruelty of nature. But in Minnesota you can't sue anybody for cold-related negligence, because the legal system would be gummed up for decades.

Unfortunately, when a boy walks through the door with black fingers and ears, his mother is likely to interpret it as an emergency situation, and emergency situations require a trip to the ER. In reality it's not that bad; the skin thaws and the circulation comes back eventually. Except when it doesn't, in which case the affected extremities need to be amputated.

In The Boy's case, he had such a severe case of frostbite that the doctors weren't sure they could save all of his fingers. While we were waiting for his fingers to thaw, I tried pointing out that plenty of people lived productive lives with missing fingers—Jerry Garcia, Rahm Emanuel, Jesse James, Matthew Perry, Frodo—but The Wife did not appreciate my attempt to see the bright side of the situation.

As it turned out, The Boy got to keep all his fingers and only lost a little chunk of his left earlobe. To this day it is hardly noticeable, just a little crescent of missing flesh that looks odd from certain angles. The more tragic downside to this episode was that The Boy's mother began insisting he wear even more clothing to school in order to prevent future bouts of frostbite. You'd be amazed at how many layers of shirts and sweaters can be stacked onto a little boy's body. But it only became a real problem when The Boy was wearing so many clothes that he couldn't reach the zipper of his coat, or fold his arms to pull off his gloves. In effect, his mother began sending him off to school entombed in a protective shield that he could not remove by himself, so my leave-the-clothes-in-the-garage strategy no longer worked. He was trapped until he got to school, and had to enlist the help of his friends and teachers to release him from his polyester prison.

I don't quite know what the lesson is here. The point, I guess, is to avoid living in a state where a child's flesh can freeze while they're waiting for the school bus. Come to think of it, this is just good, common-sense advice in general. With any luck, your son will never get caught stashing his clothes in the garage, and you can avoid the whole uncomfortable conversation about how many fingers a person really needs to live a normal, productive life.

CHAPTER 31

If you are a father involved in the process of raising a boy, it will inevitably fall on your shoulders to explain to your spouse whether certain behaviors The Boy engages in are "normal" or not. This task will be doubly difficult if your spouse didn't have a brother, because without witnessing first-hand all the grotesque and frightening things boys do in their free time, your spouse will have a hard time understanding why the answer to her question—"Is that normal?"—is inevitably "yes."

I speak from experience here, because I did some truly awful things when I was a boy, things I would never want my wife, or anyone else, to know about. But the truth is, every boy engages in all sorts of disgusting, borderline criminal behavior, and this behavior—much of which is so unmentionably gross that most men would prefer to take their secret shame to the grave—serves as a common bond among men. It is the part of a man's nature that no woman would ever understand, and every guy knows this—which is why no man will ever admit that he once drank his own urine, say, or farted in a bottle and smelled it, or tried to have sex with a farm animal.

Given that the range and scope of male degeneracy is so broad, it is difficult to explain to women that most of their behavioral "concerns" are absolutely unfounded. When my wife asks, "Is it normal that he sucks the inside of a tater tot out first, then eats the crunchy part?," how do I explain to her that not only is it normal, it's utterly boring in its normalcy—that no matter what he does with a tater tot, it will fall within the range of normal behavior? He could shove it in his ear, jam it up his nose, squeeze it between his butt cheeks, squish it with the heel of his hand, throw it, flush it, peel it, snort it, feed it to the cat, stash it in his pocket, use it as fish bait, or spit on it and give it to a friend—and all of it would be perfectly normal. In fact, where tater tots and other foodstuffs are concerned, you'd have a hard time identifying anything that isn't normal.

What most people don't understand is that coming up with new ways to indulge their questionable judgment is how boys develop their imaginative powers. There's a reason the law doesn't prosecute children the same way it does adults, and it's because children—especially male children—often behave like deranged little psychopaths.

Take myself as an example. As an adult, I am a productive, tax-paying member of society, as well as a husband and father. Most people, I'm sure, see me as a well-adjusted person of sound mind and exemplary character. But that wasn't always the case. The true story I am about to tell you is one of those shameful episodes that I have never shared with anyone, and I only do so now to make a point—that even the most upstanding citizen in your town might, at one point in his life, been a degenerate monster.

It all started one summer day when my friend Eddie and I were bored and looking for something to do. Eddie lived next door, and was one of those goofy-looking kids who grew up to own four Chick-Filet franchises and earn a seat on the city council in El Paso, Texas, where fate eventually delivered him.

Eddie and I were eleven years old at the time and living in Tulsa, Oklahoma, which was, to us, the most boring place in the world, especially during the summer, when it got so hot that the tar they use to patch cracks in the street would get all gooey and stick to our feet. Sometimes, playing with tar was the best entertainment option available to us. We'd spend hours poking soft, squishy tar bubbles with a stick and smearing it all over the road, often in the form of words that we were not allowed to say out loud. People wonder why video games are so popular with boys. Well, it's because of places like Tulsa.

We didn't wear shoes outside in those days; we didn't need to, because walking barefoot everywhere meant our feet were protected by calluses so thick that we could walk across a field of broken glass and not feel a thing. Besides, we spent a significant amount of our time playing in a marsh near our housing development, a place we referred to as "the mud hole."

The best thing about the mud hole, besides the mud, was that it supported all kinds of animal life—mostly frogs, snakes, minnows, and crawfish, but occasionally we pulled a bullhead catfish out of the muck. Frogs were our favorite, because they were slow and easy to catch, and because there seemed to be an endless supply of them. At night, the marsh got so loud with croaking that it was positively scary. But during the day, we owned the place, and explored every square inch of it.

One day, we had collected a few frogs and were trying to figure what we could do with them. We'd already done so many things with them—race them, run them through a maze, play catch with them, paint faces on them—that we were having trouble coming up with new ideas. Eddie had even considered eating one, just to see if it could survive the trip through his stomach and intestines, but he chickened out in the end.

The day before, Eddie's dad had bought a brand new bicycle pump, which we had just used to inflate our bicycle tires well beyond the recommended pressure. This confluence of events—captive frogs and a new bicycle pump—led Eddie to wonder what would happen if we used the bicycle pump to inflate the frogs. I thought it was a great idea, so we put five frogs in a discarded box we found along the side of the road and took them home to conduct our experiment.

At Eddie's house, we grabbed the pump and took the frogs out back, where no one could see us. At some level, we knew what we were doing was wrong, but when you're eleven years old, the wrongness of a thing just makes it that much more appealing. Eddie attached the needle used to pump up basketballs and footballs, and tested it by pumping the black plastic handle a few times. The air coming out of the needle made a satisfying hiss, and indicated to us that our crazy idea might not be so crazy after all. I scooped one of the frogs out of the box—a skinny green fellow speckled with black dots, about half the size of my hand—and held it while Eddie stuffed the needle end of the pump down the frog's throat. To complete the seal, I closed my fingers around the frog's mouth and held the needle tight while Eddie pumped. As Eddie pushed the plunger down, I could feel the frog expanding in my hand, and I watched as the frog's belly grew and his body began to bloat into a little green balloon that filled most of my hand.

"It's working!" Eddie shouted.

Then, without warning, the frog exploded in my hand, spraying me with frog blood and goo. Too much air pressure had blown a hole in the frog's side, and he died more or less instantly—or at least that what I like to think.

Admittedly, most people would probably recoil in horror at such a scene. But we were boys, so our reaction was somewhat different.

"Cool!" said Eddie.

"Sweet!" I concurred.

"Grab another frog," said Eddie.

"Don't fill him so fast this time," I instructed.

"No, let's fill this one faster!" Eddie said. And, since Eddie was in charge of the pump, that's what he did. And, just as you might expect, the second frog exploded faster and more impressively than the first.

Exploding frogs turned out to be less fun than we expected, though, because after you've popped them, frogs are useless. Also, I did not want to hold another frog while Eddie manned the pump, and Eddie did not have the stomach to hold one of the frogs himself while I pumped. So we re-strategized. Instead of pumping the frogs up until they exploded, we tried pumping them up only until they were fat and bloated. From holding the first two frogs I had a pretty good idea where the line between full inflation and explosion was, so I instructed Eddie to pump until I told him to stop, and no more.

Much to our delight, the frogs did not deflate when we took the needle out of their throats. They just sat there, unable to move, filled so full of air that their legs couldn't even touch the ground. We tossed them back and forth a few times, catching them ever-so-carefully, like a water balloon that could rupture at any moment. When we got bored with that, we decided that it might be fun to line them up on the fence and shoot them. Eddie had gotten a new Crosman PumpMaster BB gun for his birthday and was eager to aim it at just about anything. He was a lousy shot, so the birds and squirrels in the neighborhood were relatively safe. But a stationary frog the size of a baseball, perched on a fence at roughly eye level—that was a target even Eddie could hit.

Unfortunately, shooting frogs with a high-powered BB gun didn't turn out to be as much fun as we thought, either. All that happens when you pump a Crosman six times and shoot an inflated frog is that the BB goes straight through the frog, making a soft little thud, and the frog deflates and dies. It doesn't jump in the air or get blown to smithereens; it's really quite anti-climactic. We were looking for something more . . . dramatic.

Having discovered that frogs could be successfully filled with air, Eddie thought we should experiment by trying to inflate other animals. We quickly discovered, however, that one of the nice things about frogs is that they don't put up too much of a fuss when you stick a pump needle down their throat. Guinea pigs and hamsters squeal a lot, it turns out, and cats just run away. Snakes are hard to hold still, crawdads don't fill up with air at all, and turtles—well, who knows what happens with turtles? You can pump air all day into a turtle and nothing will happen. It's like they have some sort of built-in release valve that protects them from the idle whims of bored little boys.

The one animal on the block that we hated the most was Mrs. Lutske's chihuahua, Sparkles. Sparkles was a manic, yippie little dog who barked non-stop, all day, just for the fun of it. Mrs. Lutske named her Sparkles because at all times the dog wore a specially-made silver vest decorated with shiny spangles. In the wintertime, Mrs. Lutske even made little Michael Jackson gloves for the dog to wear. It looked ridiculous. I mean, chihuahua's don't have much dog dignity left as it is, but to take away the rest by dressing them like a Las Vegas hooker. Well, that's just cruel.

Anyway, Eddie and I, now deeply into our animal-inflation experiment, naturally began to wonder what might happen if we inflated Sparkles to make her bigger. Full of air, with her chest puffed up, would she look like more like a bulldog? Was it possible to improve such a scrawny creature with a few simple plunges of an air pump? Or perhaps a Chihuahua could be inflated into a rough facsimile of a football, with little leg handles to help you catch it? These were the questions swirling around in our head when we snuck into Mrs. Lutske's yard and tried to inflate her little yippy-yappy dog from the rear.

At the urgent-care clinic, while one nurse was sewing up the gash in my hand and another was applying gauze bandages to sop up the blood from a dozen or so puncture wounds caused by Sparkles's sharp and savage little teeth, my father stood nearby, arms folded, with a skeptical look on his face.

"So tell me again what happened?" my father pressed. "Why did Mrs. Lutske's dog attack you?"

"I have no idea," I lied. "Eddie and I heard her barking and we thought she might be in trouble, so we went to check on her."

"That dog barks constantly," my dad said. "It's never not barking. Why, today, of all days, did you take a sudden interest in its welfare?"

131

"We thought maybe it needed some water," I improvised. "It was kind of hot out."

"So you climbed the fence to give the dog some water?"

"Exactly," I said, sensing that I was getting some traction with this story.

"Because you couldn't see from the other side of the fence whether Mrs. Lutske had left a water bowl out for her precious dog, which she loves above all things. Or whether the pond in her backyard was full of water that the dog could drink if it were really thirsty. Is that it?"

"Look, all I know is that we were trying to help Sparkles," I said—which, technically speaking, was not a lie, since our intention was to help Sparkles be less of a chihuahua.

My dad stared at me with that look of his, the one that said in silence much louder than it could have in words, that he did not believe a word I was saying.

"But when we climbed the fence, she attacked us," I added. "Viciously."

"With no provocation whatsoever?"

"None," I said. "I'm telling you, that dog is crazy. I think maybe she has rabies or something. Now that I think of it, she was kind of foaming at the mouth."

"Rabies?"

"Or something like that. I mean, what would make a dog attack someone like that?" I said.

"Indeed, what?" my dad intoned.

"We're lucky it didn't go for our throats," I added, doubling down on the lie.

"For a while there, all we could see was teeth and claws and those big buggy eyes, all swirling around like that Tasmanian devil character in the Bugs Bunny cartoons. Only this wasn't funny. We were scared."

"Well, you'll be happy to know then that Mrs. Lutske is probably going to have to put ol' Sparkles down."

"What do you mean?"

"I mean that, by law, any dog that bites someone other than its owner, regardless of the reason, must be euthanized."

"What does youth-enize mean?"

"It means the dog has to be killed—executed, put to death," my father said matter-of-factly.

"For good?" I asked.

"Well, for the public good," my dad said. "It's not so good for the dog."

Suddenly, I found myself in a moral quandary. If it was true that Mrs. Lutske was going to have to put Sparkles down, should I confess the truth so that the dog could live? Or should I stick with the lie, even if it meant that an innocent little dog would lose its life? I know now what the right choice was. But back then, my fear of being punished was worse than my fear of a guilty conscience, so I stuck with the lie.

"That seems a little extreme," I ventured.

"Maybe," my father said. "But we can't have vicious Tasmanian devil dogs terrorizing kids in the neighborhood, now can we?"

"I guess not."

"Think what might happen if Sparkles were allowed to live. Someone else might get bitten, or worse."

"True."

"So that's it for Sparkles, then?"

"I guess so."

And that was that. We never saw Sparkles again. The neighborhood was strangely silent from that day forward. But that silence spoke to me and Eddie every day, reminding us of what we'd done. Every time we walked past Mrs. Lutzke's house, she gave us the evil eye through her kitchen window. And every time we pumped up our bicycle tires, we were reminded of the shameful experiments we had tried, as well as the unfortunate fate of Sparkles, the annoying chihuahua. It didn't stop us from devising other experiments in the name of science and curiosity, but it did make us think twice about conducting those experiments on creatures with teeth.

So you see, it is possible for boys to engage in behavior that might be considered by some to be psychotically cruel, and still have them grow up to be respected, responsible members of society—as I certainly am. Devious and demonic behavior—especially between the ages of eight and twelve—is no indication whatsoever of the sort of person who will emerge from such experiences, no matter how horrifying they may seem to the uneducated eye. In fact, it is arguably necessary for boys to engage in such behavior while they are young, so that they aren't tempted to do it when they are older. I don't have any science to back this statement up, just a working knowledge of what happened to Jeremy Timmins.

Jeremy Timmins was boy I went to high school with who got straight A's, joined every club, and was beloved by all the teachers for his polite, respectful demeanor. Everyone else hated Timmins. He made the rest of us look bad. But he ultimately redeemed himself—making everyone else look very good—by setting fire to a barn full of chickens when he was twenty-four years old. He spent five years in prison, had to pay a $10,000 fine, and was basically run out of town when he was released because he could not handle all the jokes people made about how he ought to open up a barbecue restaurant or Kentucky Fried Chicken franchise.

The point is, Timmins should have burned down the chicken ranch when he was twelve, so that he could claim it was a horrible accident and cry about how awful he felt that so many innocent chickens died because of his stupidity. At twelve, that kind of thing gets you a slap on the wrist from the authorities, and maybe you get grounded for a month by your parents, which they reduce to two weeks because they're sick of you moping around the house complaining of how bored you are. And, had Jeremy Timmins burned down the chicken ranch when he was twelve, the chances that he would want to repeat that experience at the age of twenty-four would have been extremely low. Nobody burns down a chicken ranch twice in their life; it just doesn't happen.

CHAPTER 32

At some point, unless you want to take matters into your own hands and educate them at home, you're going to have to enroll your boy in school. Public or private, it doesn't matter, because all schools are the same, and they're all designed to make boys miserable. The desks are laid out in neat rows, there's hardly any place to put your stuff, snacks aren't allowed in class, and all they want kids to do is sit still and be quiet all day, or else. Girls may be able to withstand this kind of torture, but young growing boys? No way. The only thing worse would be strapping them to a chair and making them watch PBS all day long. They can do that in college if they want—but even then, it should be a choice.

My wife and I had our share of run-ins with teachers and administrators over the years, not to mention babysitters, coaches, camp counselors, and all the other busybodies who wanted to tell us what was "wrong" with our child, and what we should do about it. Out of politeness, one has to listen to these people. But after you're done listening to them, it's hard not to tell them to fuck off and mind their own business.

Take The Boy's fourth-grade teacher, Mrs. I-Forget-Her-Name. One day she called us in to discuss The Boy's progress in school, or lack thereof, and to suggest a "course of action" that might help him achieve his goals. They weren't his goals, of course, they were hers. But she was the teacher, so, even though she was a complete idiot, we had to listen to her.

"Thank you both for coming in," the teacher whose name I cannot remember said. (They always thank you right before they tell you your kid is a fuck-up.) "As you're no doubt aware from your son's latest report card, he is not working up to his capabilities at the moment. He is a very bright boy, there's no doubt about that—but he has some focusing issues, and sometimes says or does inappropriate things to let his teachers know that his needs are not being met. The purpose of this meeting is to devise some success strategies we can use going forward to help your son achieve his full potential."

"What makes you think our son has potential?" I asked.

She seemed a little confused by the question—but, as I said, she was an idiot. "All children have potential," she answered. "Identifying and nurturing their aptitudes is what the school experience is all about."

"What are my son's aptitudes?" I asked. "I'd like to know, because to be honest, I don't see a whole lot there."

"I'm sure that's not true," she said, laughing a little nervously.

"As far as I can tell, The Boy is as average as far as the eye can see," I said. "He did manage to come in second in the neighborhood football pool last week, but that was mostly luck, because who in their right mind would pick the Eagles over the Patriots? Am I right?"

At that point, my wife interjected, "What my husband is trying to say is that our son does not seem to have found his passion yet."

"Well, he is only in fourth grade, so I don't think there's anything to worry about in that department," she replied. "The larger issue is that his attention appears to wander quite a bit in class. During in-class assignments, he is often not on task, and when I try to, uh, realign his priorities, he resists—sometimes quite inappropriately."

"He's a daydreamer, no doubt about that," I said. "Try getting him to mow the lawn!"

"Could it be that he is just bored?" my wife asked. "He has been identified as gifted, after all, and I know that gifted children sometimes find the pace of a conventional classroom a bit slow."

"I don't think his intellect is the problem," she said. "I think it's his predisposition toward movement and disruption, combined with his attitude."

"What's wrong with his attitude?" I asked.

"He says he hates school," the teacher said.

"Who doesn't hate school?" I asked.

"Well, we try to foster a mutually supportive learning community here at Randolph Heights, so when a student verbalizes his dissatisfaction at such a high . . . volume . . . it detracts from the school's mission."

"He doesn't talk to us much about these things," my wife said, "but one of the things he has told me is that he thinks you favor girls over boys. Is that true?"

"That is categorically not true," the teacher objected.

"Well, that's not exactly what he says," I pointed out. "What he really says is that you hate boys. And in particular, you hate him."

The teacher was flustered. "I have no idea how he arrived at that conclusion," she said, rather huffily. "I run a completely gender neutral classroom. Everyone is treated the same."

I looked around the room and could see that the walls were decorated with pictures of unicorns and flowers. Pretty much everything in the room was as neat and tidy as a photo in a magazine. Even the pieces of chalk in the chalkboard tray were lined up in a neat row, as were the erasers, and the woman's desk was immaculate. The only thing on her desk was a cup full of colored pencils; otherwise, you could have served dinner off it.

"How come you don't have any posters of dinosaurs on the walls?" I asked. "Or construction equipment? Boys love construction equipment."

"I don't know what you mean."

"What I mean is, when my son is busy daydreaming, there isn't much around here for him to look at," I said, glancing around the room. "Daffodils wouldn't hold my interest, either."

"That's not the point," she said. "The point is that time in the classroom is precious, so students need to be focused on the task at hand. Posters of dinosaurs, or whatever, would just be another distraction."

"He also says that recess is too short," my wife said.

"Well, due to state standards on instruction time and certain budget issues, we have had to limit recess to fifteen minutes a day."

"Fifteen minutes a day?" I gasped. "That's barely enough time to choose up sides."

"We don't 'choose sides' here," the teacher said. "Recess activities are all non-competitive and all-inclusive."

"Well, there's your problem right there," I said. "Boys need to run around a little. They need to tackle each other. They need to compete. How else are they going to learn if they're good at anything or not?"

"There are other kinds of skills," the teacher said.

"Such as?"

"Such as cooperative skills," she said. "Learning to work with one another to achieve a common goal."

"That's what a sport is," I explained. "It's a bunch of guys working together to kick the snot out of a bunch of other guys, who are working together to prevent getting the snot kicked out of them."

"There are ways to achieve the same goal without anyone getting 'the snot' kicked out of them," she said, as if snot-kicking were a bad thing.

"And I'll bet all of them are pretty boring," I said. "Trust me, if no one is getting the snot kicked out of them on the playground, no right-thinking boy is going to have much fun."

"We'll just have to agree to disagree on that," the teacher said, trying to turn the subject back on our son's work in the classroom. "Now, as far as your son's academics are concerned, I have to ask, have there been any problems or issues at home that might be affecting his performance at school?"

"Well, his pet ferret died a couple of weeks ago," I said. "But we stuffed it, and now it sits on his dresser."

"We haven't had any deaths in the family, if that's what you mean," my wife added. "And everything at home has been quite good lately, if you don't count that botched re-pavement job on the driveway," she said, glaring at me pointedly. "Or the crooked tiles in the bathroom. And who could forget the whole 'let's polish the floor ourselves' fiasco? Three times he had to put varnish down and re-sand it because it was uneven. Three times! And by uneven, I mean it had clumps and lumps an elephant could trip over. We have the usual arguments about who should be doing the dishes and whose night it is to control the TV remote, of course, but other than that, things are great at home."

"I see," she said, looking suddenly solemn. "May I suggest then that perhaps you consider exploring the option of behavioral therapy for your son? That, combined with the proper medication, often yields positive results in these types of situations."

"Medication?" my wife said. "What kind of medication?"

"Well, there are all different kinds," she said. "Only a physician can determine which one is best for your son. But we have found that many of the newer pharmaceuticals are quite effective in curbing hyper-activity, particularly in boys."

"Hyper-activity?" I said. "I thought you said he was bored."

"Bored and fidgety," she said. "And disruptive."

"So your advice is to sedate him?" my wife said.

"Not sedate," the teacher said, "rather, bring the chemical makeup in your son's brain and body into proper balance."

"What's proper and balanced about locking boys up in a room for eight hours a day, forcing them to sit still, and only letting them move for fifteen minutes a day?" I asked. "It seems to me that being bored and fidgety—and disruptive—is exactly the proper and healthy response to that type of situation."

"This is school, not a gymnasium," the teacher said, suddenly sounding a bit testy.

"Yes, but schools used to have gymnasiums," I countered. "And they used to give kids time to play in them."

The teacher looked frustrated, and it seemed that her testiness was turning into anger. "Nevertheless, things are what they are here, and everyone has to learn to how to manage themselves in their environment."

There was a long pause during which my wife and I sat and stared stone-faced at the teacher, and she sat like a statue staring at us. A few strands of hair were dangling loose on the side of the teacher's face, and I could tell she wanted to grab the runaways and tuck them back into the helmet she had fashioned out of her straight blonde locks. We seemed to be at an impasse. No one knew quite what to say. It was so quiet that I could hear the second-hand on the clock ticking away the time, in increments that sounded like one second every half-hour or so. No wonder my son had a hard time getting through the day, I thought. He spends all his time trapped in a quantum wormhole where time barely moves, and each tick of the clock is a relative eternity.

After about twelve hours of tick-tocking teacher-time, I could take no more. I turned to my wife and said, "I'm bored. Let's go."

"So am I," my wife agreed.

Then we got up and left.

That wasn't our only run-in with this particular teacher, of course. She was full of all kinds of advice about what we should or shouldn't be doing to make her job easier, all of which we ignored. I only share this particular incident to illustrate the sorts of problems parents of boys inevitably encounter in school.

CHAPTER 34

The problem, as I see it, is that today's schools are run by women, for girls, and if you're a boy who doesn't want to sit still and do your homework all day, you're screwed. The game is rigged. National statistics bear this out. I read somewhere that close to two-thirds of the people in college today are women, and most advanced degrees—particularly in business, law, medicine, and teaching—are being earned by women. Pretty soon the entire world is going to be run by women. Only one of two things can happen then: either women are going to eliminate men altogether, or they are going to create a world in which men are only allowed to be one of two things: movie stars or slaves. There will be no room in the world for ordinary men. Instead, slave-men will stay home all day patching ceilings, unclogging drains, fixing faucets, painting bedrooms, re-arranging the furniture, and otherwise keeping the house habitable for their female masters. That whole "equality" thing will be a quaint artifact of the past. Women who want to have children will just go to their local sperm bank and make a withdrawal. To maintain their power, female parents will genetically pre-select girls so that not enough men are left in the world to mount a revolt. In most neighborhoods of the future, I predict, there won't even be enough men around to get a decent poker game going. Maybe a golf foursome, but only on Sunday, after all the housework is done. Even then, the women will probably install cameras all over the course to make sure men aren't smoking cigars and peeing in the bushes. Mark my words, it will be a dark time for men.

Where the grand plan to eliminate men is going to falter will be the inevitable realization that in order for all of these hyper-competent power queens to feel superior to someone, they're going to need a bunch of average, under-performing men around to make them feel superior. If they got rid of men entirely, they'd just be left with a world full of over-achieving super-gals who have no one to compete with but themselves. They'd end up having their SAT scores and salary printed on their business cards, and get upset if they Googled their name and saw only thirteen pages of praise. They'd start looking for under-served causes to champion, such as the lack of old-fashioned bakeries or people who have suffered salmonella poisoning from handling their pet lizard. At the playground, they'd fight over whose daughter learned Dvorak's Violin Concerto first and who plays it better. Even worse, that wonderful feeling they had growing up—that they were better than everyone else—would disappear. It would be replaced by a nagging anxiety that everyone else is secretly better than they are, and these feelings of inadequacy would motivate them to do crazy things, like run triathlons and work ninety hours a week instead of eighty. Maintaining a sufficient number of lazy, ambitionless men in society would relieve the pressure for women to perform at such an insanely high level, because there would always be a dude in sweats and a backward baseball cap walking down the street who would make them feel better about themselves. The unfortunate part is that citizens of the she-world of tomorrow won't discover this truth until it's too late, and having a perfect score on the SATs isn't even good enough to get their daughter into cosmetology school.

Granted, it may be a while before this hellish, estrogen-powered apocalypse arrives. In the meantime, it is a father's responsibility to teach their son how to compete with girls. Playing by the rules set up by girls is a losing strategy, of course. Girls love to study, do their homework, read books, help people, organize community projects, and sell cookies. All of these things are rewarded in the modern classroom in gross disproportion to their true value. I mean, five dollars for a box of Girl Scout cookies? C'mon.

Since girls are all about excellence and achievement, and out-competing them in this arena is unlikely, the most intelligent thing boys can do is concede the battle for intellectual supremacy and stake their claim to everything average and below. Let girls take the high road, which is more difficult and time-consuming anyway. Boys need to own the middle and low roads, which account for about eighty percent of everything in this world.

What boys have going for them is that, in America, excellence and popularity do not go together at all. In fact, the more excellent something is in America, the less people tend to like or appreciate it. Consider McDonald's hamburgers. McDonald's sells more hamburgers than any other restaurant in the world. But would anyone ever argue that McDonald's sells the best hamburgers in the world? No. The best hamburgers in the world are made by chefs in hoity-toity restaurants who pump them up with all sorts of exotic, expensive ingredients. But nobody gives a shit about those hamburgers. The only hamburgers people buy in huge quantities are from chains like McDonald's, Burger King, and Hardee's, all of which have mastered the art of mediocrity to a degree unparalleled in Western civilization. Nothing about these hamburgers calls attention to itself; qualitatively, everything about them is sub-standard. The buns are spongy and tasteless; the lettuce is wilted; the tomatoes are sliced so thin that you can see through them; the onions are translucent little bits of vegetable matter, the "meat" is little more than ground up intestines and gristle; the cheese is plastic; and the ketchup and mustard they serve with them is mostly red- and yellow-dyed sugar sauce.

And people love them. Tomorrow, if McDonald's started selling hamburgers made from organic grass-fed Angus beef, whole-grain buns, and crisp fresh vegetables, their stock would go down faster than a melted McFlurry. Nobody wants to eat that crap. And so, boys need to pay close attention to this valuable lesson of the marketplace: average is okay. In fact, average is better than okay—it's the key to winning hearts and minds everywhere.

The same principle applies to other areas of commerce. Pizza, peanut butter, beer, soup, cars, movies, books—it's all the same. In each case, the most achingly average product in the category is also the best-selling product.

The reason for this is that people like shitty stuff. To put it another way, people secretly distrust anything that claims to be too good, and they dislike anything that pretends it's the best. Sure, half the restaurants in the country claim to sell the "best" hamburger in the world, but that's okay, because everyone knows it's bullshit. But when, say, an automobile manufacturer claims that it builds the best car in the world, and you buy one, and it still breaks down, you feel like a chump. Worse than that, you feel totally ripped off because you paid $70,000 for that car, expecting greatness, and it still turned out to be piece of shit. And there you are, stranded on the side of the road, hazard lights blinking, waiting for a tow, and hundreds of people are whizzing by in their Subarus and Kias thinking, whoa, I'm glad I didn't shell out for one of those lemons. Look at that poor sucker, standing next to that supposedly fantastic car, helpless and angry because he believed what everyone said about that car: that it was way better than anything else with four wheels and an engine. Bet he wishes he bought a Chevy now. Because if he bought a Chevy, and it broke down, he'd feel a whole lot better. Why? Because anyone who buys a Chevy expects it to break down. So when it happens, they don't say to themselves, Jesus H. Christ in hell and what the fuck, this isn't supposed to happen. They say, oh well, this was bound to happen, because it's a Chevy. They also don't get embarrassed standing on the side of the road next to evidence that they're a gullible idiot. Nor do they get $4,200 repair bills that a guy in a starched white coat tries to convince them is not a "cost," but rather an "investment." Because, you know, it's such a great car.

People hate that kind of bullshit, which is why they buy more Chevys than Jaguars.

The truth is, people talk all the time about the importance of excellence and quality, but at the end of the day, more of them reach for a Bud than a Guinness.

You want to be ignored, irrelevant, and poor: produce an excellent, artsy, independent film that only people with a Master's degree can understand. You want to be rich and famous and wealthy? Make an Adam Sandler movie.

You want to end up playing for nickels at the bottom of a subway platform, go to Juilliard and study the oboe. You want to bank big coin and sleep on a mattress made of money? Drop out of school in eighth grade and start a rap group.

The only girls who understand this gravitational pull toward the bottom of American life are prostitutes, pole dancers, and pop singers who show a lot of skin. Every other female in this country is busy trying to be an über-professional something-or-other, or climb the corporate ladder, or start their own business and become a multi-millionaire by selling purses and hats and jewelry that women in Africa made out of pampas grass and elephant turds. Either that, or they're selling herbal supplements and organic sex toys in a pyramid scheme that includes all of their friends and everyone they ever met in line at Target.

It doesn't matter. For boys, what matters is that they need to find ways to take advantage of the fact that all girls want to be perfect. The best part is that no matter how smart or beautiful or competent they are, women are pre-programmed to think they're not good enough, which only makes them strive harder to achieve the perfection that eludes them.

In school, boys can take advantage of this weakness by continually reminding girls that they are not as smart or beautiful as they think they are. This will infuriate the girls, and they will work harder than ever to be smarter and more beautiful. This is favorable for boys in at least three ways:

First, the girls who are trying harder to be smarter and better will monopolize the teacher's time, engaging them in conversation and asking them all sorts of questions—making it much more difficult for the teachers to monitor and harass boys for whatever they happen to be doing.

Second, it results in a lot of pretty girls, whose beauty and cuteness improves all the way through high school and college. (Though, admittedly, it begins a slow decline after that.)

Third, when all the girls in class are competing to be valedictorian, it opens up the playing field of averageness, leaving whole swaths of marginal competence for boys to exploit.

The benefits of this approach extend well beyond high school. For instance, before women decide to get rid of men completely, or turn them into slaves, they are going to spend a long time trying to figure out what is "wrong" with men, then spend a great deal of time, money, and energy trying to "fix" them.

These are the sorts of questions they'll want answers to:

Why are men so stupid?

Why don' t men have any ambition?

Why don't men care what they look like?

Why do men prefer sports over arts and culture?

Why don't men have strong opinions about what color a room should be painted?

Why don't men appreciate women?

Why aren't men grateful for everything women do for them?

Why are men so thoughtless and inconsiderate?

Why can't men remember birthdays?

Why aren't men more verbal?

Why do men like beer and chicken wings so much?

Why don't men like to talk about their feelings?

Why do men think farting is funny?

Before getting rid of men for good, our hyper-competent, super-concerned female overlords will attempt to alleviate their mounting anxiety over the sorry state of men by establishing institutions to study male culture and funding vast reams of research on male psychology.

The great part, for men, is that these research facilities will look a lot like a Buffalo Wild Wings. For a while, we'll get to do what we already do—sit around and watch playoff sports action on multiple screens—but we'll get to do it in the name of research, and our drinks and food will be paid for by the federal female government. Sure, we might have to sit through some therapy sessions, and answer questions like, "How did you feel when the Blackhawks lost the Stanley Cup?" or "When was the last time you had a conversation with a woman that didn't end up in a fight?" But that's a small price to pay for free beer and the chance to sit around all day with your friends in a wife-free zone, serving the greater cause of science.

CHAPTER 35

ut I'm getting ahead of myself. I'm also making it sound simpler than it is. Because at about the same time it's necessary to teach boys how to effectively compete with girls, it's also necessary to start teaching them how to understand and get along with them. Girls turn into women, after all, so it pays to start early when it comes to teaching boys about the lifetime of psychological warfare to come.

By the time sixth grade came around, The Boy was beginning to show some alarming signs of intelligence. In fifth grade, he had mastered the art of averageness by getting a consistent spread of Bs and Cs on his report card, making him a solid B-minus student, which is perfect positioning for a boy who does not want to call attention to himself. A B-minus average does not raise any unreasonable expectations about future performance, but it isn't so awful that a job delivering pizzas is out of reach. Under my tutelage, he had learned how to game tests by deliberately answering a few questions wrong, and when it came to writing, I taught him all sorts of ways to twist and bend and snap sentences to make it look like he was trying to say something insightful or profound without actually saying anything at all, a tactic that gave him credit for "trying" to have some original thoughts without suffering the embarrassment and scrutiny that comes with evidence of actual thinking.

In sixth grade, however, The Boy began coming home with more As on his report card than Bs—a serious breach of our mutual understanding that As were for Annettes, Amys, and Anna-Maries. He understood perfectly well the implications of getting "better" grades. Anything above a B put him in competition with a bunch of ruthless, over-achieving do-gooders in pigtails, all of whom had been weaned since birth for the rigors and demands of higher education. He didn't stand a chance in that arena, and he knew it. Yet, despite it all, his grades continued to improve. When I confronted him about it, he claimed that he was not working any harder. In fact, he said, he was working less—but no matter how hard he tried not to excel at school, his teachers kept giving him better grades.

"I swear, dad, I'm not doing anything different," he explained to me. "I don't know what's happening. I think everyone else is just getting stupider."

"Are you still sitting in the back of the class?" I asked.

"Yes."

"And are you keeping your participation to a minimum? Only speaking when the teacher addresses you directly, and only then in a mumble no one can hear, using as few words as possible?"

"Yes."

"Are you still disrupting class two or three times a day by whispering to the person next to you?"

"Yes."

"Is the person you're whispering to a boy or girl?"

The Boy could not look me in the eye. "A girl," he said.

"What's her name?"

"Leslie."

"And is Leslie what you would consider a 'smart' girl?"

"Yes. Sort of. I mean, she's nowhere near the smartest girl in class, but she's pretty smart."

"Does she laugh when you talk to her?"

"Sometimes."

"When you talk to her, do you try to make her laugh?"

"Sometimes."

"Does she laugh at things you didn't even intend to be funny?"

"Sometimes."

"I think I know what's going on," I said. "I think, without maybe realizing it, you are getting better grades to try to impress this girl, so that she'll like you more."

The Boy got a quizzical look on his face. "What? That's crazy!"

"It's not crazy at all," I explained. "The subconscious mind is a powerful thing, and it can make us behave in ways that are unexpected and sometimes dangerous. What's happening here, I think, is that your subconscious mind is trying to send certain signals to this girl that you aren't even aware of."

"What are you talking about?" The Boy protested. "Like my mind is sending some kind of radio signal without me knowing about it?"

147

"Exactly!" I said. "And it's also clouding your judgment to the point where you are unwittingly performing better in school. I know it's hard to believe, but sitting next to this girl is accidentally making you smarter."

"Even though I'm working less?"

"Well, my guess is that you aren't working less. It just feels like you're working less, because sitting next to this girl has worn down your resistance to schoolwork."

"That can happen?"

"It can."

"So how do I stop it?" The Boy asked. "How do I keep this secret subconscious part of my brain from transmitting messages to her?"

"First of all, you have to stop sitting next to her," I explained. "Identify the laziest, most bored boys in your class and go sit next to them. Chat them up, just like you did that girl, and pretty soon their responses will dumb you back down to normal. It may take a while, but it's worth it, because you don't want to risk getting on the Honor Roll. Then your life will be over, trust me. If you make the Honor Roll, every girl in school will come gunning for you."

After this talk, about a week went by before I heard anything else about it. We had just eaten dinner, and I was about to sit down and watch an episode of Everybody Loves Raymond, a show I like because it's obvious that everyone does not love Raymond, but he isn't aware of it, so it feels like they're letting you in on the joke. The show is much funnier once you realize that the title is ironic, and everyone really thinks Raymond is a whining little pussy. Before I could find the right remote, however, The Boy came over and spoke to me in the low, hushed tone we use for secret conversations that he doesn't want his mother to hear.

"Dad, can I talk to you about something?" he asked.

"Sure, son, what is it?"

"Well, I did like you said and stopped sitting next to Leslie in class. And it worked, sort of, in that I'm feeling less enthusiastic about school now. The problem is, at recess, this girl, Leslie, keeps following me around."

"What do you mean by follow?"

"I mean, as soon as class lets out for recess, she stands at the door and waits for me to come by."

"Then what?"

"Then she follows me wherever I go."

"Does she talk to you?"

"Constantly," he confirmed. "While we're walking, she asks me all kinds of questions. The weird thing is that she doesn't even wait for me to answer them. She just asks them, one right after the other, and answers them herself."

"Give me an example," I said.

"Well, yesterday I was headed over to the sand pit to see if this kid Jimmy could make it across the monkey bars and back without falling. Some of the guys had a betting pool going, and the over-under was 5-to-2 that he would make it, because someone said they saw him practicing after school a couple of weeks ago. But this kid Otto told me just before recess that he and some other boy had smeared vegetable oil on the monkey bars to make them slippery, so I should bet on Jimmy not making it across. So I bet ten dollars that he wouldn't make it, and I wanted to watch and make sure I got my money."

"And?"

"So we're walking toward the sand pit, and she's walking next to me saying things like, 'Do you like s'mores? I'll bet you do. You strike me as the kind of person who would like them. Most people do. But I don't, because they have a high glycemic index, due to the massive amount of sugar in them. Did you know that sugar is as addictive as heroin? It's true. I saw it in a documentary my parents were watching. Do your parents watch documentaries? Mine do. I wish they didn't, but they do. Do you know what a 'teachable moment' is? That's what my mom says every moment should be, but I don't see how that's possible. I mean, how do you make every moment teachable? Really? Even if you're in the bathroom? And of course, you can't learn anything when you're asleep. Are you a vivid dreamer? I am. Sometimes my dreams are so vivid I think they're actually real. In the dream! Last night, the dream I dreamed was so real that I actually pinched myself in the dream to make sure it was real. And in the dream it felt like it was real. Then I woke up, and was really sad because in the dream I lived on a big ranch and had three horses and a dog named Boo. Has that ever happened to you? It happens to me . . .'"

"Okay, I get the idea," I said.

"It gets worse," he said.

"How so? What happened when you got over to, what did you call it, the sand pit?"

"Well, that's the thing," he said. "We never made it to the sand pit."

"What do you mean?"

"I didn't even realize it, but while she was talking, she was somehow secretly steering us to the corner of the building, away from everyone on the playground. Then, just when we reached the corner of the building, she pulled me around to the side where no one could see."

"Then what?"

"Then she kissed me."

I bolted upright in my Barco-lounger and almost spilled my beer. "She what?"

"She kissed me."

"Did you kiss her back?" I asked.

"What? I don't even know what that means," The Boy said. "How do you kiss someone back?"

"We'll save that discussion for another day," I said. "How many times did she kiss you?"

"Just once. And it was pretty short. Then she ran away."

"The hussy!" I blurted.

I knew this day would come, but I didn't think it would come so fast. I'd read that girls these days are much more aggressive toward boys, but I didn't think the predation would start until junior high or high school. And, given my son's predilection for video games and computers, I secretly hoped that it might never happen at all.

"This calls for emergency tactics," I explained. "Here's what you need to do. It's not pleasant, but it is necessary, so listen carefully."

The Boy leaned toward me and indicated with his finger that my voice was getting too loud. Lowering my voice to a whisper, I said, "Here's what you need to do. Next time she corners you on the playground, you need to pull her around that corner before she pulls you."

"Okay," The Boy said, looking a bit confused.

"Then you need to kiss her before she kisses you," I said.

"Really? How is that . . ."

"Trust me."

"Okay."

"But here's the part you're not going to like," I said. "When you're kissing her, you need to stick your tongue in her mouth."

"What! Are you crazy?" The Boy exclaimed. "That's the most disgusting thing I've ever heard!"

"I know, but it's the only way," I said.

"But think of the germs," he protested. "And what if she just ate something? Or what if she's chewing gum?"

"Just trust me," I said. "If her lips are closed, just jam it in there. Pretend her mouth is the bottom of an ice-cream cone if you have to."

"But she just got braces, Dad. I could shred my tongue on those things. It sounds way too dangerous."

"You only have to do it once," I explained. "After that, she won't want to go near you."

"I don't get it," The Boy protested. "There has to be a better way." He was thoroughly confused, he admitted, and did not see how kissing this Leslie person was going to prevent her from following him and trying to kiss him again.

"This will work because that girl is a predator," I explained. "She's in it for the hunt, and she wants to be in control. Take the control away from her, let her know that you are a more aggressive predator than she is, and she'll go away. She targeted you because she thought you were easy prey. Let her know you're not, and she'll go find someone else to bother."

"You're sure this will work?"

"Trust me," I said. "It will work. However, I must caution you that when you get older, it might not work so well. In fact, the very same tactic can have radically different results."

"I'm confused again," The Boy said.

"As you should be," I replied. "I'd be concerned if you weren't confused."

"None of this makes any sense to me," The Boy said, sighing.

"Me neither," I said. "Let's change the subject. Did you get the ten bucks they owed you from that bet?"

The Boy hung his head and looked at the ground by his shoes. "No. They tricked me," he admitted. "The monkey bars weren't greased, so Jimmy had no trouble going down and back. I lost the money."

"Hmmm. That's the trouble with inside information," I said. "You never know if you can trust it." I reached for my wallet and pulled out a ten-dollar bill. "Here you go," I said, handing it to him. "Lesson learned."

The Boy put his hand up. "I can't accept that, Dad," he said. "It would ruin the lesson. I need to feel the pain of my stupidity, so that I'm smarter about it next time."

I couldn't believe it. "Whose kid are you?" I said. "You're turning down free money?"

"It's not free, Dad. It comes with a price," he said. "I need to learn my lesson."

Slowly, I folded the ten-dollar bill and put it back in my wallet. "You've been talking to your mother, haven't you?" I said. "Here's an insider tip: Before you talk to your mother about the wisdom of wagering, come talk to me first. I'll bet you ten dollars the outcome will be better if you do."

"It's a bet. Now pay up," he said, extending his hand.

"What? Why?"

"Because when I talked to mom about it, she gave me twenty dollars: ten for the money I bet, and ten for the money I should have won. So you're wrong: the outcome was better after I talked to her. Now pay up."

Stunned, I pulled the crumpled ten out of my wallet and gave it to him. "I guess you're my son after all," I said. "Well played."

The following day, The Boy came home from school looking a little weary. He'd been up all night thinking about what I'd said, and what he had to do to repel the girl at school. He wasn't sure he could go through with it, what with all the physical contact involved, but he resolved to try his best, he said, because there didn't seem to be any better options. He had already tried ignoring and insulting her, and had twice refused to share his Doritos with her at lunch, but the girl just laughed whenever he said something "mean," and seemed to enjoy it whenever he got flustered around her. Sometimes it was difficult to tell what she was really thinking, though, because her mouth never stopped moving, he said. Words tumbled out of her at a phenomenal rate, filling the air around her like a cloud. The more he ignored her the faster she talked, often filling in both sides of the conversation, like someone playing chess against themselves. The weird thing was that nothing he did seemed to bother her—and that bothered him. So this tongue thing was worth a try, he reasoned, because nothing else was working.

At school, when the bell rang for recess, The Boy had followed my instructions to the letter, he said. True to form, Leslie was waiting for him by the door, and when he walked by her, she swooped in by his side and started talking a blue streak. Again, just as she had done the day before, she casually nudged him near the corner of the building as she talked, seemingly oblivious but clearly planning to re-enact the terrifying scene of the previous day. This time, when they got to the edge of the building, The Boy did what I told him to do, he said, and pulled her around the corner. She was a little surprised, he said, but didn't say anything. Then, when they were safely out of sight, he closed his eyes and put his lips on hers, he said, even though the thought of it made him want to barf. Then, to quiet the voices of disgust in his head, he tried tricking his mind with the ice-cream-cone imagery I had suggested, and stuck his tongue into her mouth. To his horror, however, she did not recoil or run. Instead, she stuck her tongue back into his mouth! He began to panic, he said. Everything turned into a white blur in his mind, then he ran away from her, toward the playground swings. To make matters worse, after the final bell rang and he was closing up his locker, some other girls came up to him and made all kinds of woo-woo sounds and saying that they heard that he and Leslie were now "dating." He wasn't sure what that meant, he said, but it didn't sound like she was scared of him. Quite the contrary. Hence, the low mood.

I didn't know quite how to counsel him on this matter, since I had been certain that the tongue trick would work. It rarely failed me when I was growing up. In junior high and high school, every time I stuck my tongue in a girl's mouth, that was the last I saw of her. I had hoped that my son could benefit from my experience, but the plan had somehow backfired. So I said to him the only thing I could say under the circumstances. "I hate to be the bearer of bad news," I said, "but I think you're stuck with her for a while. That's how it happens sometimes. Now you have to wait until she gets tired of you, or until she finds another boy she likes more."

"How long will that take?" he asked.

"Depends," I said. "At your age, it should only take a week or two. But at my age, this kind of thing can drag on for twenty or thirty years, maybe more."

The Boy nodded, accepting his fate like a man destined for the gallows. "She said she was going to call me later," he said. "Do I have to answer the phone?"

"I'm sorry son, but yes, you do," I said. "Otherwise you will have an angry girlfriend on your hands, and that's no fun at all."

"What will we talk about?"

"It doesn't sound like that's going to be a problem," I said. "Your job now is to listen, or at least pretend to listen. Once you get good at pretending to listen, you can usually get other things done while they talk."

"Okay, thanks, Dad," he said, and trudged upstairs to his bedroom.

"Oh, and son, there is good news in all of this," I added.

"What's that?"

"Well, now that you don't have to impress this girl anymore, you can work on lowering those grades."

CHAPTER 36

By now it should be obvious that being a good father is not about exercising power and control, nor is it about having all the answers. It's about knowing your limitations, setting a good example, and faking the rest. And, to be honest, this is the area where I struggle the most.

As I mentioned in the beginning, I entered this whole fatherhood thing with serious misgivings about my ability to come up with wise, "fatherly" advice when it was needed most. I feared situations where my son would look to me for answers about life's most nagging questions, and I would have nothing of value to offer. But that's not the half of it, as it turns out. Women are always complaining about how depictions of women in movies and on television lead people to have unrealistic expectations about how a real woman should look and act. But the standard of fatherhood established by The Media is just as oppressive for men, if not more so.

In the old days, TV dads like Mike Brady and Bill Cosby were guys other fathers could relate to. They were successful professionals with hot wives and lots of wise-cracking children, which is the way it should be. But in the last couple of decades, the ideal TV dad has transformed into a figure whose extraordinary level of personal achievement is way too high for any of us mere mortals to match.

It all started with Tony Soprano. Here was a guy with barely a high-school education who ran an entire mob enterprise, lived in a mansion, and somehow managed to stay married even though he hung out in a strip club all night. The man was a lady-slayer, too, even though he was fifty pounds overweight and had the table manners of a gorilla. Women threw themselves at him, and if for some reason they didn't, he hired women to throw themselves at him. The man was a father and excellent provider for his wife and children, but he was also a player—a man who got whatever he wanted, whenever he wanted it.

I ask you: How is an average father like me supposed to live up to that?

Then there's Walter White, the mild-mannered chemistry teacher turned meth kingpin of Breaking Bad. Walter is a guy who would do anything for his family—which, in his case, means raising the money for his cancer treatment by inventing the world's purest form of methamphetamine and establishing an international drug cartel to sell it. For the sake of his family, he risks everything, often facing situations that could potentially be far more dangerous than cancer. And he's incredibly successful at it, even though he has almost no social skills, a severe lack of charm, and no sense of humor whatsoever. All he has going for him is a great product and the guts and determination of a father who loves his family—hardly the credentials one supposedly needs for success in this world. But it works for Walter. At one point, the man has so much money that he has to keep it in hay-sized bails inside a storage facility, or hidden in duffle bags under his house. Any time he needs a little extra cash, he just grabs a wad of bills and off he goes. Wouldn't that be nice?

Again, how is a regular guy like me supposed to live up to that kind of role model? I mean, in addition to making you feel like a failure, a show like Breaking Bad forces you to ask serious questions about yourself. For instance, do I love my family enough to engage in regular gun battles with a Mexican cartel? Absolutely not. Would I spend my days in a haz-mat suit dealing with deadly chemicals just to keep my customers satisfied and grow my expanding drug empire? No, I would not. I'm simply not that good a man, and never will be.

The feelings of inadequacy I have are consequently profound. I never feel like I'm doing enough for my family. I never feel like I'm making enough money. And, most importantly, I know I will never feel the satisfaction of that glorious day when my son finds out what I really do for a living, and learns that, in reality, I'm a bad-ass motherfucker who nobody in their right mind messes with.

That's never going to happen for me. My son knows what I do for a living, so his indifference to me and my accomplishments is permanent. He's never going to discover that I secretly run guns for a motorcycle gang or play high stakes poker to pay the bills. No, he's always going to think of me as a moderately overweight UPS driver who wears brown to work and drives a big, ugly truck.

Surprisingly, I'm better in the advice department than I thought I was going to be. And the most valuable piece of advice I've given my son over the years is that it's okay to make mistakes, as long as you learn from them. And if you're not making mistakes, you are not exploring the limits of your talent and capabilities. Business titans the world over all say that the more mistakes you make, the more you learn, so I've accelerated my son's education considerably by encouraging him to make as many mistakes as possible. He's found it particularly instructive to make mistakes in situations where he knows what the right thing to do is, and it would be very easy to make the correct choice—but, in the interest of learning practical lessons about life, he screws it up anyway.

Take the day he replaced the sugar in one of his mother's cookie recipes with salt. He knew it was the wrong thing to do, but now he knows for a fact what an awful idea it is. Once, he dropped a jar of jam on the kitchen floor, and, instead of cleaning it up like a "normal" person, he smeared it all over the floor and let it dry. Big mistake. Trust me, he'll never do that again. And he knows he's not supposed to go into the gun safe, or load one of my rifles and take it out of the house. But that hasn't stopped him from making a serious dent in the neighborhood's squirrel population. Nor has it stopped him from bringing squirrels home for his mother, when he knows full well that the only wild animals she will even consider cooking are deer, fish, and the occasional rabbit.

Making mistakes this frequently and deliberately goes a long way toward teaching a boy what he can and can't get away with. But again, this is one of those truths that is lost on the public school system, which punishes kids for their mistakes with an angry red pen, and creates an atmosphere where nothing less than perfection will be tolerated. Many schools these days even have a "zero tolerance" policy for many infractions. Bringing "weapons" to school is one of the things they have no tolerance for—but what they classify as a "weapon" is laughable.

Once, The Boy was suspended from school for a week for having a Swiss Army knife in his pocket. This was my "fault," because I gave him the knife and told him to carry it with him at all times. You never know when you're going to need to use the little magnifying glass to start a fire or fry some ants, I told him, so it's best to have the knife with you at all times. This is just common sense. But when his teacher found out that he had a "knife" in his possession, she freaked out and sent him to the principal, who suspended him because the school's "policy" doesn't allow for human beings to make judgment calls about how dangerous a kid with a pocket knife really is.

When I found out about this, I called the principal and let her know, in no uncertain terms, that if my son wanted to kill her, he could do it in any number of ways using common school items. He could jam a pencil in her eye, slit her throat with a pair of scissors, staple her lips shut, poison her with rubbing alcohol, smother her with a t-shirt, slam her head against her desk, make her trip and fall, shatter a window and use a piece of glass to slit her wrists. If she thought taking away my son's Swiss Army knife was going to make the school safer, she was sadly mistaken, I told her.

The next day, I drove The Boy to school so that he could carry my great grandfather's broadside sword into show and tell. "Now this is a weapon," I told him. "Make sure your principal sees it too, because I don't think she's ever seen an actual instrument of death. Oh, and tell her that the dark spots on the blade are the dried blood of Confederate soldiers who had the misfortune of crossing paths with your ancestors, and that your family has a zero tolerance policy against stupidity."

This was an error in judgment on my part—a mistake, if you will— that my son ended up paying the price for. I didn't realize how truly clueless his teacher was until she locked down the school, called the police, and had my son escorted off the premises. And I didn't realize how stupid the police were until they held my son in a juvenile detention facility for twenty-four hours. And I didn't realize how lame-brained the criminal justice system is until they slapped me with a $1,000 fine and made my son do a community service project on public safety. My "mistake" in this instance was in believing that we still live in America, where it can be presumed that an eleven-year-old is not going to decapitate his teacher with a sword, even if he has the technique and capability to do so, and even if some secret part of him wants to. My son's mistake was in doing a little too much "show" and not enough "tell," which apparently led to some confusion. We all learned something from this little debacle, though—mainly that America ain't what it used to be, a country where weapons of all kinds are cherished and admired, and a boy can walk around with an itty-bitty knife in his pocket without alarming the authorities.

CHAPTER 37

The Boy stopped being cute somewhere around the age of twelve. It's hard to say exactly when it happened. One day he was my little buddy and I was his hero and all was right with the world. The next day he was an insolent, back-talking little shit with smelly feet and a bad attitude.

How this transformation took place, I do not know. I gather from our friends, however, that the phenomenon is not confined to boys. Parents of girls also report that, at around the age of twelve, their cute little princesses somehow turned into gossiping, back-stabbing little she-witches. Apparently, it's a thing.

The change took me by surprise. Until then, my relationship with The Boy had been a good one. I told him what I thought and what to do, and he listened and did it. It was a good arrangement.

But after the change, he was a completely different person. He no longer cared what I had to say; in fact, he was sometimes openly contemptuous of my opinion. Suddenly he was an expert on every subject, and knew the answer to everything even before the question was asked. Whereas before I only had to yell at him three or four times get him to take out the garbage, now it took a dozen or more tirades for him to even acknowledge that the "garbage" existed.

"Let's call it what it is, dad—waste," he'd say. "Most of what you call garbage is just wasteful excess packaging. Reduce the amount of packaging and you reduce the amount of waste. The problem is, if I just take the garbage out, like you're asking, I'm basically enabling you and mom to generate more trash. There's no incentive for you to change your habits. But if I let the garbage pile up, you might think twice the next time you decide to have Red Baron pizzas for dinner."

I think this is why teenagers are so attracted to stories about vampires and werewolves. To teenagers, these stories aren't absurd fantasies involving mythical creatures overcome by forces they can't control; they are literal depictions of what happens when a torrent of raging hormones meets a malleable adolescent mind. No one is safe once the teenager has changed. It trails chaos and mayhem wherever it goes. It feeds on parental suffering. What was once your innocent little boy is now a hairy monster with bloodshot eyes and a thirst for pain—your pain. Once the rage has passed, the pubescent beast may return to its original form for a while, showing glimpses of the little angel you once loved. But it doesn't last long. Anything can set it off again—a simple request, an innocent question, a harmless suggestion—and then the devil dog within him takes over again, destroying whatever tranquility had existed before and replacing it with a shit-storm of stress and worry.

Teenagers see these movies and take comfort in the fact that they aren't the only ones who imagine snapping a teacher's neck with their jaws. Parents see them and wonder where they can buy a few silver bullets and an iron stake blessed by a priest. How either of them survives is one of those evolutionary mysteries for which there are no easy answers.

CHAPTER 38

The death of a child is always tragic, of course. When a child dies and a prick like Donald Trump lives, it can seem as if life has no true meaning, and that all any of us are really doing on this Earth is caretaking a sack of blood and bones, waiting for death to come.

But the *near-death* of a child is an entirely different matter. Sometimes, the best thing that can happen to a kid is to come alarmingly close to death and survive. Boys, especially, love cheating death as dramatically as possible.

My son and his friends, Zacc and Todd, liked to play in a nearby creek that ran next to a local soybean farm. The creek was natural, not man-made, which meant that its banks swelled during the springtime, turning its usually peaceful trickle into a raging torrent of whitewater, complete with menacing whirlpools that could easily suck a child underwater and drown them in seconds. On days when the water was especially high, one could almost hear an albino banjo player plucking out a dirge of doom for those who had lost their lives underestimating the temperament of this gentle stream. It was on one such day that my son and his friends, having nothing more deadly to do, decided to build a raft.

We didn't have any wood, so I suggested that they use some foldable lawn chairs as a platform, fold them flat, then attach a dozen or so empty plastic milk containers to the sides to make them float. Each boy made his own raft, and christened it with an appropriate name. Zacc and Todd named their rafts the "Nina" and "Pinta" respectively, having just finished a section in school on Christopher Columbus—albeit one that sought to "clarify" the historical record by pointing out that Columbus was a gold-crazy megalomaniac who terrorized the natives by hacking their ears and hands off, used their women as sex slaves, and killed millions of them by introducing small pox and other diseases to the New World.

Perhaps that is why my son, rather than naming his raft the "Santa Maria," chose to call his "The Black Pearl," after the legendarily doomed pirate ship in *The Pirates of the Caribbean*. He wanted to grow dreadlocks and get a gold tooth, just like his hero, Jack Sparrow, but I had to draw the line somewhere. The wool coat, boots, sword, and triangle hat were enough. If he wanted to introduce even more realism into his journey, he could also carry a telescope, a map, and a bottle of rum, I told him—but there was no way his mother was going to green light the gold tooth and dreadlocks. A parrot, maybe, and possibly a small cannon—but that was as far as either of us was willing to go.

After much arguing and pirate-swearing—including a particularly eloquent rant that cursed me to an eternity of suffering at the bottom of the sea—the boys set off on their journey. They dragged their rafts behind them until they got to the water's edge, where they assessed the level and speed of the water and decided that they were going to need a few long sticks to help guide them down the stream. They searched along the stream bank for tree limbs straight and sturdy enough to do the job, but ended up returning to our house and stealing three brooms. Aware that his mother would be angry if she discovered all of her brooms missing, the boys thoughtfully sawed off the broom heads and left them behind.

Thus equipped, they set out on their journey.

The first hundred yards or so went as planned, in that their plan was to travel about the length of a football field, then come ashore, hike back upstream, and do it all over again. But the snowmelt that year, combined with some heavy rains, had swelled the stream so much that the water was flowing much faster and stronger than usual. By the time the boys reached the hundred-yard mark, they were being carried along at an exhilarating speed by a deep, powerful current that seemed to have another destination in mind. They tried to slow themselves down by planting their broomsticks in the streambed, but the moment their sticks hit bottom, the stream grabbed them and ripped them out of the boys' hands. With no way to steer or stop, the boys were at the mercy of the stream—and the stream that day was not in a merciful mood.

What the boys soon discovered was that their humble little stream eventually connected up to the much larger and faster Zumbro river, which eventually spills into the mighty Mississippi. Shallow but swift, the water level on the Zumbro was also higher than normal, making its rippling rapids that much more treacherous.

At first, the boys found it exciting to be pulled by natural forces they could not overcome toward places they had never seen and were not, under any circumstances, allowed to go. Their rafts were floating well, and the scenery whizzed by like scenes from a movie. Field after field of freshly planted soybeans and corn flew past, their neat and tidy rows stretching to the horizon. A herd of dairy cows that had ambled down to the stream for a drink thought it curious that three young humans were yelling "mooooooo!" as they floated by. And several ducks along the way wondered how these interlopers were even moving without webbed feet to propel them.

But move they did. Every once in a while, at a bend in the stream, they would attempt to steer their rafts toward shore. Once, Zacc and Todd tried to hold hands in order to pull their rafts together, hoping that their combined weight and mass would slow them down enough to grab a branch or rock. It did not. Zacc held on to Todd's hands so tightly that he pulled Todd off his raft and into the water, forcing Todd to hold onto the lawn-chair-and-milk-carton watercraft for dear life the rest of the way. Chances to make it to shore came and went so many times that the boys felt like they were being taunted. They knew they had to stop somewhere, somehow, but the hope that it might happen before their rafts fell apart was growing fainter with each passing field.

The boys knew they were in "big trouble," and that we, the parents, were going to "kill them" when we found out what had happened to them. Soon, their fear of certain death changed the entire goal of the adventure. Having achieved their first objective—to build a watercraft that would float the length of a football field—their new goal was to figure out how to get home without their maniacally protective (yet equally homicidal) parents ever finding out.

As The Boy explained afterward, "We were just trying to save our skins, dad. You can't blame us for that."

Where the stream on which they were floating connects to the Zumbro, there is a waterfall that drops about six feet into a churning bowl of foam, which spills over a field of boulders and down into the river itself. Until then, the boys' makeshift rafts had somehow managed to stay afloat, even though Zacc and The Boy had lost several milk cartons along the way. All three of them were soaking wet by the time they reached the falls, and all except The Boy had reached their capacity for adventure and wanted desperately to go home.

As they approached the waterfall, they could hear the rush and roar of it grow louder. The sound seemed to come from everywhere, as if the falls had already started to swallow them. To the boys, it was the sound of certain death. In their minds, they were about to go over Niagara Falls without a barrel. As further punishment for their transgressions, their bodies would be smashed on the jagged rocks below and pummeled by several million tons of angry water. Bits and pieces of their dismembered carcasses would then float away. Fish downstream would feed on their rotting flesh, and their bones would sink to the bottom, never to be found.

So when they went over the falls, their screams were real. They thought they were going to die. When they didn't—when the bloated stream lobbed them down into the pool below, and nudged them up against some large rocks they could hold onto, allowing them to grab some purchase with their feet and stumble out of the water onto dry land—they were shocked. Then they were ecstatic. As they watched their milk-carton rafts get tossed over the rocks and down into the Zumbro, they felt they had cheated death.

"Wooo-hoo, that was amazing!" yelled Zacc.

"That was awesome!" agreed The Boy. "Man, we have got to do that again!"

"Guys, I think my ankle is broken. Or my leg. Or something," Todd said in a somewhat less enthusiastic voice.

Blood was oozing out of a cut on his right leg, and though it was difficult to see, a small piece of fractured bone was pushing up through the skin. Todd tried to stand up, but the moment he put weight on the injured leg, he cried out in pain and crumpled to the ground.

"That looks bad," Zacc observed. "Does it hurt?"

"Of course it hurts, you idiot!" Todd yelled.

"We've got to get some help," said The Boy, sensibly sizing up the situation.

"Yeah, but where are we?"

"I don't know, but there's got to be a road or a house around here somewhere," The Boy said. "You stay here. I'll go scout around."

Half an hour later, The Boy returned with a disheartening report. "There's nothing around here. It's just woods and fields as far as the eye can see," The Boy said.

"Maybe on the other side of the river?" Zacc offered.

"Yeah, but how are we going to get Todd over there?"

"Good point. Maybe we should just leave him here to fend for himself," Zacc joked.

By this time Todd was in so much pain that he couldn't even protest. He just lay on ground, wincing and moaning, sucking in air through his teeth. His breathing was shallow. He was wet and cold. The sun was going down, and soon it would be dark.

"We need to make a fire," The Boy said. "Maybe someone will see the smoke. And if it gets dark, we're gonna need a fire anyway."

"How are we going to start a fire?" Zacc asked. "We don't have any matches."

"I found this when I was walking around," The Boy said, holding a purple butane lighter in his hands. He flicked it and an orange flame shot out. "We just need to find some wood."

Unfortunately, most of the wood within fetching distance was either wet or green, or both. Zacc and The Boy scrounged around for twigs and sticks they could use as kindling, but didn't find much. At one point, The Boy was collecting pine cones (he'd heard they could burn), when he heard Zacc scream. The Boy ran toward the sound of the scream, and he found Zacc lying on the ground next to a dead log. Zacc had been kicking the log and breaking off pieces when he had inadvertently stuck his hand into the face of what he guessed was a mother rattlesnake. The snake bit his hand, he said, and he could feel the poison flowing up his arm.

"Dude, I got bit," Zacc said, alarmed.

The Boy had read that in this situation, you were supposed to slice two "x"-shaped cuts into the victim's skin, then suck the venom out with your mouth and spit it out. He did not have a knife, though, because his teacher had confiscated it. The sharpest thing he'd found so far was a popsicle stick.

"Can you walk?" The Boy asked.

"Yeah, but I feel kind of woozy," Zacc replied.

"Go wait by Todd and keep your hand below your head," The Boy instructed. "That way, the poison will take longer to get to your brain."

Zacc nodded that he thought this was a good idea. "Dude, if I die, you can have my skateboard," Zacc said.

"You're not going to die," The Boy said. "If it gets really bad, I'll cut your arm off. That way, the poison won't spread."

"Thanks man, you're the best," Zacc said.

The Boy grabbed the small stack of wood that Zacc had already collected and carried it with him back to the patch of grass where Todd lay bleeding and barely conscious. Zacc was sitting next to Todd, holding his hand and moaning, "It's bad, man, it's bad."

By then the sun had already gone down and dusk was fading into night. Having escaped certain death in the river, The Boy found it ironic that at least two of them were now facing death on dry land. He also found it stupendously unlucky, and wondered how it was possible for them to go from an innocent rafting adventure to an all-out episode of *Survivor*. It was even worse than *Survivor*, he thought, because there was no camera crew around to helicopter them out in case of an emergency.

Using pieces of his shirt, some pine needles, shreds of bark, and an old Burger King box he'd found in the woods, The Boy somehow started a smoky, sputtering fire. As The Boy tried to keep both the fire and his friends alive, he wondered what he should do next—what he *could* do next. There were no good options left. He could leave his friends there and walk back upstream, which would eventually lead him home. But he had no idea how far they had floated, and his impression was that they had floated quite a long way—so far that he had absolutely no idea where they were. By the time he got back, Zacc and Todd could be dead—or worse, they could die and their bodies could be carried away by bears. He didn't have a flashlight, though, so disappearing into the black void beyond the fire wasn't a very appealing proposition. The only thing he could do—really the only option available to him—was to sit and wait, and hope someone found them. But even if help arrived, it didn't matter, he reasoned. All three boys had already resigned themselves to a grisly death at the hands of their irate parents. One way or another, they were all going to die.

The smartest thing they did was start a fire, because that's how we found them. When the boys didn't come home that evening, Zacc's dad and I figured that they had probably gotten a little carried away with their rafting adventure. In any event, we reasoned, they were probably somewhere near the stream, trying to work their way back home. The boys didn't know it, but there was a campground about a quarter of a mile away from where they had landed. While Todd's dad and our neighbor, Ed, worked their way downstream, our job was to work our way upstream and meet them in the middle. We were of course concerned that they might have drowned, but we let our wives worry about that. As men, we knew there was no sense in imagining a catastrophe until all forms of denial have been exhausted. So deny we did, and went about our business.

"Happy" isn't the word I'd use to describe the boys' reaction when they saw us. Relieved and somewhat grateful, perhaps, but they were also ashamed and scared. The Boy considered being rescued by his father a personal failure. Even on the way to the hospital, he continued to insist that he had the situation "under control," and that he had been prepared to set Todd's leg with a splint, if necessary. As for Zacc, his plan had been to make his friend drink lots of water to "dilute the poison." He of course hoped that he wouldn't have to amputate Zacc's arm, but he was prepared to do that as well, though he hadn't quite figured out the logistics of such a surgery in the wild. He had been "working on it" when we arrived, he said, and felt certain that he would have come up with a solution eventually.

As it turned out, Todd did have a compound fracture in his leg, having smashed it on a rock. He had to wear a cast for six weeks, but of the three of them, Todd got the most mileage of out of their story, the heroism and danger of which had been exaggerated to the point where some girls at school had actually begun talking to him.

Curiously, when Zacc reported to the doctor that he thought he only had about fifteen minutes to live, the doctor informed him that he had not been bitten by a snake at all. "You might have poked your hand on a nail, or cut it on a branch or something, but there's no snakebite," the doctor insisted.

Zacc was crushed. He felt certain that he had done battle with a poisonous creature whose toxic venom was now coursing through his bloodstream, attacking his central nervous system, making him weak and deranged.

"Your mother says you're up-to-date on your tetanus shots, so there's really nothing more to do," the doctor added. "You're good to go."

When The Boy and I arrived home, there was a tearful reunion between mother and son. I enjoyed a brief moment as the "hero" of the story—the one who had tracked The Boy down in the dark and delivered him safe and sound to his mother's waiting arms. She, of course, wanted to know "how this happened," so that it would "never happen again."

The Boy explained that all they wanted to do was go rafting a little ways down the creek and come back. He also explained that I had come up with a "great idea" to make the rafts out of lawn chairs and milk jugs, and that I had helped them build the things. "Dad tied the jugs on real tight, so it was actually pretty safe," The Boy explained. I, too, was proud of the engineering involved, but noted that in the future, we should come up with a more effective steering mechanism.

I did not expect my wife's reaction. "You showed them how to build these rafts?" she asked in a way that was less of a question than an accusation.

"Uh, yes," I replied.

"You tied the flotation devices on with your handy 'sailor knots'?"

"As tightly as I could," I answered.

"Then you let them go out there and sit on these contraptions, in the water, without any life vests, without telling anyone, and with no supervision whatsoever?"

"That's more or less accurate," I said.

"What the hell were you thinking?!" she screamed.

I considered my response carefully. "Isn't the point of 'rafting' to put the raft in the water?" I reasoned. "I mean, what's the point of making a raft if you can't use it?"

"You are such an idiot," she said, shaking her head.

"But it was you who said the boys could build a raft in the first place!" I objected. "Right there in the kitchen, The Boy asked if they could make a raft, and you said 'yes'. All I did was help them."

My wife took a deep breath and said, "When I said they could build a raft, I did it with the understanding—the absolutely certain knowledge—that a raft would never get built. They do this all the time! They come up with some sort of crazy project, but after half an hour of trying to figure out how to make it work, they give up and go back to playing video games. It's harmless. Unless of course their father helps them, in which case it becomes inconceivably dangerous and life-threatening!"

"So this is *my* fault?"

"One-thousand percent."

"Are we even going to discuss The Boy's punishment?" I asked.

"No, because he did nothing wrong!" she yelled.

The Boy smirked at this, but he did it behind my wife's back. Only I could see it. I'm still not quite certain how all the blame got heaped on my shoulders. It wasn't the first time, of course, or the last. But in the end, I don't regret what I did. To this day, in private moments when his mother isn't around, The Boy will admit to me that the "day on the river" was one of the best days of his life—precisely because he almost died, but didn't.

CHAPTER 39

It is perhaps worth noting that The Boy losing his cuteness and charm coincided somewhat directly with a period in my marriage when things were not going very smoothly. And by "things," I mean everything. It seemed that way at the time, anyway. Because it seemed to me that as soon my son stopped being a cute and lovable little cherub, I too became somewhat less lovable in my wife's eyes, which in turn made me love her somewhat less, because she's not the sort of person who is very cute when she's mad. Or very loveable. In fact, when she's mad at me and I'm mad at her, the whole idea of love seems absurd. When her head is spinning around and the dishes are flying and a stream of unintelligible nonsense is spewing out of her mouth, the last thing on my mind is love. In those situations, survival quickly rises to the top of my concerns, followed by the formulation of an exit strategy, the dollar amount of the property damage, what I'm going to do for dinner, where I'm going to sleep, and how long it's going to be before I can watch TV again.

As The Boy approached his teenage years, these emotional eruptions became more frequent. Often, what set her off was something little—something I barely noticed. In certain moods, for instance, a harmless joke could lead to a six-hour rant-and-pout.

One evening, The Wife served flat-iron steaks that, to be charitable, were somewhat overcooked. She observed, clearly and rationally, that the meat was a little "tough." My son grunted and said, "Maybe. A little." And I quipped, quite cleverly, I thought, "You think this is tough? She brought the gravy in on a meat hook!"

At another time in our marriage, that line would have gotten a laugh. Or if not a laugh, a playful slap on the arm to let me know that I was being "bad," but in a cute and charming way. On this particular evening, however, The Wife slammed her fork down and yelled, "That's it! I'm sick of you two criticizing my cooking! Every night, I put together as good a dinner as I can manage under the circumstances, which are never ideal, and you two sneer and snipe like a couple of, well, teenagers. If you think it's so easy, from now on you can cook for yourselves!" Then she stomped off and locked herself in the bedroom.

The Boy and I sat in silence for a few moments as the din of the slamming door reverberated through the house.

"What was that about?" The Boy asked.

"I have no idea," I said. "I think she's upset because I made a joke about the steak."

"The truth hurts."

"Well yes, but in these types of situations, I'm supposed to step back and analyze my part in it. You know, to try to see it from her point of view."

"How do you do that?"

"Well, for instance, from her point of view, the joke about the gravy might not have gone over so well because, as you can see, we do not actually have any gravy at the table. So, in her mind, comparing the toughness of the meat to some even-tougher gravy was pointless, because there's no gravy to compare it to. So, again, in her mind, maybe she thought it was unfair of me to make fun of something that doesn't even exist—to, in effect, criticize her for something she didn't do—which, in this case, is make any gravy."

"Why didn't she make gravy?" The Boy asked.

"I don't know," I said. "Because if there ever was a steak that needed gravy, this is it."

"Well, I thought it was funny," The Boy said, chewing his meat in an exaggerated way to let me know that I had been right: the meat was indeed quite tough.

"Looking at it from her point of view, though, I can see how the gravy joke may have felt like a stretch, like I was working too hard for the laugh. And she might not have gotten it, because in her mind she was maybe thinking, 'What is he talking about? He's nuts. There is no gravy.' So it might have worked better if I'd said something like, 'If you think the steak is tough, it's not half as tough as your mother.' You know, wrap a complement into the joke rather than a criticism. Or I could have gone a completely different direction and said, 'Well I for one prefer tough meat. Nine out of ten dentists recommend tough meat for strong jaws and beautifully sculpted cheekbones. Which you definitely have, honey, because your cooking is so . . . *healthy* that way.'

Again, staying positive and complimenting her instead of criticizing her—that's the takeaway here, I think."

"What if she just thought you were being a dick?" The Boy said.

"What do you mean?"

"I mean, what if she thought you were being a dick for the sake of being a dick?"

I tried to envision what that would look like from her point of view, but could not. "I don't think that's it," I said. "When you've been married as long as your mother and I have, you just know things about each other." I explained. "It's a kind of intuition. And my intuition says that she's just mad about how I phrased the joke. And she has a point: If I'd put a second or two more thought into it, I might have been able to phrase it in a way that worked better for that particular moment—and might even have been funnier. So it was thoughtless of me not to be more careful about my joke, and that's on me." (These were issues we'd been discussing in couples therapy, so I was more aware of the dynamics of the situation than I might have been otherwise, even though I think our therapist is completely full of shit.)

"What now?" The Boy asked.

"We wait until she apologizes," I said. "The fact of the matter is that she flew off the handle over nothing, and as soon as she realizes that, I think she's going to feel pretty awful. When she does finally apologize, my job will be to comfort her, let her know that I still love her, and that I forgive her for ruining dinner."

"Sounds good," The Boy said. "Can I go do my homework?"

"Sure, but only for half an hour," I said. "Any more than that and you start to over-think things. And we both know how dangerous that can be."

CHAPTER 40

As I mentioned, this all happened during a period when The Wife and I were going to couples therapy twice a week. Therapy was something The Wife said we needed, because, she said, our lines of communication had broken down and, instead of supporting each other with love and affection, we had settled into a routine characterized by long stretches of boredom interrupted by periods of mutual and sometimes volatile hostility.

The suggestion that we attend therapy took me by surprise, because I thought we were doing fairly well, considering that we weren't divorced yet and most of the people we knew were more miserable than we were. I thought the pattern we had settled into was called "marriage," and that there wasn't much to be done about it except slog through the shit and hope there was a pony in there somewhere.

I refer, of course, to the old joke that was said to be Ronald Reagan's favorite. And I mention it here because our therapist used it as one of our first exercises, to determine how The Wife and I think about and deal with adversity.

The joke, for those who don't know it, goes like this:

The parents of twin boys were concerned that their sons had developed extreme personalities—one was a total pessimist, the other a total optimist—so their parents took them to a psychiatrist.

First the psychiatrist treated the pessimist. Trying to brighten his outlook, the psychiatrist took him to a room piled to the ceiling with brand new toys. But instead of being pleased, the little boy burst into tears. "What's the matter?" the psychiatrist asked, baffled. "Don't you want to play with any of the toys?" "Yes," the little boy bawled, "but if I did, I'd only break them."

Next the psychiatrist treated the optimist. Trying to dampen his outlook, the psychiatrist took him to a room piled to the ceiling with horse shit. But instead of wrinkling his nose in disgust, the optimist let out an unexpected yelp of delight. He then clambered to the top of the pile, dropped to his knees and began gleefully digging out scoop after scoop of shit with his bare hands. "*What do you think you are doing?*" *the psychiatrist asked, just as baffled by the optimist as he had been by the pessimist.* "*With all this manure,*" *the little boy replied, beaming,* "*there must be a pony in here somewhere!*"

Our therapist asked each of us which boy we identified with most, the optimist or the pessimist? I had heard that joke so many times by then—from various salesmen and business people—that I already knew the answer. My wife had never heard the joke before, though, so she had a somewhat different interpretation.

The correct answer, I knew, was that we were supposed to identify with the optimist, because his attitude helps him make the best of a bad situation. The reason this was Ronald Reagan's favorite joke was that it explained how he, the great communicator, viewed the world. And, since all of us want to be as much like Ronald Reagan as possible, it is how *we* should view the world.

I raised my hand first, so the therapist called on me to speak. "I identify with the optimist," I said, "because let's face it, life is a giant pile of shit."

The psychiatrist didn't reveal what he thought of my answer one way or the other, which I thought was rude, because I'd clearly gotten the question right. Then it was my wife's turn to speak—and, to my astonishment, the therapist's head started bobbing up and down like a chicken at feeding time, indicating that he agreed with what my wife was saying, even though it was total nonsense.

"That's the stupidest joke I've ever heard," she began. "You say it was Ronald Reagan's favorite joke? Well, that explains a lot. First, let's look at the so-called 'pessimist' in this story. He is confronted with a room full of toys, and breaks into tears because he is afraid he might break them. I get it: we're supposed to think that any boy in his right mind who is given a room full of toys would naturally want to play with them. But the setup of the joke suggests that this might not even be possible. The toys are piled to the ceiling, after all, and a little boy is about five feet tall. So, even if he did try to play with one, he'd have to pick one from the bottom of the pile, which might cause an avalanche and bury him. The boy may have assessed the reality of the situation and, for the sake of his own safety, declined to play with them—in which case the boy is being a realist, not a pessimist. Also, what if the toys were made of glass? They might shatter and cut him to ribbons, in which case the boy's concerns are perfectly legitimate.

"As for the other boy, the optimist, I don't even know where to begin. Here is a boy who, faced with a room full of horse shit, starts digging into it with his bare hands in the belief that he might find a pony. All health considerations and common sense aside (he couldn't find a shovel?), this boy isn't optimistic, he's completely delusional. The fact of the matter is that there is no pony under all that shit; he just hopes there might be, and is willing to dig through the shit all day on the thin ribbon of prayer that his effort might be rewarded. He is not going to find a pony, though, so he's really just fooling himself.

"Also, the optimist part of the story very cleverly fails to evaluate this boy's attitude after eight or ten hours of futile and fruitless shit-shoveling. What happens when he empties the room of all that shit and must confront the fact that there is no pony? What then? Is he such a resilient optimist that he will be happy without a horse? Or will he be fuming angry because his parents and this psychiatrist wasted his time, toyed with his emotions, and forced him to spend all day digging through a giant pile of horse dung for nothing? I'm guessing the latter.

"So, to answer your question about which boy I identify with most: I don't identify with either one," she said. "Why? Because the story itself is horseshit, and I just spent the last ten minutes digging through it to tell you why. I think everyone involved in this story is crazy, especially the parents and the psychiatrist. Truly, the person I identify with most is the person who had to fill those rooms full of toys and horse shit, just so some idiotic psychiatrist could bill the parents $250 an hour to conduct a ludicrous experiment. What did that person make? Ten bucks an hour? Is that why Ronald Reagan liked that joke so much? Because somebody got a shitty job out of it? I mean, I thought the man was a moron before—but now that I know this was his favorite joke, I realize that he was a delusional moron. Because of him, it's not Morning in America anymore, it's Mourning in America!"

As I said before: complete nonsense. But the therapist thought her interpretation was "interesting" and "nuanced," and deserved more discussion. I couldn't have disagreed more, of course, but he insisted. He wondered why I couldn't admit that her interpretation had some "legitimacy," and I said how could her interpretation possibly be legitimate if it included the words, Ronald Reagan is a delusional moron? Wasn't that proof enough that her opinion was bogus, given that Ronald Reagan was, as everyone knows, one of the greatest men who ever lived?

Let me backtrack a moment to say how disappointed I was that Dr. Everly—that was his name—didn't help us out more in these situations. When The Wife first suggested therapy, she wanted to go with a female therapist, but I nipped that in the bud right away. If the therapist was female, I knew she would take my wife's side and that they'd double-team me. So I insisted on having a male therapist, so that he'd have my back and we could double-team The Wife. Given my wife's skills in the argumentation department, I figured that'd be a fair fight. But no, Dr. Everly did his best to be "impartial," which meant that my wife's opinion on things ended up getting way more credit than they deserved. He maintained that he was on the side of our "marriage," and that he wanted to help us find ways of communicating that improved our day-to-day lives and inter-personal satisfaction with our relationship. I wasn't sure that more communication was the answer, and on one occasion I told him so.

"If we get into arguments every time we try to communicate, doesn't it stand to reason that the answer to our problems might be in finding ways to communicate *less*?" I reasoned.

"You see, this is the kind of thing I have to deal with all the time," my wife interjected. "It's pretzel logic from the word go. What am I supposed to do with that?" she asked, exasperated. "Say yes, you have a point, why don't we both shut up and eat our dinner?"

"That's not a bad idea," I said. "She always wants to talk during dinner—to go over the details of the day, discuss our son's problems in school, remind me of all the things in the house that still need fixing, etc. At the end of the day, all I want to do is enjoy the wonderful meal she's made—assuming it's a night when the meal is, in fact, wonderful. But even if it isn't, I'd rather eat in silence than fill the room with all that negativity. That's how my parents did it, and they were married for more than fifty years."

During therapy, whenever I voiced my opinion and, as I did here, backed it up with facts, The Wife would just put her head in her hands and mutter, "Oh my god."

After a year of therapy, The Wife and I gradually came to an understanding that I wasn't going to change and neither was she. So, according to Dr. Everly, we only had two options: Continue to put up with each other or get a divorce. Either way, he didn't think he could help us anymore, and didn't want to try. A divorce would have been expensive and messy, so we did the reasonable thing and decided to continue putting up with each other. The big difference this time was that we'd been through a year of marriage counseling, so neither one of us expected that things would change anytime soon. Once we let go of the expectation that our marriage could "improve," everything did in fact get better, an outcome that I could not have predicted and do not understand, though I suspect it had something to do with the fact that we stopped trying to "communicate" and just started talking to each other. Talking is much simpler than communicating, and considerably cheaper, which is why I prefer it. Personally, I can talk all day long, especially if I'm not under any pressure to communicate anything, especially anything involving "feelings." Less is more when it comes to communication, that's my feeling. Unless Ronald Reagan says it, in which case it pays to perk up and listen.

CHAPTER 41

In retrospect, however, one of the reasons our marriage improved during this period was that I made a special effort to stay away from the house as much as possible. One way I accomplished this was by taking The Boy on a lot of camping trips. During the summer, especially, we headed for the pine-scented comfort of the North woods, secure in the knowledge that wherever we went and whatever happened, The Boy's mother could not yell at us. I might yell at The Boy, and he might yell at me, but at least we'd be spared the humiliation of being yelled at by his mother, whose words can stab and sting in ways ours cannot. Compared to the darts and daggers that come out of her mouth, our words are nothing but nerf balls and marshmallows. One cannot win a battle with nerf balls and marshmallows, so the next best option is to head for the hills. Besides, her quilting club started meeting in our living room every Saturday afternoon, so there was no point in sticking around. "Stitching and Bitching" is what The Wife calls it, and that about sums it up. No man should be within earshot of that crowd. Those women are smiling, needle-wielding vultures, every one.

Fathers camping with their sons is one of those time-honored traditions that everyone must undertake, because there is no other way to teach a boy the survival skills he might need if, say, the world is suddenly engulfed in apocalyptic mayhem. Under such circumstances, it may be impossible to make a trip to the grocery store, and armed militias may prevent a person from taking refuge in their home. A boy needs to know what to do in such situations, and camping provides an ideal opportunity to develop the skills they might someday need.

Sadly, I did not do any camping with my father when I was young. My father did not believe in camping. He was an "indoorsman," he claimed, and thought spending time outdoors, away from the TV, was an idiotic waste of time. Besides, he said, the thought of spending whole days and nights dealing with me was more than he could bear. I wanted to right this generational wrong with my son, so I made a special effort to learn as much as I could about the wilderness experience, so that I could share it with The Boy, and the two of us would have a bond that my own father and I never quite forged.

Camping, I learned, is an opportunity to shed the comfortable trappings of civilization and reconnect with nature on a primal level—to experience, if only for a few days, the life our forebears lived, a life unencumbered by suburban minutiae and steeped in the purity of the land and water and sun.

For these and other reasons, I developed a philosophical opposition to the sort of camping that has become fashionable in our national parks. The most egregious violators of the "camping spirit" are those people who arrive in a fifty-foot mobile home outfitted with a refrigerator, kitchen, shower, movie theater, gymnasium, hot tub, and a small herd of Pomeranians. These are the sorts of people who pull into a parking space, hook up their electricity, roll out two-hundred square feet of Astroturf, aim their satellite dish at the skies, and start popping the champagne corks. To me, these people are like those families who traveled around during the Depression with all their earthly belongings stowed in the back of the truck, except that they aren't depressed, they've usually got two or three other homes, the tonnage of stuff they bring represents only a fraction of their total belongings, and they don't eat their dogs in desperation, they braid their hair and feed them *foie gras*.

Only slightly less pathetic are the people who cram as much as they possibly can into their Subaru Outback and tie five bicycles to the roof, then pat themselves on the back for "getting away from it all," while it's obvious to anyone with eyes that they've brought it all with them.

What all of these people have in common is the mistaken belief that in order to maximize one's enjoyment of the great outdoors, one must try to minimize the aggravations and nuisances that inevitably result from abandoning the place where all your stuff is kept. Nothing could be further from the truth, however. To enjoy camping to the fullest, one must immerse oneself in the experience with a pure head and heart. One must let go of the shackles of civilization and revel in the simple act of survival. That's the only way to appreciate how our ancestors once lived, and it's the only way to understand why they eventually invented flush toilets and central air-conditioning.

That's why, when The Boy and I started camping, all I brought with us were the essentials: two sleeping bags, a canteen, and a box of matches. Admittedly, the matches were a nod to modernity that we could perhaps have done without, since our forebears made due with flint and stone. But considering the other sacrifices we were making, I decided to allow us the luxury of a lighted match.

It took a bit of explaining for The Boy to understand why our camp setup was so much less cumbersome than that of other campers around us. When we arrived at our campsite and I opened the trunk of the car, he was amazed.

"Where's our tent?" he wondered. "And where's the food? I'm kind of hungry."

"Tents are for sissies and people who can't bear to leave home," I explained. "We're going to sleep under the stars and live off the land, just like our ancestors did. Trust me, it's going to be an adventure."

"Are you serious?" The Boy inquired.

"Of course I'm serious," I said. "Camping is not a joke—at least not for us."

"You know, there was a Wal-Mart a few miles back," The Boy suggested. "We could drive back there, load up on supplies, and come back."

"Wal-Mart?" I scoffed. "We're not going to Wal-Mart. We're going camping, which means that for us, Wal-Mart and everything else having to do with life 'out there' no longer exists for us. We are here, now, and we have to make do with what we have."

"Which is . . . nothing?"

"Not nothing. We've got sleeping bags, a canteen full of water, and matches," I said. "Most important, we have our wits and imagination, our intelligence," I emphasized, pointing to my forehead. "Our ability to think, to anticipate, to react—that's what separates us from animals, and it's what we're going to use to survive out here. At least for the next few days."

"Does mom know about this?"

"Your mother wouldn't understand," I said. "She thinks she's slumming it if the hotel doesn't have a restaurant or a pool."

"What kind of crap-ass hotel doesn't have a restaurant or a pool?" The Boy wondered.

"That's not the point. The point is, your mother isn't here. You're with me, and when you're with me, we're going to do things my way. You could never learn the things I am going to teach you from your mother. But you have to learn them from somebody, and that somebody is me."

"Okay. So what are we going to do for dinner?"

"We're going to catch our dinner," I explained. "There's a stream just a little way up that trail, and I'll bet it's teeming with trout. We'll catch ourselves a few, load them up on a stick, and roast them over an open fire. You can't get any better eating than that."

"But we didn't even bring a fishing rod," The Boy protested. "How are we going to catch a fish?"

"Do you think our ancestors had a Zebco spinning reel and eight-pound-test fishing line? No. They made their fishing line out of things like sawgrass and horsehairs. We can do that too."

The Boy was skeptical as we headed off up the trail to find the stream, clearly marked on the map with a squiggly blue line. When we got to the stream, though, it was more like a small creek, and it was almost dry. Only a trickle of water ran through the bottom of the streambed, and it was clear from looking at it that we weren't going to pull any fish out of it.

Back at the car, The Boy was smug about the fact that he'd been right and I'd been wrong about the possibility of having fish for dinner. Every boy has to have his victories, though, so I let him enjoy this one.

"What now?" he asked, in a tone that suggested I did not have an answer. He was wrong.

"It's called foraging," I explained. "I brought along a book that describes all the edible plants in this region. All we have to do is walk around and find them."

I grabbed the book—How to Identify Edible Foods in the Wild—from the back seat and opened it. I flipped through the pages and showed The Boy all the food possibilities stocked in the forest around us: pine nuts, acorns, amaranth seeds, persimmons, dandelions, blueberries, raspberries, watercress, cattail roots, and more. According to this book, there was a veritable grocery store of goodies out there, and we could easily survive on the calories and nutritional value they provided. "Never go hungry again," the book said, a shout of encouragement that filled me full of hope and reminded me that I was, in fact, getting hungry.

"Look at this," I said, showing The Boy a page of the book. "I think we should look for these—their called paw paws, and it says they taste like a mix of bananas and mangos. That's practically a milkshake!"

Okay, I admit that I might have been over-selling it a bit, but I had to get The Boy excited about the prospect of finding food in the forest, and I hoped my enthusiasm might rub off on him. Unfortunately, The Boy had his smartphone with him.

"Dad, it says here that the paw paw grows in Texas and Oklahoma, and you can only find them in August. We're in Minnesota, and it's late June."

So we scratched paw paws off the list. But there were still plenty of other foods to be found. Under protest, The Boy agreed to at least try to find something to eat in the wild, but only because he was so hungry, he said. I pointed out that the ground was covered with pine cones, so we might not even have to go very far. As it turned out, however, all the pine cones in the campground had been picked over by squirrels and chipmunks—or, more likely, other foragers like us—and most of the pine cones deeper in the forest were crumbled or rotten.

We stomped through the woods for more than an hour, but couldn't find anything that matched the pictures in the book. The book specifically said, "Don't eat anything you can't positively identify as edible," so we left the giant and probably poisonous mushroom caps alone, even though they looked tasty, and we only nibbled on some little black berries we found, because they tasted like turpentine and stung the tips of our tongues.

As desperation began to set in, and the hope of finding something edible was rapidly fading, we stumbled on to something that wasn't in the book but I knew from experience was edible: a honeysuckle bush. Excited, I showed The Boy how you could pluck a honeysuckle flower, bite the end off, and—just like the name suggests—suck the flower's sweet honey juice into your mouth.

The Boy was interested for about thirty seconds, but after sucking about half a dozen flowers, he spit out the last one in disgust. "Great, so I just ingested about a tenth of a teaspoon of honeysuckle juice, which amounts to maybe three calories, which will allow me to live another, oh, ten minutes. Dad, I think it's time to give in to the supe-riority of Western civilization and go buy us a burger."

A hamburger sounded good at that moment, I had to admit, but I was not ready to give up. A larger point about the value of patience and persistence needed to be made, and giving in to temptation wasn't the answer. The only way to learn how to overcome adversity is to face it square on and accept the challenge, knowing it isn't going to be easy, but also knowing that your persistence is going to be rewarded. That's what Ronald Reagan's pony story is all about—slogging through the shit until you find what you're looking for. Every spiritual leader from Jesus to Ghandi says something along the lines of "it's darkest before the dawn." What does that mean? It means that when you're feeling hopeless and lost and are about to give up, that's when God pops out of the clouds and shows you the solution to your problem.

In our case, we needed something to eat, and soon. Both of us were feeling the raw gnaw of hunger in our guts, the very same hunger that our forebears felt hundreds of years earlier, that ache of encroaching mortality that drove our ancestors to plow and till and conquer the earth. After you've spent the day trudging through the forest looking for scraps of food to chew on, a certain clarity sets in. Everything sud-denly begins to make sense. In that situation, it's almost impossible not to think: Hey, wouldn't it be great if we could just drive up to a window and order whatever we wanted, and have some cute teenager hand it to us three minutes later? It's the logical solution to the prob-lem of a forest with no food in it: a building full of food that can be dispensed at a moment's notice to anyone who needs it.

But that was precisely the temptation I was trying to avoid. Of course it would have been easier to hop in the car and go to Burg-er King. But we weren't out there in the wilderness to do the "easy" thing, we were there to reconnect with the essentials of existence from which modern life insulates us—to scrape away the layers of comfort and allow ourselves to feel the brutal primacy of nature. It had taken us hours to get to the moment of despair in which we now found our-selves. Going to Burger King, just because we could, was exactly the wrong thing to do at that moment. No, what we needed to do at that primal moment was believe that a solution would present itself; all we had to do was wait for it.

At first, I thought nothing of the little chipmunks that were scurrying through our camp. They were everywhere, scavenging for little bits and pieces of food, and they weren't afraid of people. In fact, they were quite friendly. They'd hop on the picnic table five feet away from us and beg for food with their twitchy little eyes. If they didn't get anything, they'd skitter away and come back twenty minutes later, after making the rounds from campsite to campsite.

On that evening, as darkness approached, I began to see those chipmunks in a different light—a light that I thought at the time came from God, but may in retrospect have been the park ranger's flashlight.

"Hand me that stick," I whispered to The Boy. He reached down and grabbed a fat stick about three feet long from the pile of wood next to the fire pit. I signaled for The Boy to move slowly and stay quiet. A brown chipmunk with black stripes and a fluffy little tail was sitting on the picnic table, observing us without a care in the world. I pretended not to look at it. I wanted the chipmunk to think that I was just another non-threatening human with a three-foot stick in his hand. What the chipmunk didn't know (and I was counting on), was that I, as a human, had the power, using only my imagination, to transform the stick in my hand into a deadly weapon. Feigning to the right, as if I were going to put the stick in the firepit, I suddenly raised it over my head and brought it smashing down onto the picnic table where the chipmunk sat.

Somehow, despite my trickery and speed, the chipmunk saw it coming and darted away, dodging the first blow. I saw him jump from the table to the seat across from The Boy, and instantly took aim once again. The chipmunk was too fast for me, though. As my second blow landed, the chipmunk leapt off the picnic table and skittered across the campsite and disappeared. As soon as he was gone, another one showed up to find out what all the ruckus was about. I ran after it too, taking aim and smashing the ground with my stick again and again as the chipmunk zigged and zagged through our camp. If I could only kill five or six chipmunks, I thought, we could roast them on a stick and they'd make a fine meal. That's clearly what God wanted, I was convinced, because he had provided the chipmunks in the dire hour of our need. What other possible interpretation was there?

"Is there a problem here?" the park ranger asked as he shone his flashlight in our direction. By then it was almost dark and all I could see through the beam of his flashlight was the intimidating outline of his uniform, especially his hat, which had a broad, flat rim that looked like a flying saucer in the dying light of a desperate day.

The Boy was about to say something, but I clamped him on the shoulder to let him know that I could handle the situation.

"Nothing at all, sir," I said, trying to be polite. "Just trying to scrounge up a little dinner."

"Didn't you bring any food?" the ranger asked.

"Didn't need to," I said. "We're roughing it."

"What were you planning to eat?" the ranger inquired.

"Well, we couldn't catch any fish, and couldn't find many plants to eat in the forest, so I thought maybe we'd take a few of these chipmunks off your hands. We're hungry, and there seem to be a lot of them around, so it could be a win-win for everyone, don't you agree?"

"Hunting and consuming the wildlife is not allowed in state parks," the ranger intoned.

"I'm sure that's true under normal circumstances," I said, "but I'm trying to teach my son here a thing or two about surviving in the wild."

"I don't see a tent," the ranger said. "Where's your tent?"

"As I said, we're roughing it, and as such have elected not to indulge in the creature comforts of home, because if we wanted those comforts, we'd have stayed home. Am I right?"

"I can't allow you to camp here overnight without a tent," the ranger said. "A line of thunderstorms is moving in. I'm responsible for the safety and well-being of everyone in this park, so I'm afraid I'm going to have to ask you to leave. Either that, or you can hit the Wal-Mart down the road, get properly equipped, and come back. It's your choice."

Out of the corner of my eye I could see The Boy mouthing the word "yessssss," and pumping his fist.

"Are you sure that's necessary?" I asked.

"I'm afraid so. I can only allow people to be so stupid, then I have to step in and save them from themselves," the ranger said, pointing his flashlight around our campsite. "And it looks to me like we've reached that point."

At Burger King, The Boy and I discussed our options and elected to ride out the storm in a nearby hotel, which had a pool and Jacuzzi, but not a restaurant.

"In mom's book, we'd still be roughing it," The Boy pointed out. "And weren't women the foragers in the old days?" he said. "No wonder we couldn't find anything to eat. We're men. We're hunters. And look, we found some meat," he said, pointing to the Whopper in his hand, "so we've done our job."

It wasn't the way I wanted things to turn out, but at least we didn't have to eat a chipmunk. When you're really hungry and you get a double-stack Whopper with cheese in your hands, the idea of living off the land doesn't have quite as much appeal. Though I hated to admit it, civilization does have its advantages.

CHAPTER 42

From that day forward, The Boy and I were fully equipped to survive not quite in the wild, but certainly in a state campground or national park with campsites, showers, and toilets. The Boy made these amenities a condition of his cooperation. He appreciated my desire to teach him something useful, he said, and agreed that if the apocalypse came, such skills might come in handy. To ease my anxiety, he also said that he had other plans in the event of a global apocalypse. As attractive as it may be to head for the hills under those circumstances, he was prepared to take his chances in the city. His reasoning was simple: Most human food and resources are clustered around where people live, so in a city ravaged by apocalyptic mayhem, it would not be difficult for one person to scrounge enough food and water to survive. Our adventure in the woods only confirmed his suspicion that survival in the wild was harder than it sounded, he said, and in a Darwinian struggle for survival in the city, he was betting that he and his friends would win. Why? Because they were young and agile, and if they traveled in a pack, everyone would be afraid of them. They'd carve out their turf and survive by being scrappy and resourceful. If anyone tried to muscle in on their turf, they'd simply kill them, using a cache of automatic weapons they would have acquired by raiding all the gun stores in town. But first, any intruders would have to run a gauntlet of booby-traps, including trip wires and IEDs, and dodge a fusillade of weapons, including spears, arrows, Molotov cocktails, and hand grenades. Don't worry, he said—he and his friends already had a plan.

In the meantime, he said, he was unwilling to endure the hardship of another potentially foodless night, and thought we could have more fun if we lowered our standards a bit and tried camping the way other people do it. Reluctantly, I agreed to his demands and purchased an astonishing amount of gear from Wal-Mart, including a tent, inflatable mattresses, a Coleman stove, two large coolers—one for drinks, the other for food—and a whole kitchen's worth of cooking supplies, including pots, pans, utensils, spoons, spatulas, and a French coffee press. Somehow I ended up piling $741.43 on my Visa card, telling myself that it was an investment in my relationship with my son. This is why the Walton family is the richest family in the United States—because they have made it impossible to live off the land without spending hundreds of dollars in one of their stores.

Having purchased all of the aforementioned gear, I quickly discovered that one of the problems with modern camping is that activities requiring little or no effort at home suddenly demand a Herculean amount of sweat and toil. It didn't take long to devise a handy formula for calculating the amount of energy required to complete any given task while camping this way. The formula I began using is this: Everything is ten times harder.

For instance, many campers think it's a swell idea to cook eggs, bacon, and pancakes for breakfast. Why, I don't know. This is easily the most complex meal in the breakfast pantheon, requiring as it does refrigeration, dairy products, the mixing and stirring of ingredients, multiple cooking pans, and extensive cleanup of pans crusted with burnt fats and proteins. It also involves bacon grease, which, when it cools, congeals into a disgusting glaze of aromatic goo that wafts through the piney woods and attracts every scrounging rodent within a two-mile radius.

It's madness. And yet, every morning in campsites around the country one can hear the sizzle and spit of frying bacon and hear the clank of tin and plastic as people stand in line to wash their egg-encrusted dishes under a spigot of cold water. Then they do it all over again for dinner, cooking up steaks and burgers and hot dogs, greasing up yet more pans that must be washed and stowed. Do they have nothing better to do with their time?

Because we both hate cooking and cleaning, The Boy and I quickly agreed on one thing: That it was ridiculous to participate in such a gastronomical catastrophe when modern technology provided such a vastly superior alternative. As The Boy was quick to point out, a can of Red Bull and a protein bar takes about twelve seconds to prepare, and can be consumed in less than five minutes. What could be easier?

With our daily intake of food, drink, and caffeine taken care of in the most efficient manner possible, The Boy and I were free to spend our time enjoying the great outdoors.

I won't bore you with the details of our wanderings. Suffice it to say that there were a lot of trees and rocks and mosquitos. And dirt. Lots of dirt. Some horse turds, too. Oh, and a few squirrels and birds.

CHAPTER 43

No matter what one does during the day, the highlight of any camping trip is of course the conversation around the campfire at night. That's when time slows down and one's thoughts turn to larger, more eternal truths. For millennia, stories that help make sense of the cosmos have been shared around those flickering flames, binding the generations through time and space. And so it was with us, my son and I, as the glow of the fire danced off our faces and the rest of the world receded into the darkness beyond.

On one trip, when The Boy was thirteen, I felt it was time to share with him what I knew about the mysteries of women and sex. The Boy was never too happy about being unplugged from his Xbox for very long, and didn't have much interest in women, but he *was* developing an interest in sex. Mostly it was the mechanics that intrigued him, and access to online porn had given him a graphic illustration of what went where, though he still had some questions. He was particularly curious about one thing: He wanted to know when his penis would be ten inches long.

I had to break it to him gently. "Your dong is never going to be ten inches long," I explained. "Six or seven, tops, and maybe as short as five. The only people who have ten-inch johnsons are porn actors and rock stars."

The Boy stared into the fire, a look of concerned confusion on his face. "Then how do you get into some of those positions? I mean, it looks to me like the Cowgirl and the Saddle Straddle require at least eight or ten inches. And I don't even see how the Chattanooga Express is even possible with a dick that small. And the Louisville Lunger? Forget about it."

"What is a Louisville Lunger?" I asked, but he ignored me.

"I'm also curious: Is a Flying Camel even possible? I've only read about it, never seen it, but it sounds like at the very least it would take some serious practice. Have you ever tried it?"

"What?"

"And what about a Davey Crockett? I have to say, that one sounds pretty gross."

"I have no idea what you're talking about," I admitted.

"They're sex positions, dad. Haven't you ever had sex?"

"Yes, I have, several times," I said. "But I don't go around naming it."

"You have all kinds of names for a penis. Why not name the stuff you do with it?" The Boy said.

"I'm not sure I've done any of that stuff," I said. "Then again, maybe I have, but I just didn't know it."

"Trust me, dad, you'd know if you've done a Davey Crockett."

"Where did you get all this?" I asked. "How do you know all these names?"

"The Internet," he said. "It's ninety-percent porn, you know. Me and Zacc have seen all kinds of things—things you can't unsee. Things no one should see."

"That sounds scary."

"Sick is more like it."

"Like what?" I asked.

"Well, there's the Monkey Wrench, but that's pretty tame."

"What's that?"

"That's when a girl pulls your dick down and gives you a blowjob from behind," The Boy said matter-of-factly. "That's another one that requires a long penis."

"Sounds painful."

"It probably is. Who knows?"

"What else?"

"Are you sure you want to hear this, dad? Trust me, it's not for the faint of heart."

"Yes. What else?"

"Okay. Well, there's the three-way pump-and-munch. It takes a while for everyone to get their turn, but supposedly it's worth the wait."

I felt myself wretch a little. "That's the most disgusting thing I've ever heard," I said. "Who would ever do that?"

"Johnny Sins does it all the time," The Boy said. "It's one of his things."

"Who is Johnny Sins?" I asked in dismay. "Is he a friend of yours?"

"No, he's a porn star."

"And you know his name?"

"Of course I know his name," The Boy said. "The guy is famous."

"Okay, what else?" I asked, not at all sure I wanted to hear the answer.

"Are you sure, dad? I get the feeling this is making you uncomfortable," The Boy said.

"Yes, I want to hear it. As your father, I feel it is my responsibility to understand what sort of things you are seeing on the Internet. Everyone says parents are supposed to monitor their children's Internet usage, and that's something we've been very lax about."

"Trust me, you don't want to monitor me and Zacc," The Boy laughed. "We go to some crazy places."

By "crazy," it sounded to me like he meant that he and Zacc traveled to the most deranged, demented, disgusting corners of the Internet and camped there for hours on end, witnessing the most depraved human behavior imaginable. But I had to at least pretend that none of what he was telling me was outside the realm of my own experience. Fathers are role models for their sons, after all, and sons want to believe that their fathers have been around the block once or twice. Which I have, of course—it's just that my block never had twenty-four-hour access to free porn.

"How crazy?" I asked. "What's the craziest thing you've ever seen?"

"That's a tough question," The Boy replied. "I've seen some pretty crazy things."

"Like what?"

"You're sure you want to hear this?"

"Absolutely."

"Once I tell you, you won't be able to un-hear it," he warned. "It'll be stuck in your head forever."

"That's okay, I can handle it."

The Boy took a deep breath and looked up at the stars, which were clouded by a thin plume of smoke from the campfire. He rummaged through the dumpster of depravity that was his teenage brain, and when he retrieved the appropriately deviant thought he was looking for, he exhaled and said, "Have you ever heard of Brazilian fart porn?"

"That does it!" I screamed. "I don't want to hear any more. But I will tell you this, young man, you are never going on the Internet again, do you hear me?"

The Boy laughed. "I don't know what you're so worked up about," he said. "We don't look at that stuff anymore. It was a big deal back when we were eleven, but we got bored of it and have moved on."

"Moved on to what?" I asked.

"Minecraft."

"Sounds disgusting," I said. "From now on, I'll be watching your Internet usage much more closely, you can count on that."

"Hey, it's your funeral," The Boy said, stirring some coals with a stick.

I felt like I was losing my composure, and I knew I had to keep it. But how?

When I was a kid, finding an old *Playboy* that a friend's older brother brought home from college was a rare coup. Sure, we pored over those pages for hours at a time, examining every airbrushed slope and curve. But now *Playboy* isn't even considered porn anymore—it's a men's culture magazine. And if, as kids, we ever got our hands on a *Penthouse*, we studied it like the Torah, seeking insight into the darker mysteries of womanhood and the forbidden pleasures that awaited us on the other side of eighteen.

But even when I got to the other side of eighteen and those types of pleasures were no longer forbidden, they were still maddeningly inaccessible. No one wanted to have sex with me, even though I made it abundantly clear that I was available and willing, possibly even desperate. I didn't even lose my virginity until I was twenty-one, and that was such a strange and humiliating episode that I was not eager to repeat it for some time. In truth, the "idea" of sex I'd had as a boy never matched the reality I experienced as an adult. When I married, sex with The Wife seemed promising for a while—until she got pregnant, after which her desire and need for sex disappeared and was replaced by an aching desire and need for me to fix a lot of stuff around the house.

I could see quite clearly that, at the age of thirteen, my son's idea of sex had already been distorted so far out of proportion that whenever he got to compare it to the real thing—in high school, or college, if he went—there was no way real sex would ever live up to his inflated fantasy of it. Before our trip, I had planned to gently introduce the subject of sex and have an awkward two- or three-minute discussion of it, then never speak of it again. But now that we were deep into the subject, around a campfire, where life's truths have been passed from one generation to the next for millennia, I felt compelled to explain to him the difference between real sex with someone you love and the sex he'd seen on all those porn sites.

"Son, I need to explain a few things to you," I began. "At your age, it's normal to be interested in sex, and it's normal to fantasize what it will be like when you are married and have a wife with whom you can share that sacred bond. However, I'm concerned that your travels on the Internet may be giving you an unrealistic idea of what sex is like in the real world."

"What do you mean?" The Boy asked.

"Well, pornography is a form of fantasy," I explained. "No one's wanker is ten or twelve inches long, and women in the real world don't have bodies like that."

"Are you saying those women aren't real?" The Boy asked. "That they're digital?"

"No, just that real women don't look like that."

"Kent Pearson's mom looks pretty close," The Boy said. "She works out two hours a day and had a boob job last year."

"I'm not saying there aren't beautiful women in the world," I said. "There are. It's just that the likelihood that you are ever going to meet one is extremely slim, and the chances of you ever getting her clothes off and in bed are even slimmer."

"Mark Lefke says some chicks will just give you a blow job in your car," The Boy said. "So you don't even need a bed."

"That's not the point. The point is, women are not objects for men to have sex with, they are living, breathing humans that men have to get to know and love before they engage in sexual relations. That's the part pornos don't mention."

"Okay, so let's say you get to know a girl and love her and want to have sex with her, what else is different?"

Now we were getting somewhere, I thought. The Boy is finally interested in the difference between reality and fantasy. "Well, for one, sex in real life doesn't last nearly as long as it does in porn," I explained.

"How long does it last?"

"About fifteen to twenty seconds," I said.

"Twenty seconds?" The Boy sneered. "Are you kidding me? Ryan Driller can go for an hour, at least, and Tommy Piston, that guy never stops."

"It's all in the editing," I explained. "They splice the same twenty seconds of footage together and repeat it over and over to make it look like they're having sex for an hour. Trust me, twenty seconds is average, and no man can do it for more than thirty seconds. It's just not possible."

"Are you sure?" The Boy said, incredulous.

"Look, you shared some uncomfortable information with me earlier. Now I'm sharing some uncomfortable information with you," I said.

The Boy thought for a moment, then posed the question, "If sex is over so fast, why does everyone treat it like such a big deal?"

"I have no idea," I said. "That's what I'm trying to get at. In reality, sex is not a big deal. It's hardly a deal at all. It's like a glorified sneeze. It happens, then it's over and you go back to watching television."

"The Internet sure makes it look like there's a lot more to it than that," The Boy said.

"But there's not," I said. "And the sooner you understand that, the better. When the time comes for you to have sex with a real person, preferably your wife, the last thing you want to do is get your hopes up too high. It's much better to keep your expectations low, then you won't be so disappointed."

"Okay. What else is different?"

"Well, in real life, people don't take their clothes off like they do in the movies," I explained. "And they turn the lights out so it's dark. Obviously, in a movie they need light so that you can see. If they were filming real sex, you wouldn't be able to see anything, because it would be pitch black."

"Anything else?"

"The other thing is that people don't make any sound in real life. In reality, sex is very quiet. In the movies they make all kinds of noise and they hire people who used to be gymnasts to get into all kinds of weird positions. No real person could do all that. No real person would want to."

The Boy stirred the fire some more with his stick, which was glowing red and hot at the end. "Okay, good advice, dad. Anything else?"

"The other thing no tells you is that having sex is pretty rare. After you've conceived a kid, we're talking once a year, maybe. Usually on your birthday."

"Really?" The Boy said, wrinkling his nose. "I read that the average couple has sex fifty times a year. And if you're gay, it's double that."

"That's insane," I said. "You're pecker would fall off."

"Just telling you what I read."

"On the Internet, no doubt."

"Of course," The Boy said. "Where else can you find stuff to read?"

"Well, now you know the truth," I said.

"Thanks."

"You're welcome."

"Should we change the subject?"

"Please."

"Okay," The Boy said. "I noticed that you only use a few alternative names for a penis. You should expand your vocabulary a little. Magic Wand, Captain Winky, Spunknozzle, Mr. Thrusty, Love Noodle, Plonker, Spam Javelin, Spurt Reynolds, Chicksickle, Joyprong, Purple Pointed People Poker—those are all good ones to use too."

"And you know these how?"

"Zacc and I used to memorize them for fun," The Boy said matter-of-factly. "Back when we were ten."

CHAPTER 44

My son's frightening exposure to all manner of sexual deviance naturally triggered my parental concern for his mortal soul. My wife and I did not drag The Boy to church as often as we should have in his formative years, and I feared that our neglect in this area was beginning to show. Clearly, The Boy did not fear the spiritual consequences of his actions, because no one who knows that their immortal soul will burn in hell for eternity would ever expose themselves to all that sinful filth.

I was raised to believe that God is always watching you, waiting for you to slip up, and when you do, He wastes no time in punishing you. Or worse, He does wait, and punishes you when you least expect it. Life is much easier once you realize that everything you do and think is being monitored by an all-knowing entity with the power to make your life miserable if you don't do as He commands. When the choice between right and wrong comes up, you choose right, no questions asked. When temptation rears its ugly head, you ignore it. When your body says yes but your conscience says no, you take a cold shower and try to think about something else. And when porn appears on your computer screen, you momentarily feel sorry for the girls in the photos, then click out of the website, delete your search history, and go look up some fantasy football statistics.

My son, it appeared, was not aware that his extensive knowledge of pornography would likely result in a fistful of payback from the Almighty. What form this punishment might take, or when it might happen, I couldn't say. All I could tell him for certain was that God's punishment would come, so it was stupid to pile it on by looking at even more smut. I also needed to warn him that if he ever got the chance to use the knowledge he'd pickup up on the Internet in real life, God would certainly be watching.

"God sounds like a pervert to me," The Boy replied when I warned him about the likely consequences of his actions.

"Don't say that," I admonished. "He can hear you."

"But didn't God invent sex?" The Boy protested. "And didn't He make people—not to mention animals and fish and insects—want to have sex all the time? And didn't He do all of this knowing full well that he was going to have to watch it all from his perch up in the sky? Doesn't that mean God is the biggest pervert in the world? I mean, does anyone watch more sex than God?"

"It doesn't work that way," I explained.

"How does it work?" The Boy wanted to know.

"You can't judge God by human standards," I offered.

"But God can judge us by His standards?"

"Yes, that's His job," I said.

"But no one can live up to God's standards, right, so isn't that a giant trap?"

"It's a paradox, not a trap," I explained.

"Okay, what about the whole 'Thou shalt not kill' thing. Doesn't God kill pretty much everything? So where does He get off telling people they can't kill, when that seems to be about all He does? That sounds like hypocrisy to me."

"God is not a person," I countered. "He is, well, God."

Then, out of the blue, The Boy said the unthinkable. "Dad, you don't really believe all that God nonsense, do you? The whole idea that there is some guy in the sky with a giant video camera recording your every move is just ridiculous, don't you think?"

"It's not ridiculous. That's the way it is," I insisted, shocked that he could think otherwise.

"And on top of it all, He seems like the biggest douchebag in the world. Why does anyone care what God thinks, especially when all He seems to care about is preventing people from having fun? And there's another one of your paradoxes: God makes it possible for people to have fun, and makes them want to have fun, then tells them no, they're not allowed to have fun—they have to go to church and be bored and worship Him instead? I'm sorry, but that's a complete dick move, if you ask me."

"God does not want to prevent people from having fun," I said. "He just wants people to prefer certain kinds of fun over others."

"Same difference," The Boy said. "It's like taking a kid into Baskin Robbins, showing him all the fantastic flavors, then making him choose vanilla."

"In my defense, vanilla is an excellent flavor," I said. "And the reason I made you eat vanilla ice cream in your youth is so that you could appreciate the other flavors as you got older."

"Whatever. It doesn't matter to me anymore. I've decided I am an atheist."

The very word, *atheist,* sent chills up my spine. It's one thing to question God's methods; it's a whole other, entirely unacceptable thing to declare yourself a non-believer.

"You don't mean that," I said.

"Yes, I do," The Boy insisted.

"How can that be?!" I cried. "What could possibly lead you to believe that God does not exist? Look around you. How could any of this exist if God didn't make it exist?"

"Duh, dad—it's called *science?*" The Boy said, exasperated. "Evolution? Natural selection? Chaos theory? Quantum mechanics? Science explains it all."

"Science is just a bunch of theories. It's not the truth," I said. "The truth is in the Bible, which is God's guide to the world. Besides, science can't tell you the difference between right and wrong, or good and evil. You need God for that."

The Boy laughed. "Dad, even I know there's no such thing as right and wrong, or good and evil. Those are all just social constructs."

"I don't even know what that means," I said. My face was flush and I could feel my heart beating in my chest. I didn't know how to respond to this kind of blasphemy.

"It means they're ideas invented by people, not God," The Boy said. "It's all about power and control. Take religion. All religions are just social constructs created by a bunch of guys who wanted to exert power and control over everyone else. It's the same with government. Power, control, and money—that's all any of them care about."

"When did you get so cynical?" I asked.

"It's not cynicism, it's reality," The Boy said. "We learned all about it in my Social Studies class."

"It sounds to me like your Social Studies teacher is both an atheist and a communist."

"And a radical," The Boy added. "And probably a few other things. She's really super smart."

"She?"

"Yes. All my teachers are women," The Boy said. "Men don't teach. Everyone knows that."

"But God is a man," I reminded him. "And He teaches."

"By the way, which God are we talking about here?" The Boy asked.

"The one true God," I said.

"But which one is that? There are more than a thousand religions in the world, and each of them have their own god, and lots of them have multiple gods," The Boy said. "It's a bit confusing."

"There's only one God," I insisted. "Everyone knows that."

"You want to know what I think?" The Boy said. "I think the word 'God' is just a word, a syllable, a sound that people make to refer to stuff they can't explain. Nothing else makes any sense."

Our discussion about God did not go anywhere useful after that. Every time I told The Boy the way it was, he told me why it wasn't that way, and around and around we went. Pretty soon I realized that he was just arguing with me for the sake of arguing. Deep down, I knew, he believed the same things I did, even if he insisted that he didn't. Everyone knows that children learn their belief systems from their parents, so my son had to have learned his from my wife and me. School, it seemed, was just polluting his mind with nonsense and encouraging him to ask questions that should never be asked in the first place. Supposedly intelligent people are always going around questioning whether God exists or not. It's boring. In my opinion, the question "Does God exist?" is the stupidest question in the world. The answer is obvious: yes. End of discussion. Arguing otherwise is just a waste of time—time that could be devoted to the study and appreciation of God's handiwork.

Something strange happened while The Boy and I were discussing the matter, however. Somewhere in between his explaining to me what a "tautology" is and why American exceptionalism is a myth, I began to question my own relationship with the Lord. More specifically, I began to wonder if my son's sudden turn away from God was God's way of punishing me for not taking him to church more often, and for not insisting that he study the Bible. And might it also be a punishment for me sleeping in on Sundays and failing to attend church more regularly myself? If I knew the Bible, wouldn't I have better arguments at my fingertips when The Boy's questions needed answering? And wasn't that my fault? Because, to be honest, I've never actually read the Bible. I tried once, but got bogged down in the "be-gats" in Genesis, and never got past them. All of my other knowledge of the Bible comes from sermons in church, where my sporadic atten-dance, I had to admit, might have left a few holes in my knowledge of the Good Book. And if I didn't know the Bible as well as I should, wasn't it possible that I didn't know God as well as I should? And if I didn't know God as well as I should, could I continue to call myself a good Christian? Or was I, in reality, a so-so Christian, a pretender who went around claiming more knowledge of God than I really had? And if that's the case, wouldn't God find ways to put me on the right path toward believing in Him more?

But then my thoughts began to morph and twist in a way that was unfamiliar to me. Why, I began to wonder, does God care if I believe in Him or not? After all, He knows He exists, so why does it matter if I or anyone else believes He exists? God doesn't need me to affirm his omniscient all-knowingness, does He? Or does He? No, He can't. Because if God needs me to believe in him to affirm his existence, it would mean that God isn't quite as great as He would have us believe. Could it be that God only exists if you believe in Him? And that He doesn't exist if you don't believe in Him? And that neither me nor my son are right about the question of God's existence? Or that we're both right—that God both exists and doesn't exist, depending on your per-spective?

Suddenly I realized that this sort of tortuous thinking is why my own father insisted that I refrain from asking questions. "Just do as you're told," he always said, and if I did, he was much less likely to hit me. The rules were simple. But by not following these rules in raising my own son, I realized, I had allowed The Boy's questions to fester and grow like a fungus or a boil, or some sort of illegal, immoral weed.

CHAPTER 45

Out of respect for any family members who might someday read this, I am going to skip The Boy's fourteenth year altogether. Nothing good or constructive can come of it, because it was a hellish year full of frustrations and disappointments, not the least of which was the unfamiliar creature my son was becoming.

They say parents love their kids no matter what, but that doesn't mean they necessarily like them. And I'll freely admit that in his fourteenth year, I didn't much like The Boy. He had gone from being a charmingly misinformed thirteen-year-old to being a defiant, argumentative know-it-all who thought it was now his job to set us, his parents, straight.

Other parents, I'm told, are blessed with sullen, non-responsive teenagers who stay in their room all the time, out of the way, where no one has to interact with them. We weren't so lucky. Our son came home from school each day pumped full of new knowledge that he couldn't wait to try out on us. What seemed to excite him most was the fact that everything he learned in school contradicted what we were trying to teach him at home. This is somewhat understandable, considering that teaching is one of the lowest-paid, most thankless professions around, which means that only people who are okay with not getting paid or thanked go into teaching, and people like that are just plain stupid.

The trouble is, these people are running our schools and passing their stupidity on to our children. Sometimes, it would take me hours to correct the disinformation he picked up at school, and then even more time explaining to his teachers why they didn't know what they were talking about. Honestly, his history teacher didn't even know that Christopher Columbus discovered America. She told her class some confusing, cockamamie story about how the Vikings discovered America first, then the Chinese—the Chinese!—and that Columbus himself never even made it to our shores. According to her, the closest he got was somewhere in the Bahamas. It sounds ridiculous, I know.

What she could not explain was why anyone in America would go to the trouble of writing songs and naming a holiday after someone who spent all his time on a beach in the Caribbean? It doesn't make any sense.

But that's just one example. There are many others, as the battles with The Boy over his continual mis-education happened almost daily. When Saddam Hussein was captured, for instance, his political science teacher kept insisting that Iraq never had weapons of mass destruction, and that the war itself was a "mistake." His science teacher kept insisting that climate change is caused by burning too much coal and gasoline, when it's pretty clear that the climate on Earth has been changing ever since it was created, some six-thousand years ago. This woman couldn't even admit that love is real: The Boy said she explained to him that love is nothing more than a chemical reaction in the brain—an "oxytocin feedback loop," she called it—that tricks people into feeling like they're on drugs. When people fall in love, she told him, they essentially become addicted to each other.

What kind of hippie nonsense is that? Who teaches kids that love is some kind of drug, rather than a sacred gift from our Creator?

A drug dealer, that's who.

Even I watched Breaking Bad, so I know how desperate teachers can get. I'm willing to bet there are a lot of science teachers in this country who thought Walter White had the right idea. And what better way to build a customer base than to teach kids that they can find love in a pill? Don't get me wrong: I admired Walter's entrepreneurial spirit and dedication to product quality, and thought he made many good business decisions. But I suspected that my son's science teacher was up to something far more sinister, because anyone who has been in love knows that it feels nothing like a drug. Unless, that is, your drug of choice tears a whole in your chest and makes you feel guilty all the time and makes you wonder why you even bother, because nothing you do is right, even though your intentions are good and you can think of nothing else except how to make the person you love happy, since she is so obviously miserable.

No one would buy a drug that makes you feel that way. So I figured the drug she was selling might actually make you feel better than love—and if that was the case, I should try it, if only to help clarify for my son the difference between the two. Unfortunately, every time we had a parent-teacher conference with the woman, she claimed she had no idea what I was talking about when I asked if I could purchase a little of what she was selling on the side. She claimed not to be "selling" anything, just educating—but that's exactly what you'd expect a teacher/drug-dealer to say, so I figured there must be some sort of secret password or hand signal she used to identify her customers. I asked my son about it, but he said he didn't know anything either—which, again, is exactly the response you'd expect from someone who is guilty of buying drugs at school from their teacher and doesn't want their parents to know about it.

These and all kinds of other shenanigans were the icky substance of that fourteenth year. But the most stressful part of it all was my son's sudden and inexplicable interest in politics and world affairs. Every day, he'd come home with another emergency alert about how the world is coming to an end. One day it would be all about global warming, then he'd start railing about nuclear proliferation, loss of biological diversity, deforestation, pollution, poverty, sustainable agriculture, honeybees, drought, fracking, bird flu, antiobiotic-resistant diseases, genetically modified organisms, biological warfare, income inequality, religious fanaticism—it was like having Rachel Maddow in your living room and not being able to turn her off.

Every day, he'd work himself up into a state and cry "Dad, we have to do something!" But no matter how many times I explained to him that most of the things he mentioned were president Obama's fault, and that the simple and obvious solution to all of it is to lower taxes and get government out of the way so that capitalism can work its magic, he wouldn't listen. He'd come back at me with some Marxist nonsense about how capitalism is the problem, and that companies without enough regulatory oversight—like Exxon—were the ones most likely to cause the greatest amount of damage. I don't know how many hours I spent trying to explain to The Boy how the world really works. The fact that we have stock in Exxon, for instance, so whatever Exxon does to raise its stock price is in our best interests. Or that poor people are poor because they're lazy, not because they lack resources or have to fight racism. Or that a farting cow generates more greenhouse gases than a Cadillac Escalade.

The really annoying part was when he kept insisting that we take some kind of "action" to help save the planet. The Boy was full of suggestions: Divest our Exxon stock, install solar panels on the roof, buy only organic foods and "eco-friendly" products, drive a more fuel-efficient car, recycle more, donate money, volunteer our time—ridiculous ideas that only a mush-minded liberal would take seriously. I tried to explain to The Boy that the world has been on the brink of catastrophe for a long time, and will continue to hover on the brink of disaster no matter what we do—so why do anything? I told him the story of the Russians back in the 1970s and 1980s. How life was back in the Cold War, when the U.S. and Russia had their nuclear weapons pointed at each other and it seemed like the world could go up in smoke at any second. And I explained how Ronald Reagan solved the whole mess with his golden tongue and how he tore down the Berlin Wall with his bare hands. We didn't have to do anything to solve that problem, I explained, except elect Ronald Reagan president.

"All you need to know about politics is to vote for Republicans and against Democrats," I told The Boy. "Everything else takes care of itself."

Unfortunately, fourteen was an age when The Boy seemed to know everything and nothing at the same time. I would say something sensible like that, and he would reply with some bizarre question totally out of left field that had nothing to do with anything.

"Have you heard of microbeads, dad?"

I kid you not, that was a question.

Microbeads? Of course I don't know anything microbeads, because they don't exist and don't have anything to do with anything, so why the hell would I know anything about microbeads? And why would I care? He went on to explain something about how these little plastic beads, which are too small to see, are put into toothpaste and detergent, and are now showing up in rivers and lakes and streams around the country, gumming up our waterways. And that they're becoming a real problem, even though no one can see them and you wouldn't even know they were there unless some smartass fourteen-year-old told you so.

His point, as I understand it, was that the microbead problem exists because there are companies that don't care about the environment and will do whatever they can to make a profit, and that the only way they'll stop putting microbeads in toothpaste and detergent is if the government swoops in and says they can't. In this case, he said, the companies were the problem, and government—by the people, and for the people—was the only solution.

My wife was much more forgiving whenever this kind of nonsense came out of his mouth. She'd say something like, "That's interesting, dear, we should take that into consideration," or "Yes, it's a shame what some people will do for the sake of profit."

But that, in my opinion, was not an adequate response. One of my responsibilities as a father, I felt, was to help The Boy develop a life philosophy that he could use to guide his actions in the future as a man, father, husband and citizen. But if he kept talking about things like microbeads, I worried, people were going to think he was insane. Microbeads, I explained, are a perfect example of an imaginary problem created by liberals to make it look like something as innocent as toothpaste is really a threat to the environment, and that more government regulation is the solution to this imaginary problem. It's the same with global warming. Liberals act like it's a big problem, but when you get right down to it, all you need to do if the world is a few degrees warmer is wear shorts and a nice cotton shirt that breathes. It's a simple, common-sense solution, with no government involvement—and that's the way it should be.

Besides, if these supposedly irresponsible companies caved and removed these invisible beads from their products, and suddenly everyone's teeth and dishes started looking dingy and gray, what then? Are we supposed to just live with dirty teeth and grimy dishes? Are gleaming white teeth just another social construct, a random cultural indicator of beauty and health invented by the advertising industry to sell a product with deadly microbeads in it? But of course that's a trick question, because microbeads don't actually exist, so why would anyone go to that much trouble to sell them? Isn't it possible that what companies like Crest and Colgate really care about is providing the public with a product that gets their customers' teeth their whitest white? And isn't it possible that their true secret agenda is to prevent cavities and promote effective oral hygiene?

My concern went much further than the microbeads, of course. I mean, what happens to a person who sees imaginary corporate conspiracies everywhere? What kind of life is there for someone who sees corruption around every corner, and who thinks that everything in the world revolves around power and money? After all, how is it possible to live in America and believe that companies do not act in the best interests of their shareholders and customers? That's the way capitalism works, and companies that don't operate that way go bankrupt. It's as simple as that. But to believe that's not the case—that every advertisement has an agenda behind it, or that every time a Coke shows up in a TV show, it means the Coca-Cola company paid them to put it there, in the hope that next time you're at the grocery store, you'll switch from Pepsi to Coke—well, to be thinking about all of that instead of just enjoying the show, that's no way to live. Anyone who thinks like that and lives in America is going to be miserable. Honestly, people like that would be better off moving to Vietnam or Pakistan, where they can spend their whole day digging vegetables out of the ground and not worrying about whatever deadly chemicals were used to preserve them in a can, or how the seeds they came from were genetically engineered to resist certain bugs. But I'll tell you this: If you're happier eating bug-infested food in a place where there's no TV reception or Internet, and where people spend their time sitting around a fire telling each other stories about their exciting day on the farm, there's something seriously wrong with you. That's why Western civilization was invented—to avoid a life like that. The point of life in America is to enjoy it and be thankful that you don't have to sleep in a mud hut or grow your own food. Why people have to complicate it with all this other nonsense, I'll never know.

That was also the year his grandmother (my mother) died, which wouldn't have been so bad if The Boy's attitude about it hadn't been so unforgivable. He couldn't just accept her death and move on, like the rest of us; he had to make it all about him. Nothing about the funeral or wake was good enough for his highness, master of all things spiritual and holy. We are Catholic, so when people die, we put them in a coffin, have a wake and service, bury them, then eat. That's how it's done. That's how we've always done it. But no, the fact that it's worked for millions of people for hundreds of years wasn't good enough for The Boy. He kept complaining about how the ceremony was "empty," how it didn't have any "spiritual significance," and how everything about it seemed canned, like everyone was just going through the motions, reading from a script. That's the whole point!, I explained. People have no idea what to do or say when someone dies, so the church provides the guidelines—the script, if you will. That's what a ritual is—something people do without thinking about it, because doing it any other way would be uncomfortable, if not a complete pain in the ass.

He Who Knows All disagreed, of course. In his not-so-humble opinion, his grandmother's funeral was useless because it didn't have enough spiritual power. It was too easy, he said. He thought it made more sense to honor the dead the way they do in Nepal (wherever that is), by hauling their bodies down the street in a colorful parade and then burning them on a funeral pyre in the middle of the town square. Such barbarity was somehow more "real" to him than purchasing a $15,000 coffin lined with satin and lowering it into the ground. I could certainly see how that approach would appeal to the pyromaniac in him, I said at the time, and how it would not register in his tiny brain what an enormous fire hazard that approach clearly was. But the fire wasn't the part that impressed him, he insisted; it was the fact that the person who must light the fire is the oldest son, or the closest person to it. (That would be me in this scenario.) His argument was that the act of lighting the fire was, ritualistically speaking, a way of helping the eldest son to accept the death of a parent by forcing them to participate in the act of purification that sends the soul off into its next life. Or something like that. Saying a few words about your saintly mother and watching her get boxed up and buried wasn't enough, he insisted. In order to accept death and grieve properly, one had to confront death head on. A Catholic funeral seemed designed to keep as much distance between the living and dead as possible, he thought, while the Nepalese ritual sought to connect them in order to recognize the sacred role of death in life. Roasting the dead in public was how that feat was accomplished, apparently, and the Catholic way was clearly inferior.

I told him that he obviously hadn't known very many people who had died, because if he had, he'd realize that putting as much distance as possible between the living and the dead is the better way to go. But he wouldn't listen. In his mind, everything about Western civilization "sucked," and everything about Eastern civilization (if you can call it that) was full of magic and meaning. I blame it all on the World Literature class he took in ninth grade. In that course, the teacher had them read Siddhartha and selections from the Bhagavad Gita. I read the blurbs on the back of both those books, and both of them sounded a little smug about how smart and profound the words inside were. Both books also pictured bald guys in robes sitting around doing nothing, so I could see how The Boy might be attracted. After all, sitting around doing nothing with his nose in a book was one of his favorite things to do.

Anyway, like I said, for all these reasons and more, I'm going to skip talking about The Boy's fourteenth year altogether. It's just not worth mentioning.

CHAPTER 46

y the time The Boy reached fifteen, I was seriously ready to ship him off to Siberia or sell him on the Internet, or do something, at least, that would give me a few minutes of peace and quiet. Is it too much to ask to sit and watch Wheel of Fortune without listening to a lecture on the corrupting values of capitalism and the perversity of packaging the American Dream in the form of a game show, where hope for a better life is just one spin of the wheel away? How many times did I have to remind The Boy that it wasn't enough to spin the wheel; the contestants had to solve the word puzzle too! There was skill involved.

He didn't care. All The Boy cared about at this point in his life was the tornado of random nonsense that was careening around his brain. How did I know it was nonsense? Because it made no sense, that's how. Most of what came out of his mouth was complete gibberish. It was like he was speaking a foreign language. He used English words, but arranged them in orders that I didn't recognize and couldn't begin to understand. I recorded some of it so that I could replay it at his wedding and embarrass him.

Here was The Boy on various topics:

On Lawn Care: "Dad, did you know that the pesticides you use to keep our lawn green are known carcinogens linked to birth defects, kidney damage, neurotoxicity, auto-immune dysfunction, and other diseases? And did you know that exposure to these chemicals in childhood can increase my risk for leukemia by seven-hundred percent? Knowing all that, dad, and knowing the risks involved, do you still want me mow the lawn?"

On Garbage: "Dad, did you know that the average American produces four and a half pounds of trash every day, or about 1,600 pounds a year? And that most of that is packaging? We could reduce our family's carbon footprint considerably if we just recycled more, composted our organics, bought in bulk, and made sure the trash bags we use are biodegradable. And all those wine and liquor bottles? Totally recyclable."

On Traffic: "Dad, did you know that while we're sitting here in this traffic jam, we're pumping out—and breathing—a toxic stew of hydrocarbons, nitrogen oxide, carbon monoxide, sulfur dioxide, formaldehyde, benzene, and a few dozen other deadly chemicals? If I get asthma or have a pulmonary embolism, or drop dead from cancer, it'll be no mystery why."

On Meat: "Did you know that the average hamburger contains eighteen insect parts, four grams of bovine fecal matter, six rat turds, and a colony of E. coli? And before the meat even gets to the store, they pump the cows full of antibiotics so that they don't get sick standing knee-deep in their own feces and vomit? And that barbecuing a steak basically just bathes it in carcinogens?

More On Meat: "Speaking of global warming, did you know that beef is the most carbon-intensive form of meat production on the planet? You know why? It's because ranchers in South America are cutting down the Amazon rainforest to raise cattle. Yep. For every pound of hamburger we eat, 220 square feet of rainforest is destroyed."

On Bees: "I think we need to include more indigenous plants in our garden to help the bees. They're dying, you know, because of America's monocultural agricultural practices and the use of too many pesticides. Which, by the way, you should stop using on the lawn, even if it does make the grass look wicked green."

On Income Inequality: "It doesn't seem fair to me that CEOs make millions of dollars while people who work in their company for minimum wage can't even afford a tiny apartment."

On Drugs and Crime: "I think marijuana should be legalized everywhere. That way, the government could regulate it, drug-related crime would go down, and people who needed it for medical purposes would have easier access."

You get the idea. Listening to The Boy talk was like accidentally picking up a copy of the New York Times. The Boy couldn't go five minutes without spouting his opinion on something, and each time he finished a sentence, he'd look at me, expecting a response. But how was I supposed to respond to ideas that I was fairly certain I disagreed with? I don't spend my day memorizing statistics and arguments on various political issues, and I don't really care about bees and poor people and drug addicts. All I know is that there seem to be a lot of people out there who are hell bent on ruining everything that's great about America and trying to make everyone who enjoys our freedoms feel guilty about it.

I like to grill steaks, for instance, which is about as basic an American right as you can get. Do I want to know how my cow was raised and what they fed it and how sick and scared it was when they slaughtered it? No, I don't. I want to hear the sizzle of its ripe red flesh on the barbecue and pop a Budweiser and forget about all that crap. I don't want or need to hear it, because my knowing it is not going to change anything; it's only going to make eating my steak less enjoyable. And why would I want to pollute my brain with information that's going to make life less enjoyable? Life in America is about the pursuit of happiness, and sometimes, to stay happy, you have to tune out all the bullshit. But with The Boy around, the bullshit flew non-stop all day long. Tuning it out was impossible. It was also embarrassing, because The Boy wanted to know what I thought about all of these "issues," and the truth was that I didn't think about them much. And when I did try to answer, he didn't like what I had to say.

Take the lawn care issue. "Mow the lawn or I'll kill you long before those chemicals ever do," was my initial reaction. But The Boy insisted that I wasn't taking his concerns seriously. So I said, quite sensibly I think, that there should be lower taxes on lawn care so that the free market could take care of the problem. He wanted to know how the free market would "take care of the problem" if the problem itself is high demand for chemicals and pesticides that create green, weed-free grass? I told him that no one knows the answer to that question, because the "invisible hand" of capitalism works in mysterious ways; all we have to do is get government out of the way and let the magic happen. He wasn't satisfied with that explanation, either. He wanted to know precisely how the magic happens. I told him I don't know—it's magic, for chrissakes!

CHAPTER 48

About this time is when I started getting the feeling that my son thought he was smarter than me. Every once in a while I'd catch him rolling his eyes or shaking his head when I said something, after which he'd mutter "whatever," and walk away. At some point he stopped arguing with me altogether. Honestly, I didn't know what to do when that happened. At least when he was jabbering on about blood diamonds or corporate corruption or the drought in California, he was talking to me. When he stopped talking altogether and became one of those sullen teenagers who shuts himself in his room all night—one of those creatures I'd secretly wished for—I became concerned about our relationship. My wife thought it was just a "phase," but I suspected it was something more.

My neighbor Larry is good in these situations, so I decided to ask him what he thought I should do.

"Sounds to me like you need to engage with The Boy on his level," Larry said when I explained the situation. "He's obviously taking in a lot of information and trying to fit it into a cohesive worldview, what the Germans call weltanschauung. He tells you because he wants to compare his nascent worldview with your mature one."

I told Larry that I wasn't sure I had one of those welterwangs, or if I did, I wouldn't know how to explain it. He said that was nonsense, that I'd been teaching The Boy what I thought every day of his life. This was no different, Larry said, except that now The Boy was looking for guidance in areas that may not be familiar to me.

"When The Boy started encountering math problems that you couldn't immediately solve yourself, did you just throw in the towel and let him figure them out? No, you might have had to study a little to remember the algebra and geometry you'd forgotten, but the point is you did it, because that's what The Boy needed from you at that time. Now, he needs something different—but it's the same basic principle. You're just going to have study up a little on what he happens to be interested in so that you can continue the conversation."

I couldn't admit to Larry that when The Boy hit Algebra, I did in fact throw in the towel. His mother stepped in at that point, and from there on out I had nothing to do with The Boy's homework, just as my father had nothing to do with my homework, and his father had nothing to do with him, period. It was part of a long family tradition, I thought, to let the eldest son struggle and sweat and fail in order to prepare him for a lifetime of struggle and sweat and failure. Besides, as we have already discussed, succeeding in school just fills people with expectations that can never be realized and aspirations that can never be achieved. It makes much more sense to keep one's expectations low in order to avoid a lifetime of perpetual disappointment. By not helping The Boy in school, I thought I was doing him a favor. But this was different, Larry insisted, because it was about continuing the conversation I had been having with The Boy since he was a toddler, maintaining the connection between father and son through the fruitful exchange of ideas. But, since most of the ideas The Boy was interested in were foreign to me, the conversation had come to a standstill. It was up to me, Larry said, to meet The Boy at his current level of intellectual development, because expecting him to snap his fingers and meet me at my level was unrealistic.

That made sense to me. So I decided then and there to find out what The Boy was curious about now and, if necessary, make the extra effort to educate myself about it so that we could discuss it.

That evening, the door to The Boy's room was closed, as it had been for the past few weeks. Until then it had seemed like an impenetrable barrier, and that all who sought to enter The Boy's domain were unwelcome. The sign on the door—"Trespassers Will Be Shot, Dismembered, and Burned to a Crisp"—may have had something to do with it. But even more disturbing than the sign was the eerie silence that radiated from the room, as if nothing were happening inside. The Boy was of course doing something in there. But what? Opening the door meant finding out.

I worked up my courage and gently knocked on the door.

"Enter and be recognized," commanded the voice inside, which had gotten lower and huskier in recent months.

I opened the door slowly and poked my head into his room. "Hey, buddy, how's it going?" I asked.

214

The Boy shrugged his shoulders. He was sitting on his bed with a magazine splayed across his lap, and did not hide the fact that he was annoyed at me for interrupting his reading. Most magazines I flip through have a lot of pictures in them, but the one he was reading didn't. Each page had nothing but columns of words on it, so I assumed it was for school.

"What are you reading about?" I asked, hoping to spark a conversation.

"The Higgs boson," he replied.

"Who is Higgs Boson?" I asked.

"It's not a who, it's a what," The Boy clarified.

"Then what is it?"

"The God particle."

"You're reading an article on God?" I asked.

"No, it's an article on the Higgs boson," The Boy said.

"Oh," I said, as if I understood what he was talking about. I figured that if he

kept talking, I might be able to piece it together. I was wrong.

"It's really an article about the Large Hadron Collider in Switzerland," The Boy said. "But the reason everyone is excited about the Collider is that it helped scientists discover the Higgs boson."

"That's very interesting," I said, trying very hard to understand why it was interesting.

"It's important because it confirms the legitimacy of the Standard Model of particle physics, which postulated fifty years ago that there was an as-yet-undiscovered particle that holds the universe together. That's why they call it the 'God particle,' because without it, we wouldn't exist."

"Hmmmm. What would the universe look like without this God particle?" I asked. "Like Las Vegas, I'm guessing."

"We'd be nothing, or maybe anti-matter," The Boy said, ignoring my excellent joke. "The universe is basically a tug-of-war between matter and anti-matter, and the Higgs boson is what allowed matter to win over anti-matter after the Big Bang. It's why things in the world have mass and weight and substance. It's invisible, though, and it's unstable, so it was extremely hard to isolate."

I had no idea what The Boy was talking about, but I tried to keep the conversation going by asking, "So, how did they find it?"

"That's where the Large Hadron Collider comes in," The Boy said. "It's a giant machine built underground in Switzerland that allows scientists to smash particles together and observe what happens, hopefully unlocking the secrets of the universe. It's funny, because some people were afraid that when they fired this thing up and started smashing atoms together, they'd create a black hole that would suck in the entire world."

I didn't like the sound of that.

"Idiots," he said. "Look, we're still here, aren't we?"

"That sounds a lot like scientists playing God with the universe," I ventured.

"No, it's more like scientists ripping God's clothes off," The Boy said, laughing. "If you believe in God, that is, which I don't."

"But how can you read about the God particle if you don't believe in God?" I countered, snaring him in his own twisted logic.

"It's a misnomer," he said. "Some guy who wrote about it forty years ago called it the God particle, and his book publisher thought it had more PR value than 'Higgs boson.' And he was right."

I wondered why The Boy was interested in any of this at all, so I asked, "Are you doing this for some kind of school science project?"

"No, I'm just reading about it for fun," The Boy said.

For fun? Now I was really confused. Who reads about physics for fun? You read the comics for fun. You read Harry Potter for fun. Physics is a school subject; no one reads about physics for fun.

"Why does this interest you?" I asked, using a question Larry had suggested.

"Well, the Higgs boson itself isn't what interests me," The Boy said. "What interests me is its implications for quantum mechanics. In quantum theory, space and time are curved, not linear, and the existence of the Higgs boson suggests that it might be possible to time travel someday. You know, like in Star Trek. Travel through wormholes, explore distant galaxies, that kind of thing."

"So you want to be an astronaut?" I asked.

"No, I don't want to be anything," The Boy said. "I just think it's interesting. Don't you?"

"Oh, definitely," I said, backing my way out of the room. "Tell you what, I'll leave you to your reading. Good talk. Interesting stuff. Can't wait to hear more about it."

"Did you come up here for a reason, dad?" The Boy asked.

"Yes, yes, I did," I said. "I just came up to see . . . to see if you were still alive. You know, for your mother's sake. I see now that you are, so I'll be going now."

The Boy rolled his eyes, shook his said, and scoffed, "Okay, whatever."

I closed the door and wondered on my way back down the hall what had just happened. Yes, we had engaged in a kind of conversation, which was good, I supposed. But I had no idea what the conversation was about other than some very scary-sounding stuff that I didn't understand, and didn't really want to. I mean, I know there are scientists out there who are experimenting with some strange and potentially dangerous things, but I don't want to know about it. If I'm going to be sucked into a black hole, I'd rather it just happen. I don't want to know about it beforehand. Because if you know it might happen, it's impossible not to think about. Once you know, there's always this voice in the back of your head saying, "Could this be the day? At aisle four in Home Depot, while I'm shopping for a belt sander, is the black hole going to open up and suck me in? Because if it is, I'd like it to happen before I get to the cash register. Otherwise, the whole trip to the store will have been pointless." Or, it might be a different voice if, say, you're headed into a three-hour business meeting. The voice might be saying, "Please, God particle, suck me into oblivion now, so that I don't have to endure this stupid meeting." Either way, it's no longer possible to just drift through life untroubled by thoughts of impending doom.

I cursed myself for listening to Larry and not my wife, who had warned me that I should just stay away and let The Boy come to me, in his own good time. "He'll be back," she assured me. "He just needs to get through this butthead phase and on to the next phase, whatever that is."

So I decided to wait.

CHAPTER 49

I didn't have to wait long, because an opportunity to engage with The Boy on a promising father/son level arose almost immediately. While I was looking at the calendar one day, trying to decide when to schedule my next trip to the city dump, it hit me that The Boy's sixteenth birthday was coming up, so he was going to need to learn how to drive. Who better to teach him than me, whom everyone agreed was an excellent driver, despite that fender-bender in the Walgreens parking lot, which absolutely was not my fault, no matter what the insurance adjuster said. The subject of driver's-ed had not come up in our household yet, but it was inevitable. So I decided it was better to get The Boy behind the wheel sooner rather than later.

One sunny Sunday afternoon, on the way back from a trip to the hardware store, I pulled into an empty parking lot and stopped the car. The Boy was in the passenger seat with his head down, playing some kind of game that required a lot of movement with his thumbs. We sat there for a minute before The Boy realized we had stopped. He looked up and glanced out the window, then resumed his game. It took him a while longer to realize that I was waiting for him to finish.

When it finally dawned on him that we weren't going anywhere, he looked up at me and sneered, "What?!"

"Get out of the car," I said.

"Why, are you going to rape me?" he said.

"What!?"

"Isn't that what happens when someone suddenly pulls you into an abandoned parking lot and starts ordering you around?"

"No, it usually means you're about to get a bullet in the head," I said. "But in this case, I want you to trade places with me. Because today, you're going to learn how to drive."

I thought The Boy would be excited. I remember the first time I got behind the wheel of an automobile. It was one of the most thrilling moments of my life. But The Boy did not react the way I expected.

"What if I don't want to learn how to drive?" he asked.

"What do you mean? Your sixteenth birthday is coming up," I pointed out.

"So?"

"So, that's when people learn to drive. It's a rite of passage. Everybody wants to learn how to drive."

"I don't."

"What are you talking about? Of course you do. Don't you want to start dating? Don't you want to feel the rumble of a three-hundred horsepower V6 at your fingertips? Don't you want to drive to your summer job? Don't you want to be able to do errands for me and your mother?"

"No, no, and no," he said. "Why would I?" he added, as if what I was saying was total nonsense.

"Why wouldn't you?"

He took a deep breath and said, "Well, dating is expensive and all the girls in my school are boring and ugly, for starters. If I don't date, I can keep my expenses down to the point where I don't need a summer job. I don't go anywhere that isn't just as easy to get to by bike or the bus or light rail. Lots of my friends can already drive, so I can always get a ride anywhere. And, as you mentioned, knowing how to drive means doing all kinds of errands for you and mom. The way I look at it, knowing how to drive has a lot of cons and not many pros. So I'd rather not learn, if that's okay with you."

"But what about the extra freedom?" I pointed out, exasperated. "Don't you want to be able to go wherever you want, whenever you want?"

"Where am I going to go?" The Boy asked.

"Anywhere. Everywhere. I don't know. All I know is that when I was your age, I couldn't wait to get behind the wheel. It was like taking control of my destiny!"

"And how'd that work out for you?" The Boy snarked. "Do you think I want to drive a truck all my life like you?"

"I don't drive a truck," I said. "I provide a valuable delivery service to hundreds of people every day. Without me, Amazon could not exist."

"That won't be true for long," The Boy said, "which is another reason I don't want to learn to drive: I just don't see the point. In ten years, driverless cars will be everywhere; no one will need to know how to drive. In fact, some people think it will eventually be illegal for humans to drive, because computer-driven cars will be so much more reliable than humans. Your job will be toast for sure, because by then Amazon will be delivering everything by drone. If I were you, I'd be developing another skill set, because the one you've got is going to be obsolete pretty soon."

"That's crazy talk," I objected. Holiday deliveries by drone would be absolute chaos, I knew, and there's not a drone in the world that can deliver a 200-pound ceramic egg barbecue set.

"No it's not—it's reality," The Boy insisted. "Google is already testing driverless cars in Los Angeles. It's just a matter of time before knowing how to drive a car is one of those skills no one needs to know anymore, like dialing a phone or reading a newspaper."

I'd of course heard rumors that some communists in California were working on a way to take our jobs. But it always sounded like a joke, because there are so many people in this country employed as truck and taxi drivers who can't do anything else, that taking their jobs away would be a disaster. A lot of these guys are not nice people, and they would not take kindly to some computer jockey in California taking their job away. There'd be riots. There'd be murders. People would die.

But it was more than that. The Boy was trying to rattle me, and it was working. What rattled me most was The Boy's prediction that in twenty years, all cars would be Google cars, and they'd all look the same. If you needed to go somewhere, you'd just tap an icon on your phone, a Google car would stop in front of your house, you'd get in, tap your destination, and the car would take you there. It would be a driverless taxi, basically, available to anyone and everyone at the tap of a finger. Kids could drive themselves to school. Old people could get the pharmacy and the food shelf. Crippled people could go for joy rides. Drunk people could get home safely at night from bars. Teenagers could do drugs and have sex in cars without endangering their lives. Texting and cruising the Internet while driving would not be a safety hazard. Plus, he predicted, with all the extra time people saved from not driving, people would get more work done, the demand for music and entertainment would go through the roof (which would be a giant video screen), and economic productivity would soar. Furthermore, accidents would go down because computers would be in perfect control. Fewer people would die. Anyone could go anywhere, anytime, and do whatever they wanted. It would be true freedom, The Boy argued, not the false freedom of getting a driver's license only to become your parents' errand boy.

To me, however, what The Boy was describing was a kind of Google shuttle hell, where everyone drove the same car; or worse, where anyone could drive anything. It did not sound very American to me. Driving a car is about as American as it gets, right? After all, what are the companies that made America great? Ford, Chrysler, and General Motors, that's who. Americans are their cars, for god's sake; it's how we identify each other on the road. If someone in a five-year-old minivan passes me on the highway, I know it's a family with little kids that need to be shuttled around all over the place. When some douchebag in a BMW sedan passes me, I know right away he's probably involved in some sort of white-collar crime that involves computers and hedge funds. If a red Cadillac with shiny chrome rims and tinted windows goes by, I know there's a drug dealer inside. If a Subaru Outback cuts in front of me, I know I'm dealing with some sort of tree-hugging, Whole Food-shopping, marathon-running do-gooder whose kid has a peanut allergy and is organizing a fund drive to raise awareness of childhood diseases that didn't exist thirty years ago because Subaru drivers didn't spend all their time whining about their kids' problems. And what about the Toyota, Honda, Kia, Mitsubishi, Nissan, and Mazda-driving masses? They're all un-American sheep as far as I'm concerned. People who drive those kinds of cars don't care about anything except gas mileage and reliability at an affordable price. There's a lot more to a car than that, though, which is what American car manufacturers have always known. When I see someone like me who is driving a three-year-old Ford Taurus, I know he's probably a solid citizen with a respectable job who has enough pride in his country to buy American. The kind of car you drive tells other people what kind of person you are, and serves as a kind of early-warning system for identifying assholes. If everyone were driving around in the same kind of car, the only differentiator would be the advertising on the side, and that would not be determined by the driver, so you would have no idea what sort of person was inside. It could be a six-year-old kid, or it could be Donald Trump. You would have no way of knowing. It would be anarchy—a world without cheap cars and expensive cars and cars that say, dude, I'm so rich and politically progressive that I can afford to rub your face in it by driving a Tesla.

In the end, much to my dismay, I was not able to convince The Boy that getting his driver's license was necessary, or even worthwhile. When I told him he would at least need one as a form of identification, he told me he had researched it and had already downloaded the form to apply for an official state identification card. And besides, he already had a fake ID that did the job.

"Check and mate," is what he said next. "Can we go home now?"

Reluctantly, I climbed back into the driver's seat and eased the Taurus out of the parking lot. Why my son did not want to get behind the wheel I did not fully understand. He had his reasons, but they did not seem reasonable to me—they seemed like the mad ravings of a teenager who has read too much science fiction and believes the fantastical worlds in his books will soon be real, so why not just wait? I feared that he might be taking drugs and thinking strange thoughts because of it. I feared that he was sacrificing his future for a dream world that would never come. I feared that he might be mentally ill.

But what I feared most was the possibility that he might be right.

CHAPTER 50

Despite all my guidance and coaching and hundreds of warnings about the consequences of doing too well in school, The Boy not only made his high school's honor roll in his senior year, he was one of the top five students in his class. Number three, to be precise, behind two aspiring super-girls who, had they not been so super, would have stranded The Boy at the top of his class.

I was not happy about the situation. But at least he did not graduate number one in his class. Because then he'd be really screwed, doomed to a lifetime of competition with the best and brightest girls in the country, all of whom would be gunning for him, trying to hunt him down and destroy him just to prove that they, not him, were the smartest of the smart. Who needs that kind of pressure? This way, at least, he could say that he was beaten by a couple of girls, so people shouldn't get their expectations up. Sure, I'm a fairly smart guy, he could say, but there are lots of girls who are smarter than me, so cut me some slack. I was glad for that. Life is a lot easier at number three, thirty, or three hundred. Sure, number one sounds great, and it's what everyone says they want, but being number one sucks, because the fall from the top of that mountain can be really painful. Just ask Tiger Woods.

My wife and I did not see eye to eye on the value of good grades and an education. To wit, she thought they had value, and I did not. To her way of thinking, our son was growing up in a different world from the one in which we were raised. Education is more important than ever nowadays, she argued, because today's jobs require more technical skill and managerial know-how. Sure, I could get by driving a UPS truck, and all my friends in high school got decent jobs as postal workers, firemen, police officers, and bar owners. But she wanted more for our son, she said (as if driving a truck eight hours a day was somehow beneath him), and he wanted more—or at least something different—for himself. Opportunities were opening up in all kinds of industries, she argued, but almost all of them required a college education. She trotted out all the statistics about how ~~r~~ who go to college earn so much more over their lifetime than peopl~ who don't. She pointed out that his chances of snaring a young lady with high earning potential diminished considerably if he couldn't meet them in class or have interesting things to say when he did talk to them. She also hit me with the old saw about how college is about "finding yourself" and "discovering your passion," so that you can "do something you love."

I disagreed. I didn't go to college, so my opinion on the matter may be suspect, but everything I've ever heard about it suggests that it's about meeting snooty girls, getting drunk, doing drugs, and racking up a mountain of debt that takes twenty years to pay off. Yes, you might get a degree that allows you to get a decent job. But it seems just as likely that an innocent, unsuspecting student with too much curiosity can get sucked into studying English, Music, or Art, and then where are they? They're deep in debt, with no way to pay off their loans, and doubly depressed because now they're over-educated and under-employed and nobody gives a shit what they write or paint or do to "express" themselves, because they were idiots to study that stuff in the first place. Sure, they may have identified a "passion," but following their passion down the yellow-brick road of occupational bliss will only lead them straight back into their parents' basement—if their parents will let them back into the house, that is.

The Boy insisted that he wanted to go to a "good" school, by which he meant one of the best, most expensive colleges in the country. I am naturally suspicious of anything or anyone who claims to be "the best," because there can only be one "best," and the law of mathematical bullshit dictates that 99.99 percent of those who claim to be the best are lying. All of the schools my son wanted to attend claimed to be the best. So, unless one of them actually was the best, they were all lying as far as I was concerned.

But before I could object, the folders and flyers and recruiting materials came streaming into our house like a river of junk mail. Literature from places like the University of Wisconsin or Notre Dame or Michigan—places that at least have a decent football team—all went into the trash. The literature that didn't get tossed was the stuff from Harvard, Yale, MIT, and Princeton, places so expensive that they can afford to have lousy football teams. How do I know they're expensive?

..cause I looked them up. All of these places cost $65,000-$75,000 a year, or approximately 120 percent of my annual paycheck. There was no way we could afford any of those schools, and I told The Boy so before he started getting his hopes up.

"No one pays full tuition, dad," my son explained, in an effort to calm me down. "Almost everyone who goes to these schools gets financial aid. And if I got into Harvard, guess what? You wouldn't have to pay anything. It would be free."

"How is that possible?" I asked.

"Because people who make under $65,000 a year don't have to pay a dime. The school takes care of it."

"Really."

"Yes."

"What's the catch?" I asked.

"The catch is, you have to get into Harvard."

"I knew it. There's always a catch."

"That's the catch with every school in the country," The Boy said. "Harvard is just harder to get into."

"How do you do it?"

"By being awesome," The Boy said. "Which I am."

I of course was raised to be suspicious of anything that sounds too good to be true. I know a scam when I see one, and this sounded like a classic case of way too good to possibly be believed.

"What if you don't get into Harvard?" I asked.

"Well, other Ivy league schools have similar deals. If it's not free, they usually have an extremely generous sliding scale. So, ironically, it would actually be cheaper for me to go to an Ivy League school than someplace like the University of Minnesota or Iowa State, because the financial aid at those schools isn't nearly as generous."

"So, what you're saying is that if you went to Harvard, it would cost the same as if you didn't go to college at all?"

"You could put it that way, I suppose."

"Could I get a bumper sticker that says, 'My Kid Went to Harvard for Free'?"

"You could," The Boy said, "but that would basically be like having a bumper sticker that says, 'We're too poor to send our kid to college, so we sent him to Harvard instead.'"

Thus began our family's ambitious campaign to get our son into Harvard University, the most exclusive school in the country.

It was a short campaign. In fact, I never got a chance to call the school president or bribe the admissions officer with a couple of crisp Benjamins, because The Boy said there was nothing we could do to help him get in. It was all up to him, he said, and besides, he'd already applied. Harvard had been on his short list for two years, he said. It wasn't something he talked about, because he knew I wouldn't "get it." And besides, he said, he wanted to make sure he even had a chance of getting in before applying, so that the whole idea didn't sound like a ridiculous pipe dream. Now that he was a senior, he had good grades (if not the absolute best), had done exceptionally well on his SATs (whatever 2237 means), and he came from a working-class family in the Midwest (a demographic they were supposedly trying to fill), where he went to public school, not some fancy private school where they wear uniforms and speak Latin and learn how to cast magic spells to help them make more money.

Plus, he said, he had a secret weapon: He was a boy.

CHAPTER 51

"There are so many girls with 4.0 GPAs and great board scores now that it's actually an advantage to be a boy," he explained over dinner. "That didn't used to be the case, but we live in a different world now."

This, I did not expect.

According to The Boy, there are so many over-achieving girls in the world now, and so many under-achieving boys, that—all things being equal, which of course they are not—it's actually easier for a boy to get into college than a girl. Fully two-thirds of the students in college now are women, The Boy claimed, and the situation is getting worse. So many women are smarter and better educated today than men their same age that the era of male servitude and slavery I have long predicted is actually happening. It's also happening much faster than I thought.

Still, one part of this statistic bothered me. Since women are trying to take over the world, I would have thought their agenda included excluding men entirely from higher education, severing the male connection to power and money. Why, then, would they start making it easier for boys to get into college, rather than harder? After all, it's a well-known fact that most college women are lesbians, so they don't need men for sex. And every time a boy gets let into a school, it means a girl did not get in. And for every qualified boy there are probably fifty more qualified girls, so it's clear that preferential treatment is playing a role.

My son planned to take advantage of this imbalance, but I had some serious concerns. If women are bending over backwards to let men into college, even though the world is flooded with over-qualified super-women, it must mean that all the pieces of the feminist plan to take over the world aren't in place yet—that it's happening too fast, even for them, so they have to slow the process down a bit by still allowing boys into college. If there suddenly were no boys anywhere, their plan would be exposed, impossible to ignore or refute. But as long as a man is president and there are still some old white men clinging to the last vestiges of institutional power, there is still work to do. They could be waiting for a woman to finally be elected president. They could be waiting for the day when there are no more male CEOs. They could be waiting for the day when you can buy a vial of sperm at the drugstore for $1.99. Whatever it is they are waiting for, they're trying to make it look as if it benefits men, by doing boys the favor of letting them into their classrooms.

It's a trap, of course. These boys are doomed to fail. Because what red-blooded, eighteen-year-old boy could possibly focus on his studies with so many women in a room? The deviousness of the plan is breathtaking.

CHAPTER 52

A few weeks went by, during which time I had a chance to research Harvard and the sort of people who go there. Harvard's website makes a big deal out of all the important and famous people who have attended Harvard over the years—presidents, CEOs, Nobel-prize winners, billionaire entrepreneurs, opinionated actresses—but it's not hard to read between the lines. What all of this said to me was that Harvard is basically a factory for manufacturing pompous elitists, people who walk around in tailored suits, drink Perrier, speak in vaguely British accents, and pay for everything with an American Express gold card. Sure, they're rich and famous and successful, but at what price? In order to be one of them, you have to become one of them. And that means you have to read their books, subscribe to their magazines, watch their TV shows, buy their clothes, eat their food, drive their cars, live in their penthouses, care about what they care about—live the way they live.

The way they live is totally different from the way we live, of course, and I worried that if my son were to spend too much time in the company of these people, he would eventually be poisoned into thinking that their way of life is better than ours. Being a rich elitist has its advantages, I'm sure, but all you have to do is watch TV to see that people with too much money have a lot of problems. And the kids are the worst. They get into drugs, have sex parties, drive at unsafe speeds, embarrass their parents, accidentally kill their friends, and generally make unwise life choices because they know, deep in their heart, that their parents can always hire a good lawyer. These are the kids my son would be going to school with if he got into Harvard, and I didn't want him getting the wrong idea that, if he ever got into trouble, we could afford to bail him out of jail. If he ever went to jail as an adult, he'd need a presidential pardon to get out. Which, The Boy argued, was yet another good reason to go there, since he would end up with a greater chance of knowing a president of our country personally.

The Wife insisted that my objections to Harvard had more to do with my fear that The Boy would change if he got in, and that he and I might grow apart. Or worse, that spending all that time around the children of rich and successful people would somehow make The Boy think less of me.

In this case, her analysis was absolutely correct, because how could I possibly compete with presidents and CEOs for parental prestige? Would The Boy come home for Christmas breaks thinking I was a loser because I couldn't afford to cap his teeth with gold or fly him back and forth on a private jet?

To ease my anxiety, The Wife reminded me that the chances of him getting accepted were still pretty slim. "If he does get in, it'll be no thanks to you," she said. "With all your stupid talk about how school isn't important and how he should keep his grades down so that he doesn't attract attention. Well, all that might blow up in your face now, because you might end up having to pay for him to go to Iowa State or the University of Wisconsin—someplace that actually charges tuition."

I'd never looked at it that way before, but now that paying tuition at an American university was suddenly a terrifying possibility, I had to admit that she had a point.

CHAPTER 53

If getting into Harvard is such a big deal, you'd think they'd put more effort into the presentation. When you win the lottery, they hold a press conference and hand you a giant check and fire up the confetti cannons and hire a reporter to stick a microphone in your face. When you get into Harvard, they send you a standard-size envelope with a single piece of paper inside in that congratulates you for being one of the lucky few—details to come. That's it.

They do it this way, I think, because that same envelope could contain a rejection letter. And, using well-known principles of anticipation pioneered on The Price is Right, all the doors need to look the same on the outside to heighten the surprise, if you win, and the grief, if you lose.

The Boy, having watched many a game show with me, knew what to do when he opened that envelope. As my wife and I awaited the verdict, he opened the letter and feigned sadness, leading us to believe that he had been rejected, then abruptly changed his expression to one of extreme joy, indicating that he had been accepted, then he took it back, saying he was kidding and that no, he had not gotten in—then, in a final gotcha, tossed the letter on the kitchen counter in disgust, allowing us to read that he had in fact been accepted.

You don't get many moments like that in life, so I had to admit that The Boy played it well.

The rest of his senior year in high school, The Boy was of course insufferable. He was only one of three kids in his high school who got into an Ivy league school (those girls ahead of him were the other two), so he was a minor celebrity at school and a major pain in the ass at home. Feeling untouchable and entitled, he neglected to do his chores around the house and began going out until all hours with his friends. There wasn't much we could do about it. Most parents can yell at their kids for goofing off and letting their grades slip, but since I didn't care about grades in the first place, and in the second place he had gotten into Harvard, we had no leverage. Other parents can also

231

threaten not to pay for college if their kids don't shape up, but since Harvard was going to pick up the whole tab, we had no leverage there, either.

Our therapist (whom my wife had continued seeing over the years, but I had dropped because he did nothing to help me) suggested that we allow The Boy to revel in his glory for a while, since he had worked so hard, and by all reasonable measures was about as successful as a young man could be. Besides, he said, we were going to have to get used to not having him around, so we might as well start now. So cut him some slack, he advised. The Wife was already cutting The Boy so much slack that she might as well have been using spaghetti noodles as rope, so I assumed that the therapist's advice was directed at me. This was confirmed when my wife relayed the information from their session and added, "He means you."

CHAPTER 54

The last big event in The Boy's high school life was the senior prom, an event he had not planned on attending, he said, because it "perpetuated stereotypes" and represented a "bourgeois tradition" that he did not believe in or want to support. In the end, though, he conceded that "circumstances" had changed—meaning, I think, that he got a date—so he was going to attend after all.

On the night of the big occasion, The Boy couldn't have been less enthusiastic. We offered to rent him a tux, but he declined, saying that he had found what he wanted to wear at a local thrift store: a seersucker jacket, black shirt, skinny white tie, and white pants. If he didn't want to go to the prom, I told him, he could always join a barbershop quartet. He did not laugh. He and a few friends rented a limo for the evening, and we were waiting for them to pick him up when there was a knock at the door.

"That must be Erin," The Boy said.

He got up to answer the door. Moments later, The Boy re-emerged into the living room with another person. "This is Erin," The Boy said by way of introduction. "Erin, these are my parents. Or so they claim."

I had been wondering what sort of girl had convinced my son to go to the prom. My guess was that she was going to be cute verging on hot, and that his principles had been compromised by the possibility of spending an entire evening with a girl who was technically out of his league. When this Erin person walked in, however, I must admit that I was confused.

The strange thing about Erin was that I couldn't immediately tell if he/she was a boy or a girl. The facial features and skin were softer and more girl-like than most guys The Boy's age, and there was some mascara and the slightest bit of cheek rouge, along with one small silver earring loop dangling from the right ear. But Erin was also sporting a neat, cropped haircut—almost a military crew cut—and wearing a classic black tux with matching black wingtips. If Erin had any breasts, they were crushed flat and hidden by the jacket. Erin's handshake was extremely firm, too, and there was no clue in the voice, which was low and breathy. Then again, Erin's fingernails were painted black with silver sparkles, so my brain was short-circuiting.

"Pleased to meet you," Erin said, shaking my hand with two assertive pumps.

The Boy was eager to make our little meet and greet as short as possible. He and The Wife exchanged some logistical details and she delivered the requisite warnings about staying safe and not drinking to excess and not doing drugs, all of which The Boy dismissed with a brief hug and a "bye, mom." Then they were gone.

After they left, The Wife and I exchanged looks of concern. She, who is usually pretty good at reading people, was just as confused as I was about which side of the aisle Erin was standing. And the implications of the answer caught us by surprise. If Erin was a boy, did that mean our son was gay? If Erin was a girl, what did that say about our son's taste in women, or his ability to attract them? The Boy had insisted that he and Erin were "just friends," and that he was only going to the prom because Erin wanted to go. But was Erin a buddy, or was Erin a ghoulish chick with a weird sense of humor? It was hard to tell, and not being able to tell was surprisingly disconcerting—like waking up one day to discover that the sun has risen in the west and is going to set in the east, or maybe south, depending on how far the earth has actually spun off its axis.

The Boy did not get home from the prom until about eight o'clock the next morning. Then he slept all day and didn't wake up until dinnertime. At the dinner table, The Boy was groggy, his hair was messed up, and he looked like he had a hangover. He didn't smell too great, either. As the pasta bowl was being passed around, The Wife began to gently inquire about The Boy's evening.

"So, did you have fun last night?" she asked.

"Some," The Boy answered.

"What did you do?"

"Nothing much. Mostly just hung out."

"It was nice meeting Erin," she said in a sing-songy voice that said, 'tell us more.'

The Boy nodded and stuffed some pasta in his mouth.

"How did you two meet?"

"In English Lit."

Tired of these short, clipped answers, and impatient for a few other kinds of answers, I decided to jump in and cut to the chase. "What your mother and I really want to know, and were not able to determine, is whether your date to the prom was a guy or a girl?"

The Boy continued to eat, but between bites managed to say, as nonchalantly as possible, "Neither."

"Excuse me, did you say neither?"

The Boy nodded.

"What are you trying to say?" I asked. "Are you trying to tell us you are gay?"

The Boy laughed. "If I was gay, I'd tell you," The Boy said. "Because the look on your face would be priceless—almost as good as the look that's on it now."

"So clarify for us," my wife said. "How can Erin be neither a boy or a girl?"

"Erin's non-binary," The Boy explained, without explaining. "Though the preferred term is 'demiflux.'"

"What are you talking about?" I said. "That sounds like one of those bladder medications they advertise on TV. Does this Erin have a bladder problem of some sort?"

The Boy sighed and said, "Non-binaries are people who don't identify with either gender. They don't feel like a boy or a girl, or sometimes they feel more like a boy than a girl, or vice-versa."

"What? That makes no sense," I said. "You're either a boy or a girl. There are no other choices. Here's a test: Which bathroom does Erin use, the boys or girls?"

"Neither. We have unisex bathrooms at school," The Boy said.

"I don't believe this," I said, staring up at the ceiling for some supernatural assistance that was conspicuously absent.

"Are you saying that Erin is androgynous?" The wife asked, patting me on the arm to calm me down.

"That's the old-fashioned term," The Boy said. "The term Erin prefers is demiflux, which is a subset of non-binary, which is the term most closely associated with androgyny. The trouble with androgyny is that is doesn't describe people's gender identifications specifically enough, and it implies gender neutrality. But in most cases, people identify with one gender more than another, and their identification can shift on a daily basis. Erin prefers demiflux because she is biologically a girl, but she identifies with her male side more often than her female side, except when she doesn't. It changes, hence the flux."

"So she's a tomboy," I said. "Why does your generation have to complicate things so much?"

"No, she's not a tomboy," The Boy insisted. "Erin prefers not to be referred to with any kind of gender pronoun—he or she—and doesn't even play sports. Erin is just Erin, and who Erin is changes, which is part of why Erin is interesting."

"So what you're saying is that Erin is confused," I said.

"Erin is the least confused person I know," The Boy replied.

"How can a girl who thinks she's a boy but can't make up her mind about it from day to day not be confused?" I said. "I'm confused just talking about her, it, him, or whatever."

"Sh-He," The Boy said. "That's the term we made up as a joke. But that's what I call Erin."

"This is ridiculous. At the doctor's office, which box does Erin check?" I asked.

"Probably female. But I wouldn't be surprised if those boxes disappear pretty soon, or if they don't add a bunch of them. When you start studying this stuff, it turns out that gender identification is extremely fluid. Only a small percentage of the population fully identifies with their birth-assigned gender, and it's only now that our understanding of gender and the language we use to describe it are starting to catch up."

I wanted to puke. "And you know all this how?"

"Duh, I took a Gender Studies class?" The Boy said.

Harvard or no, there were definitely times when I thought it might have been better to homeschool The Boy, and this was one of them. No wonder he never learned anything at his school; they couldn't even get the basics right.

"And this is the person you chose to go to prom with?"

"Yes."

"Why?"

"Erin's funny," The Boy said. "And smart. We like to hang out. So we figured, why not?"

"Why not? I'll tell you why not—because it had to have caused a scandal," I said. "I wouldn't be surprised if you get suspended or expelled. And what is Harvard going to think of that? There's just not that much room in this world for that much . . . difference. I'm sure the school has rules against this kind of thing."

"What kind of thing?" The Boy asked.

"Gender—what did you call it—fluidity."

"Dad, the school has classes in it," The Boy pointed out.

"They have sex education classes too, but that doesn't mean you can just procreate at your leisure in the hallway," I said.

The Boy snickered and said, "You haven't spent much time at my school."

"You get my point."

"Yes, but technically we were just a boy and girl going to prom. What could they say?"

"I'm sure they said a lot."

"Dad, nobody cares," The Boy said as he poured himself another glass of milk, his third. "Lots of kids at school are non-binary. It's become kind of a thing—a way for misfits to fit back in."

"Well I for one think it's a great idea," The Wife interjected. "I've always thought it was strange that girls are supposed to do one thing, and boys are supposed to do another, and if you cross the line too much—if a girl takes an auto shop class, say, or a boy wants to play field hockey—they look at you funny. I mean, who decided that the equipment in your pants is the end all and be all of who you are?"

"I'm pretty sure God had something do to with it," I reminded her. "If God had wanted everyone to have the same equipment, he would have given everyone a penis and called it a day. But He didn't. In His infinite wisdom, he saw that man needed a place to put his penis, and so he created woman. And I for one think that was a great idea."

"Gay guys put their penises in all kinds of places that have nothing to do with women," The Boy said.

"And that is the end of this conversation," I declared as I grabbed my plate and took it to the kitchen. "I'm not going to get sucked into a conversation about the ins and outs of gay sex. I'm not a prude. I know what goes on in dark allies late at night after the bars let out. I just prefer not to think about it, or know any more about it than I already do."

"Sounds to me like you know quite a bit about it," The Boy said.

"That's enough, dear," The Wife said to The Boy, who was grinning like an idiot. "I think your father has been traumatized enough for one evening."

And that, thank God, was the actual end of the conversation.

CHAPTER 55

We didn't see much of The Boy that last summer. He spent his days working at a local used bookstore, and almost every night out with friends. By the time he was ready to leave for the East coast, to Harvard, it felt almost as if he had already left. Often the only evidence he was still around was an empty cereal box and a counter covered with crumbs, as if a giant rat had invaded our kitchen and helped itself to breakfast.

His departure at the end of August was strange. The day itself seemed to come out of nowhere. I knew it was coming, but had somehow convinced myself that there was more time. Secretly, I may have been hoping that he would change his mind, that he would suddenly realize that this whole notion of going off to college in some faraway city was insane and unnecessary. There were plenty of schools within a day's drive of our house. In fact, there were half a dozen within a twenty-minute radius, and two he could walk to if he lived at home. Why did he have to go so far away? Why did he feel the need to leave his parents and strike out on his own? It felt like rejection. It felt as if we had failed as parents, and that The Boy had grabbed the earliest opportunity to escape the chamber of horrors that was his childhood home. What stories would he tell his new chums at school?, I wondered. Would he lie, or tell the truth? I knew the answer to that, of course: He would lie. But what sort of lies would he tell? How would he paint the canvas of his childhood to the children of wealth and privilege? Would he downplay the modesty of our means? Would he exaggerate the urban danger of his upbringing to gain street cred with all those ultra-capable co-eds? Would he portray me as being a worse or better man than I am? Would we, in his narrative, be loving, supportive parents, or monsters of abuse and neglect?

I truly did not know.

The Wife kept reminding me that The Boy's desire to leave home and make his own way in the world was actually an indication that our parenting had been successful. It meant that he was comfortable with himself and that he felt secure enough about his connection to his parents and home to leave it.

All the parenting books say stuff like that, though: that the worse it is for the parent, the better it is for the child. If your kid yells and screams and throws tantrums, that's a good thing, they say, because it means the child feels safe to freely express themselves. If your teenager is an insolent, back-talking little shit, that's a good thing, they say, because it means he's asserting his own independence and has the courage of his own convictions.

Still, I felt like a complete failure.

When The Boy was born, I had a plan, an image in my head of the kind of boy I wanted to raise and the kind of man I wanted him to become. But as far as I could tell, almost nothing I tried to teach The Boy had sunk in. The Boy spent his entire childhood ignoring my advice and failing to learn the lessons I tried to convey. He had grown up to become a person I hardly recognized. The Boy that headed off to Harvard was not The Boy I imagined when he was a little ball of flesh who periodically puked and pissed on me. He was something entirely different, a mutant by-product of my failure to be the father I wanted to be, and of my inability to influence his development in the ways that I had hoped. It felt almost as if he had become the opposite of what I wanted—as if God's big joke on me was to give me a boy I did not understand and could not change. How it happened, I do not know. I devoted eighteen years of my life to this project of raising a son, and now that The Boy was gone, it was over.

I also feared for his future. Just as I had tried to protect him from the voracious competitiveness of a world ruled by estrogen, I now feared that he should be protected from the teeth and claws of the privileged classes—from the dark tunnels of despair that certain paths to success often lead. Yes, he had survived the gauntlet of high school, but this was something entirely different, and I could not protect him from it, because I did not understand it. Everything The Boy was about to experience was foreign to me. The Boy was on his own in this strange new world, and there was nothing I could do to help him.

And so, in the most literal sense possible, I felt helpless.

CHAPTER 56

A few days after The Boy left for college, I fell into a deep funk. It was as if a dense, wet cloud had enveloped me, making everything more difficult. My arms and legs felt heavy. Just getting out of bed felt like hard work. And actually working—loading the truck, doing my route, delivering all those boxes and packages—well, that was torture. My back had been hurting for quite some time, and every day now my knees throbbed with pain. I tried back braces and knee braces and Ben-Gay and Advil, but after a while nothing seemed to work. I began to yearn for the dark empty quiet of sleep, and to dread waking up, because waking up meant facing the pain, and the pain meant that I was still alive—though not nearly as alive as I once was.

And then, one day, I could not move. The sadness was too heavy. The ache in my chest seemed to have its own gravitational pull, sucking me down into the bed and holding me there as strongly as if leather straps had been attached to my wrist and ankles. My eyes could not focus, and the shafts of light coming through the bedroom window felt like shards of glass being hurled through my eyeballs and into the back of my brain, cutting and slicing it to ribbons.

When I did not come downstairs for breakfast, The Wife came up to see where I was and found me curled up in the bed, shaking.

"What's wrong, dear?" she said as she sat on the side of the bed and put a gentle hand on my shoulder.

I'm not afraid or ashamed to say it now, but the sound of her voice at that moment opened up a chasm in my heart, from which arose a primeval wail that seemed to split me in half. Suddenly, uncontrollably, I began to sob. Great waves of grief and hurt tore through me, shaking my body with the force of a thousand hands. I was no longer me in that moment; I had no body, I was just a pulsing white blob of agony and regret. After a while, I tried to form some words, but nothing intelligible came out. Whatever I was trying to say got smothered in mucus and snot, as wave after wave of despair rolled over and through me, simultaneously lightening my burden and pulling me deeper into the infinite pit of sadness from which it came.

"There, there," said my wife as my sobs began to subside. "It's okay. Let it out," she said. "You really should cry more than once every twenty years, you know. That would make it a lot easier."

Somehow I found it within me to laugh at that, and a stream of snot shot out of my nose onto the pillow. Once I gained my composure, I confessed to my wife—my beautiful, understanding, loving wife— that I did not feel like I had been an adequate father to our son—that I had, despite my best efforts, failed him in all the most important ways. And now that he was gone, I told her, I would get no second chance. My failure was permanent. The only way I could see to salvage the situation, I told her, was to get a divorce, marry some fertile young nymph in her twenties, and try again.

She hit me in the arm and said, "There's something I think you should see." She then left the room for a few minutes and returned with a few sheets of paper in her hands.

"Read this," she said. "It's your son's college entrance essay. It's the reason he got into Harvard—the reason he was accepted over all those other kids in the country who might arguably have been better educated and more qualified."

I sat up in bed, took the papers from her, and began to read:

It's 5:00 a.m., and my father is already out of the house, on his way to the UPS loading docks, where he will fill his truck with boxes and packages and envelopes full of items to be delivered all over town. Many of the boxes say "Amazon" on the side, and all must be delivered in a timely manner over the next eight hours. When he is finished with his route, in the early afternoon, he will spend the rest of his day with me, or with me and my friends, showing us how to do all kinds of things—make a potato cannon, build a model rocket, shoot a slingshot, make a whistling sound with a blade of grass. Then he will eat dinner, fall into bed early, and get up the next morning to do it all over again.

My father thinks he is living the American Dream. He is not the most educated person in the world (he did not go to college), and he hasn't traveled much, but he has a job, a house, and a family, and he believes wholeheartedly that the United States in which he lives has given him—and will continue to give him—the opportunity to live this dream of his.

What my father doesn't know is that his country is lying to him. He may have lived the dream for a while, but the dream he believes in is quickly disappearing. My father doesn't realize, or even believe it's possible, that in five years, he might be replaced at his job by a robotic truck or smart drone. "They'll always need someone to carry the boxes to the door," he claims, not realizing that an engineer somewhere has likely already solved that problem, and the only barrier between him and unemployment is the time it takes to patent and produce it.

But it may not matter, because his back and knees are shot from delivering so many thousands of packages over the years. His company is no doubt aware of his advancing age and, with it, the increasing risk that he will injure himself on the job.

These days, he is in so much pain when he gets home that he can barely stand. He won't go see a doctor, though, because he is afraid of what it might cost. One CT scan and a surgery will bring my parents close to bankruptcy, he fears, and my father won't help himself because my mother's hip has been bothering her, and he is concerned that she, too, might need surgery. My parents have no savings (everything they ever made went toward raising me). In fact, they are deeper in debt than they would ever want anyone to know. They have no retirement plan, and as they approach their fifties, re-training in a different field is both impractical and expensive. They are happy, sort of, but that sort-of happiness is built on a shaky foundation of denial and a dwindling supply of hope. In truth, they have no idea how they are going to survive over the next twenty-five years. But they still believe that, because they live in America, everything is going to be okay—somehow.

My generation is not so fortunate. We don't have the luxury of believing that everything is going to be okay, because the reasons it will not are too obvious to ignore. Climate change, terrorism, income inequality, student debt, unemployment, stagnant wages, global economic instability, governmental gridlock, political corruption, drought, disease, pollution—it all adds up to a bleak future for all of us, because too many factors are either beyond human control, or are being controlled by humans who do not care much about us, the people. The future feels precarious to my generation, never certain and always on the verge of collapse. As Sept. 11, 2001 taught us when we were kids, everything can change in a day.

This is not the America my father tried to teach me about. He was skeptical of the government, to be sure, but he believed with all his heart that if you were a good person and worked hard, that was enough. Throughout my life, he tried to teach me about the importance of independence and self-reliance. Once, we went camping and he refused to bring anything, even a tent, because he wanted to teach me how to be self-sufficient in the wild. Whatever project my friends and I were working on, he always had advice about how to turn it into a business or an adventure, or both. He wasn't an entrepreneur, but he had an entrepreneurial spirit, and he spent a good portion of his life trying to instill in me the idea that all I had to do was believe in myself and everything would work out. He bought me my first chemistry set, which sparked my interest in the natural sciences. He allowed—even encouraged—me to make mistakes, and I made quite a few. He had some odd ideas about the need for a formal education (he didn't see much value in it), his advice wasn't always very good, and his teaching methods were a bit unorthodox at times, but he believed so completely in his convictions that it was hard to argue with him.

But argue with him I did. I argued with him a lot, in fact, but the only reason I could argue with him was that he, in his weird and sometimes maddening way, taught me to think for myself. I am who I am today because of my dad—and my mom, too, who tutored me and taught me the things my father could not.

I realize that I am not the usual sort of student Harvard University chooses to educate. I do not come from a rich family, I did not attend private school, and I grew up in a part of the country where people still grow corn and raise cows and drive pickup trucks with shotguns in the back. I grew up in middle America, where, I gather from the news, many people think the American Dream still survives. And it does, for some—but for many, including my parents, it is slowly slipping away. The worst part is, they don't even know it. The world is changing, and they are not prepared for it. They are trapped between the world they grew up in and the world that is leaving them behind.

They don't know what to think of teenagers who can make a million dollars just because they're good with computers. They don't know what to make of young men in hoodies and sunglasses making piles of cash playing poker on television. And they certainly can't fathom how it's possible that ambitious young entrepreneurs in states like Colorado and Washington can make a fortune selling marijuana—legally. It all sounds crazy to my parents, and I am scared for them, because they are not stupid people—they just don't know how to face the fact that the America they know and love has no more use for them.

That may sound cynical, but it's not—it's sad. Which brings me to why I want to attend Harvard University. As I mentioned, though my father was not a fan of formal education, my mother was, and she pushed me to excel academically so that I could become my best self. The reason I want to attend Harvard is that I believe it is my responsibility to help rebuild and restore the idea of America that my father still believes in. I don't believe in it, and most of my generation doesn't either—but we all want to. We all desperately want what my father has: a true and unwavering love for this country and all it pretends to stand for. The difference is that we want to get rid of the pretense. We want our belief in America to be based on something true and solid and trustworthy. We don't want to be lied to, or manipulated, or sold a bogus version of the real thing. We want it to be the real thing, the genuine article—the America the world used to believe in, and my father still does.

To be a man, my father once told me you must find out what you believe in, then be willing to fight for it if someone tries to take it away. If I'm accepted to Harvard, I'm not sure my father will even understand what that really means in educational terms. But my goal in life will be to use my Harvard education to fight for my father's vision of America, before he finds out it's a just a fading mirage—a shimmering illusion of sand and sweat and dust.

Thank you for your time and consideration. I look forward to your decision, and hope it is a favorable one.

I read the letter a few more times, then set the paper down on the side of the bed. "I didn't realize your hip was bothering you so much, and that I was so worried about it," I said.

"Okay, yes, he exaggerated a few things to make his point. But it shouldn't have escaped you that it is pretty much a love letter to you. He's basically saying 'I love my dad, and I'm grateful for everything he taught me. You see that, don't you?"

I nodded yes, and suddenly started crying again. Jesus, I thought, this has got to stop.

"So you see, you're not a failure after all. Far from it," my wife said. "Sure, there were a few things that, given a second chance, you might want to re-think. And on balance, you were a better father than a husband. But overall, I think you did pretty well, given your limitations. You should be proud."

I appreciated the sentiment, but one thing about the letter bothered me, and I couldn't stay silent about it. I drew her attention to the sentence where The Boy is saying he is who he is because of me, "and my mom, too, who tutored me and taught me the things my father could not."

"I'm not stupid," I said. "This sentence suggests that there were times—times I was unaware of—when you were teaching The Boy things on the sly, in private, without my knowledge. Is that true?"

"Of course it's true," she said. "I taught him algebra, geometry, calculus, art history, literature, poetry, and half a dozen other subjects. I was also the one who carted him to violin lessons every week, and who made sure his homework was done on time, and who went to parent conferences after you gave up on them. I also kept his schedule, made his meals, took him to the doctor, and did everything else. You had all the fun; I got most of the work."

I thought about what she said for a moment. It explained a lot, including why The Boy was always "busy" whenever I wanted to do something with him.

"It wasn't all fun," I said.

"Look, I'm not complaining," she insisted. "Parenting is a team effort, and everybody has to play to their strengths. You don't have many strengths, so it was natural for a few things to fall through the cracks, all of which I cleaned up. Oh, and don't underestimate the effort it took to undo some of the nonsense you tried to teach him. If it makes you feel any better, he wanted to be more like you. I just couldn't let that happen."

CHAPTER 57

When I started my great boy-to-man project, I didn't know how it was going to turn out, obviously. I had an image in my mind of the kind of boy I wanted to produce, and did everything I could to achieve that goal, but in the end, my wife was right: no matter how carefully I planned or what I did to help him, the little fucker found a way to screw it up.

When I think back on all the information and wisdom I tried to pass on to my son, and how he took that knowledge and twisted it and rearranged it in his own head to become The Man he is now—well, the mind boggles. Instead of the clean-cut, square-jawed gentleman I envisioned, I now have a long-haired, scruffy-bearded beanpole who is six inches taller than me and talks a mile a minute about the sorts of things that, I gather, they teach people at Harvard.

This is of course what I was afraid of—that, surrounded by a bunch of East coast elitists, and wooed by women of wealth and privilege, he'd get a bunch of fancy ideas in his head and forget who he was talking to on the infrequent occasions when he came home. Honestly, if too many of tomorrow's "leaders" think the way my son does now, I fear for the future of this country. Nowadays, his ability to over-think and complicate things is astounding. He thinks himself in circles, weighing the pros and cons of everything, pointing out all the ironies and paradoxes, marveling at the contradictions and hypocrisies, getting indignant about everyone else's stupidity, and wondering how things got so messed up in the first place. How, in the ten-thousand years of civilization before he was born, did things go so horribly wrong?, he wondered. And how, he seemed to be thinking, was he supposed to fix it all with a practical working life of only forty or fifty years?

What I'm saying is that right out of the gate, Harvard had rinsed his brain of one of the most fundamental lessons I tried to teach him as a boy. I don't know how many times I tried to tell him that in order to be a self-sufficient, independent person in this world, you have to forget about other people's problems and focus on your own. You want to help the world? Help yourself first. Then, later in life, if you have the money and time, you can think about donating to a charity or buying a hospital wing, or whatever. But until then, you have to stay focused on yourself and your family. Life is short; who has time to worry about other people's problems? What The Boy is learning now is that as soon as you lose your focus—as soon as you start feeling bad for all the people in the world who aren't Americans—your own problems don't seem so important. And when your own problems are no longer as important to you as other people's problems, they fester and bloat into bigger, worse problems. Pretty soon, your own problems are so huge that you can't ignore them anymore, and then you're in a shithole of trouble. Because now, not only do you have a few million less fortunate non-Americans to worry about, you have no choice but to start worrying about your own problems again. Then you start feeling sorry for yourself and wondering, how can I help all those non-Americans out there when I can't even help myself? Which is a very good question, but one that never needs to be asked if you just take care of your own business first and let other people worry about theirs.

Face it, I tried to teach him: you're an American. Everyone else in the world has it worse than you do, so learning about the inferiority of other counties and cultures is just going to make you sad and depressed. If you're like your mom, I told him, you'll end up feeling guilty about your American-ness and how much better you have it, and you'll start sending money to every godforsaken shithole on the planet. If there's a hurricane in Indonesia, you'll send money to help. If there's an earthquake in Nepal, you'll write a check. If someone comes to the door holding a clipboard and telling you some sob story about how all the fresh water is disappearing, or how all the bees are dying, or how we're all going to die if you don't care as much about the welfare of the planet as they do—that's right, you're going to write a check. After a while, you'll run out of checks and start putting your guilt on a credit card. Then you'll hit your credit-card limit and apply for another card, then another. Pretty soon you're carrying $100,000 of debt on those credit cards, paying fifteen percent interest, and you can't even keep up with the minimum payments. Then what good are you? Now, because you tried to help a bunch of people who can't be helped, because they live somewhere other than America, you have to take a second job just to keep up with the interest payments on those credit cards. The next thing you know, you're getting drunk every night, popping pain pills like candy, and sitting at your computer all day, yelling at people in the internet in CAPITAL LETTERS! Now you can't help anyone anymore, because you have to help yourself. But you never would have gotten into that situation in the first place if you'd just taken responsibility for your own life and cultivated a healthy attitude of self-sufficiency and independence. If you want to be your own man, then be your own man! Just don't make the mistake of trying to be someone else's man too. That way lies danger and regret. You think credit-card debt sucks your soul? Try paying alimony.

All of this and more I tried to teach The Boy, but he obviously didn't listen. Now I worry about what kind of man he's actually going to be. He uses the phrase "non-profit" a lot now—as if it's a good thing. And he still refuses to get a driver's license. He prefers tapping a little button on his phone and having someone pick him up. How he can have so many friends on stand-by waiting to cart him around, I don't know. But again, it's the same thing: instead of taking responsibility for his own transportation, he's relying on other people to get him wherever he wants to go. It's freeloading, pure and simple. That's not how I taught him, but that's how he is—and I can't fathom how he got that way.

I guess that's the big takeaway here: Whatever you do, however hard you try, and however much head protection you provide, there's something in a boy that makes them want to go out and beat their heads against a wall—a wall you warned them is there, and that you explained is very hard and unforgiving.

At this point I have to apologize to all you fathers out there who thought I might have had something more substantive and practical to say about raising a boy. To be fair, I thought I'd have more to add to the conversation as well. Having raised a boy myself, I figured I'd learned something about being a father that, if I wrote it down, might benefit others. In hindsight, I see that's where I went wrong—in thinking that I could actually help other people. That's what I get for listening to my neighbor, Larry. He's the one who suggested I "put my thoughts down on paper," so that others might benefit from my experience. He also claimed the mere act of writing it all down would clarify my thinking and help me appreciate all that I actually did for The Boy, regardless of the outcome.

I don't know if any of that is true. Honestly, there is only one thing I'm certain of, and it's the only absolutely true thing I can say to you if you are the father of a boy and are trying your best to turn him into a man. Whatever problems you're encountering, whatever setbacks you have, whatever brainless nonsense you're dealing with, whatever disappointments and aggravations and heartaches you end up enduring, just remember that it could all be much worse:

You could be raising a girl.